∽ Fugitives ∽

The clearing erupted with gunfire of all makes and models. Pistols of different calibers barked and spat hot lead at the two men fleeing toward the river. Shotguns sent waves of thunder through the air and tore apart tree trunks while chipping away at fallen rock. Fortunately, most of those shots were taken in a hurry before the men pulling the triggers could get a good look at their targets.

As he ran, Caleb ignored the panic gripping him like a cold, iron fist clamped around his stomach. He tried not to think about the bullets hissing past him or the pain that sparked in his ankles, knees, legs, and arms as he charged onto the fragile ice. The truth of the matter was that he hadn't actually planned on making it to the river before getting caught or killed.

Although Doc had followed Caleb to the edge of the stream, he stopped and turned so he could draw his second pistol. Caleb's voice was swallowed up by the roar of gunfire as Doc pulled his triggers and fired into the nearby clearing . . .

Titles by Marcus Galloway

THE ACCOMPLICE
THE ACCOMPLICE: BUCKING THE TIGER
THE ACCOMPLICE: THE SILENT PARTNER

THE
~ ACCOMPLICE ~

The Silent Partner

Marcus Galloway

BERKLEY BOOKS, NEW YORK

THE BERKLEY PUBLISHING GROUP
Published by the Penguin Group
Penguin Group (USA) Inc.
375 Hudson Street, New York, New York 10014, USA
Penguin Group (Canada), 90 Eglinton Avenue East, Suite 700, Toronto, Ontario M4P 2Y3, Canada
(a division of Pearson Penguin Canada Inc.)
Penguin Books Ltd., 80 Strand, London WC2R 0RL, England
Penguin Group Ireland, 25 St. Stephen's Green, Dublin 2, Ireland (a division of Penguin Books Ltd.)
Penguin Group (Australia), 250 Camberwell Road, Camberwell, Victoria 3124, Australia
(a division of Pearson Australia Group Pty. Ltd.)
Penguin Books India Pvt. Ltd., 11 Community Centre, Panchsheel Park, New Delhi—110 017, India
Penguin Group (NZ), 67 Apollo Drive, Rosedale, North Shore 0632, New Zealand
(a division of Pearson New Zealand Ltd.)
Penguin Books (South Africa) (Pty.) Ltd., 24 Sturdee Avenue, Rosebank, Johannesburg 2196,
South Africa

Penguin Books Ltd., Registered Offices: 80 Strand, London WC2R 0RL, England

This is a work of fiction. Names, characters, places, and incidents either are the product of the author's imagination or are used fictitiously, and any resemblance to actual persons, living or dead, business establishments, events, or locales is entirely coincidental.

THE ACCOMPLICE: THE SILENT PARTNER

A Berkley Book / published by arrangement with the author

PRINTING HISTORY
Berkley edition / October 2008

Copyright © 2008 by Marcus Pelegrimas.
Cover illustration by Bill Angresano.
Cover design by Steven Ferlauto.
Interior text design by Laura K. Corless.

ISBN: 978-0-425-22415-1

BERKLEY®
Berkley Books are published by The Berkley Publishing Group,
a division of Penguin Group (USA) Inc.,
375 Hudson Street, New York, New York 10014.
BERKLEY is a registered trademark of Penguin Group (USA) Inc.
The "B" design is a trademark belonging to Penguin Group (USA) Inc.

PRINTED IN THE UNITED STATES OF AMERICA

10 9 8 7 6 5 4 3 2 1

To Cherry,

For giving me some of the best news of my life

Author's Note

As always, I want to make it clear that this book is not trying to reflect historical fact. Instead, I consider it more of a historical tribute. Whenever possible, I have tried to maintain the actual names, dates, places, and events marking the colorful life of John Henry Holliday. From my own research as well as several other great volumes out there, I have endeavored to put together a fairly accurate picture of what it would have been like to work with Doc Holliday throughout the wilder years of his career. Of course, some liberties have been taken every so often, but I have struggled to keep Doc's essence true to form. Many of the events in this book are documented fact, and the rest is hopefully a good reflection of what Doc might have done. Since none of us were there to ride alongside Doc, it's hard to say which factual accounts are truly accurate. The following books, however, have helped me get a clearer view of the real Doc and the men who crossed his path. *Doc Holliday: A Family Portrait* by Karen Holliday Tanner; *Doc Holliday: The Life and Legend* by Gary Roberts; *Deadwood: The Golden Years* by Watson Parker; *Wyatt Earp: Frontier Marshal* by Stuart Lake; and *Wyatt Earp: The Life Behind the Legend* by Casey Tefertiller.

Deadwood

∽ November 1876 ∽

Caleb Wayfinder had seen some hard times in Dallas, but none of those compared to a winter in Deadwood. To be honest, Caleb wasn't able to make much of a comparison since this was the first time he'd stepped foot in the Dakota Territories. But setting that foot upon the hard, frozen ground was more than enough to tell him what he needed to know.

Deadwood was damn cold in the winter.

Fortunately, there were plenty of ways for a man to warm himself.

Main Street was littered with more than enough humanity to create a fog in the air from the steam that drifted from folks' mouths. Smoke rose from the chimneys of more saloons than Caleb could count. As he walked along the street and did his best to avoid getting shoved or trampled, Caleb spotted the Bella Union, the Grand Central Hotel, the Bullock Hotel, and the Gem. On this cold November day, like most of the days before it, Caleb was headed for the Hazen House. It wasn't the biggest or best place in Deadwood, but it did steady business.

Of course, any place that served liquor and hosted plenty

of working girls was bound to do good business in Dead-wood.

Caleb took his hands from his pockets so he could pull his coat a bit tighter around him. His frame was losing some of the muscle that had been there a few years ago, but that was mainly due to his focus upon his newest endeavor. Doc liked to call it "the sporting life," but Caleb didn't find much sport in riding from town to town in stinking stagecoaches or being jostled for hours on end inside of a crowded train just so they could part another set of fools from their earnings. Doc's luck was holding up a bit more than Caleb's since they'd reached the Black Hills, which could have accounted for Caleb's sour disposition.

The cold touch of iron pressed against his ribs and back served as a constant reminder of how Caleb had earned whatever luck he did have. One of the pistols had been won in a particularly good game of seven-card stud back in Cheyenne. That gun was the last thing Caleb had won in the past few months and it had been put to good use since then. In fact, all of Caleb's guns had been getting plenty of use since he'd decided to throw in with the likes of Doc Holli-day.

Caleb smirked and shook his head as he twisted around to let a disgruntled miner walk past him. Right about now, Doc was probably enjoying some hot coffee at the Bella Union. Odds were just as good that Doc hadn't even gotten up and read the newspaper yet. Since Caleb's bankroll had run as dry as a poor miner's pan, he hadn't seen too much of Doc. After a few more paces down the street, Caleb was given an abrupt reminder of what had been filling his days as of late.

"Go to hell, you damned whore!" a man with long hair and a greasy beard spat as he stumbled through a nearby doorway.

Following the loudmouth outside was a fellow who looked more like a bear than a man. He filled up the door-way with a set of wide shoulders, bowed legs, and a gut that hung down low enough to cover his belt buckle. When he spoke, the thick brown beard covering most of his face parted like a furry sea. "That's why you don't get no women, Jake! You got a filthy mouth."

Strangely enough, the loudmouth looked at the big man as if he didn't even know he was there. Jake tried to straighten himself up, but looked more like he was being held up by a rope. "Go fuck yourself, Paul. That's all I got to say to you."

Despite the formality of Jake's tone, the words he spoke were blunt enough to smack the big man in the face and take away the smirk that had been there before.

"What did you say?" Paul asked.

Jake glanced back and forth nervously. There had been plenty of other folks out there with him before, but most of them knew well enough to give Jake and Paul some room after that. Seeing that he was on his own, Jake focused as best he could and squared his shoulders to the big man.

"You heard me," Jake said. "This is 'tween me and that whore."

Without taking his eyes off of Jake, Paul turned just enough to direct his next question over his shoulder and into the saloon behind him. "You hearin' this, Stephanie?"

As big as Paul was, he was shoved aside like a scarecrow as the short, stout blonde marched outside. She wasn't dressed in much more than a slip, which wasn't nearly enough to cover her generous curves and ample bosom. Even so, she seemed to have more than enough fire in her belly to ward off the bite of the winter wind.

"That prick didn't pay!" Stephanie shouted.

Jake's only response was a shrug as he said, "You didn't hold up your end."

"There's nothing wrong with my end. You just need to worry about yourself."

"There's plenty wrong with your end," Jake replied. "There's too much of it, for starters."

"Well, you're the first man I've ever met who couldn't get his pecker straight enough to get the job done."

Jake narrowed his eyes as if he'd been rapped on the nose. The next move he made was a quick, fumbling grab for the pistol tucked under his belt. By the time his hand found the weapon's grip, Jake was being knocked off his feet.

Caleb's shoulder slammed into Jake's chest like a kick from a mule and he wrapped his arms around Jake's midsection just to make certain Jake hit the ground first. Gritting his teeth and letting out a reflexive grunt made the Indian portion of Caleb's blood boil to the surface. At least that way Caleb had something softer than frozen mud upon which to land.

Most of the air was knocked from Jake's lungs when he hit the ground. Caleb scrambled up so he was on one knee with a tight grip around Jake's collar by the time the loudmouth got his bearings.

"You son of a b—" was all·Jake managed to say before his mouth was closed by Caleb's fist.

As Caleb punched Jake in the face, he found himself hoping the loudmouth would keep fighting back. Every time he felt the sting of bone against his knuckles, Caleb thought about his recent losing streak. By the time his current occupation passed through his mind, Caleb found another bit of reserve strength to put behind his fist.

"That's it, Caleb!" Stephanie shouted. "Hit him again!"

The blonde's shrill voice was still making its way through Caleb's ears when he saw a little foot wrapped in a boot with a pointed toe slam into Jake's ribs. Before she could get another kick in, Stephanie was hauled away by the big man who'd previously been filling up the nearby doorway.

"Come on, now," Paul said as he struggled to pull Stephanie back while also avoiding her flailing feet. "The Injun's got his hands full enough."

"Just one more, Paul! I owe it to the limp-dicked asshole."

Despite the fact that he was being pummeled and was too drunk to put up much of a defense, Jake gritted his teeth and started swinging at Caleb when he heard the insult that had just been sent his way. Jake managed to land a glancing blow off of Caleb's cheek, but that wasn't nearly enough to get the dusky-skinned man off of him. The bunch of men who'd stepped up to surround Caleb, on the other hand, stood a much better chance of getting that job done.

"Let him go," a man grunted from behind Caleb.

Pulling his fist back to put Jake down for good, Caleb replied, "Step back, mister. This fight's almost done."

"You're damn right it is," the man said. His words were punctuated by the metallic click of a pistol's hammer being thumbed back.

Caleb froze with his fist still hovering next to his right ear. His eyes darted to try and get a look at what he was up against as the bitter cold seeped back into muscles that had so recently been warmed through the unexpected scuffle. Since he wasn't quick to look behind him, Caleb felt the tap of a gun barrel against the back of his head to speed him along.

"Back away from him and be quick about it," the man behind Caleb said.

Jake showed Caleb a bloody grin as he scuttled back like an overweight crab and then climbed to his feet. "Good to see you boys," he said.

The man pointing the gun at Caleb was slender and several inches shy of six feet tall. His narrow face was streaked with dirt and set into a cautious scowl. "What's happening here?"

More than happy to step forward, Stephanie didn't pay any mind to the drawn guns. "Your friend's too cheap to pay for what I gave him, that's what."

"That whore barely even spread her legs to earn her pay," Jake replied as he leveled a trembling finger at her.

"I did plenty! It ain't my fault you weren't—"

"That's enough, Steph!" Caleb interrupted before the fires could be stoked any higher. "Did you do everything he wanted?"

"Well . . . no. But that's only because he couldn't—"

"Fine. Then you'll be paid for what you did do." Looking over to Paul, Caleb asked, "That fair enough?"

Reaching behind him, Paul accepted something from within the saloon. When he brought his meaty hand back around, it was wrapped around a sawed-off shotgun. "He'll also need to pay for the damage he done to this place when he threw his fit."

Jake shook his head and wagged a finger at the big man in the doorway. Now that half a dozen others were gathered around him, he wasn't having any trouble screwing up the courage to speak his mind. "To hell with that. I want my money back. All of it! Get the owner out here. I don't need to talk to nobody that gets paid to toss good folks out on their ears."

"You won't hear any different from the owner, Jake," Caleb insisted. "You did damage and you got something from Steph. All of that needs to be paid for. Once the account's settled, you can all be on your way."

For a moment, Caleb thought that Jake might do the sensible thing. Then, after a few seconds, Jake looked around and defiantly asked, "What if I don't?"

Caleb hadn't worked at the Hazen House for long, but he'd worked in more than enough saloons to know what was at stake. If an ignorant cuss like Jake could get out of paying what he owed while also getting the best of the saloon's two best bouncers in the process, he could show all the people gathered on that street what a bunch of spineless idiots were running that place. In a business fueled by equal parts liquor and greed, that simply would not suffice.

Caleb straightened up and shifted his coat open just enough to display a few of the guns he wore. "You'll pay. One way or another, you'll pay."

Jake had been coming to the Hazen House long enough to know that Caleb wasn't bluffing. Some of the men who'd come to help him on the street, however, weren't so well informed. One of those men went for his gun as Jake snapped his head around to try and convince him otherwise.

The man who went for his gun had the scruffy look of a miner who blamed Caleb for all the worthless dirt he'd sifted through over the years. He wasn't able to clear leather, however, before Caleb snatched one of his .44s from the double-rig holster strapped around his waist.

Caleb drew and fired as he dropped to one knee. His shot missed its target, but hissed close enough to the other man's head to get him running away from the saloon.

Of the others surrounding Jake, two of them kept their wits about them enough to draw weapons of their own. A clean-shaven man in his late twenties pulled a Smith & Wesson from its holster and fired an overly anxious shot into the ground. The second was a man in his forties who let out a profanity as he pulled his trigger and sent a piece of hot lead through the saloon's front window.

"Get the hell out of the way!" Paul shouted.

That was enough to get Caleb moving to one side. Unfortunately, that also cleared the way for one of Jake's friends to fire a shot at the doorway where Paul was still standing. The big man flinched as the bullet whipped past his head and sent splinters spraying out of the door frame.

Caleb let out a breath and focused on a single target. He aimed his pistol as if he was simply pointing his finger and then he squeezed his trigger. The gun barked once and ripped a bloody gash through the chest of one of the men who'd fired at him. When he shifted his eyes toward the clean-shaven man, he saw that one's gun barrel was already pointed directly at him.

In the space of half a second, Caleb decided he was probably going to die.

Even after the eternity it took for him to blink, he hadn't prepared himself for what was about to befall him.

Clang.

That sound came suddenly and echoed through Caleb's ears like a choir of angels. The clean-shaven man's eyes rolled up into their sockets and his knees buckled under his weight. As the man dropped, he revealed another fellow standing behind him. This fellow also looked even more like a miner, mainly due to the large, dented tin pan he held in both hands. Although it was made to sift through river water, the pan had done a mighty fine job of bouncing off the top of the clean-shaven man's head.

"Nothin' I can't stand more than an unfair fight," the man holding the tin pan said.

Another shot was fired, but this one blazed into the air and was followed by a steely voice. "Next man who shoots won't live to regret it!"

Caleb relaxed his trigger finger, but wasn't about to take his eyes off Jake. He didn't have to look at the new arrival to know it was Sheriff Bullock.

Bullock was a well-dressed man, but hardly a dandy. His lean features and sharp eyes made it more than clear that he meant whatever he happened to be saying at the time. "Holster your weapons before I gather them up," Bullock said.

"Start with them," Caleb said as he nodded toward Jake and what was left of his friends.

Jake was breathing as if he'd just run all the way in from the badlands. "Those two started it, Sheriff!" he grunted as he waved toward Caleb and Paul. "They meant to gun us all down in the street."

"He wanted his money back after he was done with me," Stephanie said as she stepped forward.

When Bullock looked over at Jake, there was a hint of a smirk on his face. "That true, Jake?"

"Yeah . . . well . . . she didn't . . ."

"He couldn't—"

Once more, Stephanie was cut short as Jake hastened to add, "She didn't do all of what I wanted, but she did do something."

"Then maybe you should pay for it."

"That's all we were asking for," Caleb said.

Bullock slowly shifted his eyes toward Caleb and obviously wasn't completely happy with what he found. He then looked over at the two men who were lying on the ground. "Pay what you owe, Jake."

"Fine," Jake muttered as he dug some money from his pocket and threw it at the man filling up Hazel House's front doorway. Paul let the money bounce off his chest without blinking an eye or moving a finger to catch it.

"But that Injun better answer for what he done!" Jake said. "He killed my cousin!"

As Bullock watched, the man who'd been shot rolled onto his side and let out a pained howl. Although it had looked as if he'd caught Caleb's round in the chest, it was obvious now that the bullet had ripped through the meat under his left arm.

"That man's not dead," Bullock pointed out.

"Yeah, well, it ain't my fault if the Injun is a bad shot. He should still rot in a cell for it."

"If I put him away," Bullock warned, "then I'll also have to drag in anyone else who may have fired a shot or caused any sort of harm in this instance. Is that what you want?"

Jake thought that over for all of two seconds before allowing his head to droop forward like a wilted flower. "No."

"Then get your friend to the doctor and have him stitched up." With that said, Bullock holstered his pistol and started to walk away. He paused and asked, "You going to square up the rest of that bill, Jake?"

Jake let out a measured breath, took some money from his pocket, and cocked back his arm as if he meant to throw it just as he'd tossed the first batch. Not only did he walk the remainder of that money over to Paul, Jake even stooped down to pick up what he'd thrown before so he could hand it all over properly.

"Nice and civil," Bullock said. "Just the way I like it."

Once the sheriff had walked away, the rest of the crowd began to disperse. It seemed that watching a man bleed from his armpit wasn't nearly as interesting as what had come before. Caleb stood his ground to ward off the rest of the men who'd stepped forward on Jake's behalf. Those fellows had plenty of glaring to do, but not much else. They left without another cross word.

Paul wore a wide smile that was only partially caused by the quick grope Stephanie gave him by way of a thank-you. "Hell of a way to earn a day's wages, huh?"

"Sure," Caleb said. "If you say so."

"I hear there's a game being held tonight and you should be able to sit in. That usually cheers you up."

"It would if I'd saved up enough to last more than a few hands. Thanks all the same, though."

"Then have a word with Steph a little later," Paul said. "She's gonna be grateful for at least the rest of the night."

Caleb couldn't decide what made him feel worse: the fact that he was truly too poor to ply his preferred trade or the fact that getting some private attention from a squat, foul-mouthed whore like Stephanie actually sounded appealing.

Deadwood was on its way to becoming a real stop along the gambler's circuit. Joining that group of saloons preferred by professional cardplayers and cheats alike was something every saloon owner prayed for. The big games attracted all kinds of big fish. Some games grew big enough to draw crowds away from the more well-known establishments and pack them into a place like the Hazen House. Leaning against the bar several hours after his tussle in the street, Caleb nodded to himself and grinned.

"Admiring your handiwork?"

The question drifted through the air in a voice that was colored by a distinctive, if somewhat slurred, Georgia drawl. Caleb didn't need to look to know who'd stepped up beside him to ask that question. The smell of whiskey was thick enough to bring the slender gentleman to his attention from several feet away.

"Hello, Doc," Caleb said.

Although he was a dentist by trade and still hung a shingle whenever he needed to earn some money or build up a bit of respectability in a town, John Henry Holliday didn't look like a dentist. The clothes he'd been wearing of late had drifted more toward the extravagant end of the spectrum and tonight was no exception.

His dark blue suit was tailored to fit the Georgian's slender frame while also falling nicely over the guns that were always strapped to his person. Doc's face was sunken, but not overly so. While the cold air ripping through the Dakotas had played havoc with Caleb and everyone else in Deadwood, it had done a bit of good for Doc's consumption. His coughing fits had been slightly fewer and farther between and when he did get them, they didn't confine him to bed as had been known to happen for men in his condition.

Actually, most men in Doc's condition would have been dead long ago. When he wasn't coughing up blood or wheezing into a handkerchief, Doc was inhaling more tobacco smoke and whiskey than fresh air. Even though he'd been given a month or two to live several times in the last several years, Doc still kept a smile upon his face.

"I'd say you haven't lost your touch when it comes to spreading the good word," Doc said.

Caleb took another satisfied look around and nodded. "When it comes to poker games, I'd say you were right."

"Of course I'm talking about poker. What better word is there?"

"Did you convince anyone else from the Bella Union crowd to stop by?"

"There was no convincing required, my good man," Doc replied. "A good game is a good game. It hardly matters where the tables are set up."

"I believe there's plenty of folks in town who would disagree on that score."

"That's just because those folks own their own saloons." Doc tapped the bar a few times, which was enough to catch the barkeep's attention and get a glass of whiskey sent his way. Even though he may not have spread himself equally among all the gambling establishments, Doc was well-known at nearly every one.

After tossing back the whiskey like it was nothing but

dirty water, Doc cleared his throat and looked at Caleb. "Why don't you join us for a game? It's been a while since we've played in the same hand."

"I don't have enough to buy in, Doc. If I did, I wouldn't be spending my nights tossing drunks into the street. Now, if you'll excuse me . . ." With that, Caleb gave Doc a quick wave and then waded into the crowd that was growing inside the saloon. Caleb looked even bulkier now that his coat was off and his shirtsleeves were rolled up. Inside the Hazen House, there was too much heat pouring out of too many bodies in close proximity for the outside chill to be much of a bother.

"Howdy, Doc," Paul said as he slapped the dentist's shoulder and sidled up next to him.

"Why, Paul Vasher, whatever have you been putting my friend through these recent weeks?"

Paul looked at Caleb, then back to Doc and then took another look around before asking, "You mean Caleb?"

"When we arrived in this camp, we were both right as rain. Now, just look at the poor soul."

Scowling at the tone in Doc's voice, Paul shrugged and lowered his own voice to something just above a whisper. "Between the two of ya, you're the one that's been soaking up all the luck. Or couldn't you tell as much by comparing the two of you's attire?"

Doc looked down at his perfectly tailored suit and the silver watch chain running from one half of his vest to the other. "I see your point. I heard there was some commotion in the street earlier."

"Sure there was, but it didn't amount to much."

"Was that man a part of it?"

Paul looked in the direction Doc pointed and saw the miner who'd stepped up on Caleb's behalf. "Damn right he was. That fella dropped one of Jake's buddies before he could get a shot off. Nearly caved his head in with a gold pan."

Nodding slowly, Doc eased his hand away from the gun hanging under his left arm. "Then I'll just let him surprise Caleb. Lord knows he could use some cheering up."

"I thought you two were friends," Paul said.

"That doesn't always mean he's happy to see me," Doc replied with a smirk. "Besides, my table is filling up and I always like to get a feel for my competition before the cards are dealt. If you'll excuse me."

Paul shrugged and let Doc go. When he looked over to Caleb, he saw his fellow bouncer wasn't going to be too surprised after all.

∽∾∽

Caleb twisted at the hip as his hand snapped down toward the gun at his side. His eyes narrowed reflexively to take in the man before him the way a hawk summed up a nearby mouse. The miner was tall and a bit meatier than most of the other men who shared his trade. While a good portion of miners had been slimmed down by the lean times of their chosen profession, this one looked more like a cowboy. His shoulders weren't stooped from hunching over a section of river for days on end. His legs weren't wobbly from crouching and his eyes didn't have the anxious sharpness of a man who'd spent his life searching behind grains of dirt and thin layers of silt for the one glittering bit of hope that would put some food on his table.

The man in front of Caleb at the moment had a prominent nose that jutted from a long face. His hair was cut short, but at odd angles that gave away the fact that he'd either cut it himself with a knife or had a drunkard for a barber. Thick whiskers sprouted from his chin and upper lip, but none of those things struck Caleb as much as the gun that was slung high in a well-worn holster. Obviously, this miner was more concerned with his draw than with keeping the pistol out of his way while working the river.

"Don't shoot," the miner said as he raised his hands well above hip level. "I'm the one who dented my pan on that gunman's head, remember?"

Already nodding, Caleb shifted his hand away from his gun. "Sure I remember. Your drinks are on me tonight, friend. You want anything else around here, just let me know."

Keeping one hand up, the miner extended his other. "I'll take a drink or two, but an introduction was all I'm after."

"Caleb Wayfinder," he said while shaking the miner's hand.

"Sounds like an Indian name."

"It is," Caleb snarled.

"No offense meant. Just pointing out a fact."

After spending his entire life hearing the smug, often-times hateful comments made about his family tree, Caleb could recognize that brand of contempt from miles away. There was nothing of that sort coming from the miner's scruffy face.

"Pardon my tone," Caleb said. "It's been a hell of a day."

The miner grinned. "You don't have to tell me. I was there, remember? My name's Jack Johnson, but friends call me Creek."

"Now that sounds like an Indian name."

"Heh. It's just short for Turkey Creek."

"There a story behind that?"

"Yeah," Johnson replied, "but it's a long one. If you got the time to share a few of them drinks with me, I'm sure I'll get around to telling it."

Caleb's eyes drifted toward the poker tables that were quickly filling up. "I don't have the time. The games are getting started."

Still nodding slightly, Johnson glanced toward the tables. It was plain to see that he wasn't paying too much attention to what was going on there. Just then, one of the girls who worked the Hazen House slipped her arm around Johnson's waist.

"He's a friend of mine," Caleb said to her. "Be sure to treat him right."

The working girl was a bit on the plump side, but only to the point that it gave her more voluptuous curves. Long brown hair hung freely along her back and was splayed over her shoulders as if she'd tumbled out of bed moments ago. The smile on her face made it look like she wanted to go right back under those same covers.

"Caleb's kept more than a few rowdies away from me lately," she said. "Any friend of his is a friend of mine." Nudging Johnson playfully, she added, "That bodes well for you, mister."

Chuckling as he patted Johnson on the shoulder, Caleb told him, "I'd take her up on that if I was you."

Creek Johnson was a man and he had a pulse, which meant he was feeling the effects of the curvaceous woman's probing hands. Judging by how much he squirmed and fretted, however, he was putting up one hell of a fight to keep from being dragged away to her room.

"Actually . . . uh . . . there was something else I wanted to say to you, Caleb," Johnson sputtered.

Genuinely impressed with the other man's resolve, Caleb shifted so he could look directly at him. "Are you sure about that?"

"Yes, but this little lady's making it awfully hard to concentrate."

"You mind giving us a minute, Sally?" Caleb asked.

The curvaceous woman peeled herself away from Johnson and put on a pouting face that would have been enough to change Johnson's mind if she'd kept it aimed at him for much longer. "All right, but be quick. I don't know how long I can wait." With that, she slowly walked away. Sally made sure to keep her hands on Creek for as long as the length of her arms would allow.

Caleb couldn't help but laugh at the way Creek Johnson fidgeted from one foot to another. "You sure you don't want to reconsider? Sally's awfully popular and hasn't caused any street fights since I've been here."

"Oh, I'm not gonna let her get too far," Creek replied. "But since I've got the chance, I'd like to ask what I came to ask you."

"Sounds serious."

"It's serious to me and may be mighty profitable for you."

"A business proposition, huh?" Caleb asked.

Creek nodded. "I've only been mining for a short while,

but I've done well enough to hold my own where plenty of others in these hills have lost their shirts."

"I was starting to think you weren't a miner."

"You mean the pan I was carryin' around wasn't a big enough hint?"

"I could carry a doctor's bag, but that don't make me a doctor. I've learned to trust my instincts where reading folks is concerned."

"I bet you get plenty of instincts bouncing drunks out of places like this one."

"Actually, I got them from owning a place like this. Well," Caleb added while taking a look around, "a place better than this."

"You owned a saloon here in Deadwood?"

"No. I had a place in Dallas. I sold out to my partner so I could move along and make my fortune in gambling."

While nobody could have missed the sarcasm in Caleb's tone, Johnson knew better than to draw attention to an obviously sore subject. "Luck favors them who works for it," Creek said optimistically.

"Which brings me back to your proposition," Caleb said. "Why don't you say your piece before someone gets accused of cheating and needs to be tossed out of here?"

Johnson leaned toward Caleb and lowered his voice to a fast whisper. "There's some men moving in on my claim and I could use someone like you on my side."

"Someone like me?"

"Someone who can handle himself in a fight. I seen plenty of scuffles in and around these saloons, but most men involved run through them like chickens with their heads cut off. You didn't panic and that tells me you can use that gun of yours for something more than a decoration around your waist."

Caleb nodded as he rearranged his thoughts regarding Creek Johnson. "Go on."

"I've been doing some good business and if I do a bit more, I'll be able to get out of this mining game before it breaks me like it breaks everyone else."

"Don't you have partners?"

"Sure I do," Johnson replied. "But they're the ones I'm worried about. One of 'em's in debt up to his ears to a man down in Chinatown and the other's trying to bring in another partner who's supposed to make our money situation brighter than Judgment Day."

"And that's not a good thing?" Caleb asked.

Johnson scowled, took another look around the saloon, and lowered his voice another notch. "Not when the man saying those words is full of shit and wouldn't have any problem in siding with known killers."

"And I take it you're not excited about that kind of prospect?"

"You got that right. The men who I thought I could trust have started asking some questions I don't like. They've been asking about how we could cover our tracks if we needed to get the hell out of the Dakotas and have even mentioned meeting a few people who can't exactly be seen by the likes of Sheriff Bullock."

"And those would be the known killers?" Caleb asked. "Anyone I might know?"

"There's a few local boys who you may or may not have heard about, but there's someone else who's coming in from New Mexico way that could be real trouble."

"Who?"

After a bit of a pause, Johnson let out a sigh. "I don't know for certain. That's where I was hoping to get some help from you. If there is something rotten going on, I doubt my partners trust me enough to let it slip in front of me and I don't have the time to wait for them to get sloppy. Someone else might have better luck in seeing what's going on, but mostly I need backup."

"And what makes you think you can trust me?"

"I've asked around about you and haven't heard anything too bad," Johnson replied with a grin. "I know you're no miner and ain't friends with my partners, which means I can trust you more than I trust them."

"What's in it for me?"

"A percentage of the gold that would have gone to my partners if they hadn't tried to stab me in the back."

"And what if they do come around and expect their share?"

"A hundred dollars. Considering that we should be able to tell which way my partners are leanin' pretty damn quick, I'd say that's fair."

Caleb might have been able to win a lot more than that in a good poker game, but he hadn't made that much in all the time he'd been forced to work at the Hazen House. As he thought it over, he could see Johnson growing more uncomfortable.

"All right, one-fifty," Johnson said. "But it could get rough. If I'm right, the men my partners are siding up with ain't the most reputable. None of them will be happy to know they been found out by me."

"Keep it at one hundred," Caleb replied.

Johnson seemed pleasantly surprised to hear that. Before he could get too happy, he saw a glint in Caleb's eye.

"But if you do find yourself without these traitorous partners of yours," Caleb added, "I want to take their place. Not just a percentage of their share. I want a full share. If I'm to put my neck on the line for this deal, that's only fair."

For a moment, Johnson didn't say anything. Caleb did have plenty of experience in reading faces and even he was having a hard time figuring out what was going through the grizzled miner's head. Finally, Johnson started to nod.

"I can see I was right about you, Caleb. You ain't just some thickheaded bouncer who knows how to handle a shooting iron. That's a real smart offer. Can't say as I'm glad you came up with it, but it's real smart."

Caleb was the first to extend his hand. "So is it a deal?"

"Yeah, it's a deal."

"Great." Slapping the bar with the palm of his hand, Caleb raised his voice so that he could catch the barkeep's attention as well as be heard by most of the people in the saloon. "Give me a round for the man that stepped up for me today!"

When Johnson started squirming again, it wasn't anything like when he'd been in the center of Sally's attention. "I wanted to keep this quiet, if you don't mind."

"You already been seen talking to me," Caleb grumbled under his breath. "At least this gives a reason to anyone who's interested. Come find me here later tonight around two." A bottle of whiskey was placed onto the bar next to a mostly clean shot glass. "Here you go, friend," Caleb said loudly. "Enjoy it."

Johnson nodded and plastered a smile onto his face. Raising his glass, he looked around to find a bunch of wobbly men eyeing the bottle in his hand. They lost interest when they realized Johnson didn't intend on sharing.

"How about you bring that along to my room?" Sally asked as she sidled up next to Johnson. "We can share it without so many people watching. I still need to reward you for your bravery."

"I think I'd like that," Johnson said as he draped an arm around Sally. "Very much, as a matter of fact."

Caleb kept his eyes pointed toward the poker tables, but was more focused on what was happening at the edge of his field of vision. A subtle grin worked its way onto his face. The more he thought about Creek Johnson's business proposal, the more possibilities sprang to mind.

[3]

Doc hadn't left his chair for hours. He didn't know exactly how many hours it had been, for he didn't bother looking at his watch when he played. More often than not, he would have had too much whiskey in his system to care what time it was anyhow.

For the last several hands, Doc had barely even looked at his cards. Instead, his slightly hooded eyes gazed around the table at the other players, sizing them up carefully. To Doc's left was a skinny man named Vasily who spoke with a heavy Russian accent. He played tight as a drum and didn't drink. The next man around the table claimed to be a prominent local businessman and he had the big belly to back up his claims of easy living. Next to that one was a drunk named Ed who was easier to read than a children's storybook. Between that drunk and Doc was a woman named Alice Ivers. Everyone called her Poker Alice.

Alice had a rounded, pretty face that was framed by soft, well-maintained curls of light brown hair that fell just past her shoulders. Her eyes were kind but always on the prowl, and her hands were smoother than the silk of her expensive dress. Of the others at the table, she was the one who was dressed as nicely as Doc. When she caught Doc looking her way, she would always return his smile or shake her head at his occasional wink.

"Is it my turn?" Doc asked innocently.

Vasily kept his back straight and his voice tense when he replied, "You know it is, Mr. Holliday. Please take it."

"You seem awfully anxious. Perhaps I should fold."

"Whatever you do, do it soon, please."

Coughing once as he peeked at the cards he'd been dealt, Doc shrugged and tossed in enough chips to cover the bet. "There you go."

Vasily called without hesitation, leaving the businessman next to him to make his move. " 'Bout damn time," the rotund man grunted as he tossed in his chips.

"All right, then," Alice said. "No need to get impatient. How many cards you want, Doc?"

"Whatever you see fit to give me, darlin'."

"How about you take the guesswork out of it?"

"Jesus Christ," the businessman snapped as he shifted his bulk against his chair. "You two wanna smooch, then get a damn room. Otherwise play cards."

Doc grinned in a way that made him look livelier than all three of the other men combined. For a man in the advanced stages of consumption, that was no small feat. "Better make it two, then."

Alice flipped the cards to Doc and filled in the other players' hands. When it was her turn, she set the deck down.

"Standing pat?" Doc asked. "If I wasn't so supremely confident in my good fortune, I'd be worried."

"Worried enough to fold?" Alice asked.

Doc watched her for another second before tossing in a ten-dollar bet. "Almost, but not quite."

Vasily smirked and counted out his chips. "You drink so much, Holliday. I think it makes this too easy for me. I raise to fifty dollars."

The businessman let out a heavy sigh and raised his cards less than a quarter inch off the table.

"Everybody watch out," Doc slurred. "The big man is making his move."

Randal started to shake his head and tighten his grip on his cards as if he was bracing to toss them into the middle of the table.

"What business do you own, anyway?" Doc asked.

"Pardon me?"

"Your business, Randal. What is it?"

Randal shifted in his chair and replied, "I'm part owner of Nye's Opera House."

"Really? Is that the one that's about to be shut down from lack of interest?"

"Lack of culture is more like it."

Doc leaned back and cocked his head as if he was genuinely taken aback by what he'd just heard. "As a member of this community, I am sorely perturbed."

"You been in Deadwood less than a month, Holliday, and that's only because Sheriff Bullock hasn't drummed you out yet."

Looking over at Alice, Doc said, "There are plenty of good theaters in these parts. I hear the miners in a camp about half this size put on a dandy *Macbeth*."

"What the hell did you just say?" Randal sputtered.

Doc was quick to change his tone and stare across the table with wide eyes. "Sorry about that. My mistake." His smirk quickly returned as he looked back toward Alice. "You're supposed to call it the Scottish play."

Randal glared at Doc and then stared at his cards. Gritting his teeth, he glared at Doc some more and then stared at his cards again with such intensity that he practically burned a hole through them. Shaking his head, he tossed his cards into the muck.

Ed looked at most of his cards and then folded.

Alice did a good job of keeping herself from giggling, but couldn't help but look in Doc's direction. "I call."

Despite the confidence that was ingrained onto Doc's face, he didn't wait too long before tossing his own hand onto the rest of the discards.

"All of that just to fold?" Vasily asked. "What kind of game is this?"

"I ask that same question about the big, dusty world we live in," Doc spouted. "Someday, perhaps a bard will put the answers into a fine production for all to see. Let's just hope he gets an audience. I suppose he'd better stay away from Nye's Opera House."

Randal muttered a few obscenities and got up so he could reach across the table for Doc's throat. Before Randal could make it halfway, Doc had reached under his coat to draw the pistol holstered under his arm.

Randal froze for a moment before easing himself back onto his chair. "My apologies."

Doc kept his eye on Randal until the businessman averted his gaze and squirmed as if he wanted to crawl away. Only then did Doc holster his pistol. When he glanced over at Alice, he saw her reach for something in a pocket that was just out of sight. Doc poured himself a drink as Alice took out a slender cigar and placed it between her teeth.

"Care for a light?" Doc asked.

Alice shook her head. "It's fine the way it is."

"As are you, darlin'. As are you."

The game went on for another two hours, but it felt like a different table altogether. Ed was all but passed out most of the time. Vasily hardly said a word and Doc was able to keep Randal's temper at a constant boil. Eventually, the businessman was barely able to contain himself when Doc threw his chips into the middle of the table.

"It's getting late," Randal said after losing a pot that robbed him of all but a few white chips. "I'd like to be going now."

Seeing that Randal's eyes were on him, Doc tipped his hat and said, "By all means, sir."

Even after getting Doc's permission, Randal wasn't quick to get up. He shuffled toward the front door and dragged himself toward the street. Since most of his chips had wound up in front of Doc or Alice, he didn't even bother stopping to cash the remainders in.

"I suppose this game is over?" Vasily asked.

"I hear there's a game every now and then at the Bella Union," Doc replied. "They may not always be as exciting as this one, but they can usually get fairly interesting."

"Perhaps I will look in on you there." The Russian took his money and showed Doc and Alice a beaming smile. He then turned and headed to cash in his chips.

Doc cleared his throat and then poured some more whiskey down it.

"I do believe he'll take you up on that offer, Doc," Alice said.

While feeling the burn of the liquor work its way through his system, Doc replied, "And our friend the theater owner will probably join him if he gets the notion that he can put me in my place."

Alice did a good job of keeping her smile under control. When she got up and gathered her winnings, she looked at Doc with just the right amount of friendliness to avoid suspicion. "You've got a real talent for rubbing people the wrong way. Just be careful you don't upset the wrong man."

"Good point," Doc replied as he hacked noisily into his handkerchief. "I wouldn't want to jeopardize my bright future."

Cocking her head in response to the sarcasm that dripped from Doc's voice, Alice said, "You know what I mean."

"Of course I do. It would be a shame to break up our little syndicate at the Bella Union."

"We'd sure hate to lose you."

"You may for the next few weeks. Isn't there going to be a string of games being hosted in Kansas?"

Alice nodded. Even though she was dressed better than every other woman in or around the Hazen House, she didn't carry herself with the airs that usually went along with such trappings. And though she and Doc were both in their mid-twenties, she seemed almost motherly when she reached out to rub her hand along his cheek.

"We're all dying of something," she said. "Just because

you wear yours on your sleeve doesn't make it any more or less fatal than what's coming for the rest of us."

"On my sleeve, but mostly in my handkerchief."

"There's that smart mouth again. I swear it's a talent. Take care of yourself, Doc. And stop sulking," she said sharply. After flattening the hand that she'd rubbed against Doc's cheek, she smacked him just hard enough to catch his attention. "It doesn't suit you."

"What on earth was that for?" Doc asked with genuine surprise.

"To sober you up for the walk back to the the Grand." Alice kept her eyes on him as she turned around and headed for the front door. Her lips curled into a smile that somehow even managed to make the unlit cigar between her teeth look cute.

Doc shook his head and watched her go. Once she was out of his sight, Doc strode over to the bar and knocked on it. "Bottle of whiskey, my good man," he said to the barkeep.

"Didn't I just give you one a while ago?"

"Why yes, and now it's gone. I'll have another."

The barkeep started to reach for a bottle similar to the first one he'd served Doc, but then reached for a more expensive brand. When he turned around again, he saw Doc staring him down with eyes that were much sharper than a man in his condition should have had.

"Switching brands on me?" Doc asked. "Now I see why I prefer the Bella Union."

"Sorry, I just thought you'd prefer . . ."

The bartender's halfhearted explanation was cut short when Doc reached out to snatch the bottle away from him. Doc's other hand reached for his coat, which caused the bartender to jump as if something had stung the bottom of his foot.

"Cash these in for me," the Georgian said as he piled several poker chips onto the bar.

When he saw those chips, the bartender let out a whistle and said, "Those are the big ones. I'll have to go in the back."

"I'll be waiting right here." Doc turned so he could lean back against the bar. Spotting a familiar face, he grinned and held up his bottle.

"I hope you counted those chips already," Caleb said as he walked over and stood at the bar next to Doc.

"Are you worried I may be cheated?"

"As drunk as you are, he may assume you won't know any better."

"I just hope he also assumes he'd get a bullet through his skull if he tried to short me on my winnings."

Smirking, Caleb said, "After all the times we've pulled similar tricks, I'm amazed you can say that with a straight face."

Doc pulled in a breath and let it out noisily. "I suppose you're right. Still, I'm not about to become one of the suckers who deserve to be plucked. That is . . . if that made any sense."

"I know what you meant. Why don't you call it a night?"

"Because I'd be lying," Doc replied as he filled his glass with whiskey. "I should call it morning."

Caleb wondered if he should go through the trouble of clarifying himself, but knew that Doc was just being difficult. Before he could say anything more, the barkeep reemerged from the back room with a wad of money in his hands.

"I was just looking for you, Caleb," the barkeep said.

"What for?"

"To make sure this money gets out of here safely. Then again, I'm sure Mr. Holliday isn't in any real danger."

"You see what happens when I forget to hang a shingle?" Doc asked. "Folks forget to address me by my proper moniker."

"Moni . . . what?" the barkeep asked while scowling as if he'd smelled something rotten. "Here's your money."

Tucking the money away, Doc said, "You may walk me to the door, Caleb, but don't get any ideas. I will not allow you to take advantage of me."

Caleb walked next to Doc, but couldn't help noticing the

perplexed look on the barkeep's face. "He's drunk, Will. That's all there is to it."

The barkeep shrugged and then started making his rounds to refresh the glasses that were still being guarded by paying customers.

Once they were outside, Doc took his hand from his pocket and extended it toward Caleb. "Here's your cut for tonight's game. You keep steering men like that our way and there'll be plenty more."

Caleb took the money, but didn't look happy about it. He counted it, winced, and then counted it again. "There's too much here."

While Doc's Southern drawl tended to get thicker when he was drunk, the first touch of cold night air against his face was enough to ease it back a notch. "You've earned it. Not only did I get a fine read on that Russian, but that businessman got angry enough to drop most of what he brought straight into my lap. Does he really own half of Nye's Opera House?"

"The hell if I know."

"If you go to Alice, she'll probably toss a share your way as well. After what she won tonight, she owes it to you. And don't look so down in the mouth, either. Both of those men we played tonight will most definitely be seeking us out at the Bella Union. That," Doc said with a wolfish grin, "is when the real fun will start."

Lifting his chin to pull in a breath of fresh air, Doc nearly filled his lungs before coughing and then hacking it up loudly. The fit subsided quicker than usual and when it was through, Doc fished in his pockets for a handkerchief.

"Seems like the mountain air is doing you some good," Caleb pointed out.

"Either that or the whiskey." Doc squinted down at the money in Caleb's hand. "Another payday like that and you should be able to stake yourself in a game for a change."

"That's just the thing. I don't know if I should get into another game."

"Then stick with the arrangement as is. The two of us still work well enough together to make it profitable all around.

One of us may even save up enough to get back into the saloon owner's game again."

Caleb looked down at his own boots and grumbled, "I don't know if I want that, either."

"It's been a long night and I'm feeling more tired as this conversation wears on."

"I want to earn my own money doing my own kind of work," Caleb explained.

"I thought that's what we were doing."

"That's what you're doing. Ever since my luck turned, I've been steering the right folks your way and keeping the wrong ones from getting too close."

Doc laughed under his breath as he removed his hat and ran his bony fingers through dark blond hair. "I don't exactly need an angel on my shoulder."

"You sure about that?"

Doc stopped so he could scowl directly at Caleb without running the risk of tripping over something or someone on Main Street. "Yes. I believe I am sure about that. Why do you ask?"

"Because sometimes it seems like luck's the only reason you haven't been shot dead yet."

"You care to try yours?" Doc asked in a voice with more than enough of a steely edge to raise the hackles on the back of Caleb's neck.

Caleb squared his shoulders to Doc and stood toe-to-toe with him.

Doc no longer seemed like a man who'd spent the better part of his last several years being eaten alive by disease. The Georgian dentist stood tall and glared at Caleb with eyes that would have been at home in any predator's head.

"Most of the trouble that comes our way could have been dodged if you weren't so anxious to catch it," Caleb said.

"Are you blaming me for your losing streak? I've had my share of them, so you'll take yours like a man."

"It's not about the cards," Caleb explained. "It's about the fights and the threats and knocking on death's door so many times that it's starting to lose its appeal."

Doc shook his head. "It's not losing anything. You're not the first one to get into a scrape, Caleb, and don't tell me you didn't enjoy your last one just a little bit."

As much as Caleb wanted to step up and tell Doc he was wrong, he simply couldn't. Drunk or not, Doc was way too good at sniffing out a bluff.

"And don't tell me you miss running that saloon of yours," Doc continued. "The Busted Flush was a hell of a place. It probably still is, but you'd still be there if you wanted to keep riding that rail. Folks do what they want to do."

"Sometimes they just use the cards they've been dealt."

"If that was the case, I'd be laying with my feet up in a sickbed right about now. More likely, I'd be in a coffin."

"It's easy to be optimistic when you're riding high, Doc."

And in the blink of an eye, the edge in Doc's voice was gone. He let out a breath, which was more of a ragged wheeze, and then draped an arm over Caleb's shoulder. Doc continued walking down Main Street and dragged Caleb right along with him. "I know all about losing at cards. Why do you think I went to school all those years to learn my proper trade? Every man needs a solid place to fall."

"I can't pull teeth for a living, but there is something else."

"Here it is. Finally!"

"I may be taking part in a job that could lead to more money than I've seen in a while."

Doc let out a sputtering laugh. "That's not saying much."

"Yeah, but this could have some long-term advantages."

When Doc looked back at Caleb, he studied him carefully. "Sounds promising. Just so long as it's not some half-witted scheme put together by one of the crazed miners scurrying through this camp."

"He's not crazed, but he is a miner."

"Those fellows may have good intentions," Doc warned, "but they don't have the reliability to back them up."

"Funny words coming from a professional gambler."

"Point taken. Proceed."

"The man's name is Creek Johnson," Caleb said as he rubbed his hands together and walked alongside Doc. "He's got a claim that may get taken out from under him and he needs someone to back him up. For the job, I get a percentage of the profits and possibly a very lucrative partnership of my own."

"I'm no miner, but anyone who lives around here knows that most claims aren't worth much. A percentage of not much is even less."

"This one's valuable enough to fight over," Caleb replied. "That always means something. Even if it's not, I'm sure we can figure out a way to come out ahead where all these tempers are flaring and all this money is being tossed around. Gold or not, these men got to have enough to buy up land. Since they're not flat broke, they must be carrying at least some cash around with them."

Doc nodded and licked his bottom lip. "Another good point. Sounds like an endeavor with some potential."

"I should be able to handle myself, but I may need someone to watch my back. You spend a lot of time in saloons . . . almost as much as the miners who come to town when they're not working their claims. You could listen for a few things. You could possibly move your game to another saloon if I find out there might be someone there worth listening to."

Still nodding, Doc said, "That shouldn't be a problem. Fresh blood is good in any game. Is that the only sort of backing you may need?"

"Do you still have that gun I gave you?"

Doc flipped open his coat to reveal the pearl-handled .38 that hung under his arm.

"Gussied it up a bit, I see," Caleb said as he tapped the pistol's handle.

"Doesn't affect my aim."

"Which, I hear, has slipped since you've taken to drinking whiskey as if it was water."

Doc shrugged, closed his coat, and straightened his lapels. "I can hit a man sitting across from me at a poker table. That's mostly all I require. If I ever find myself dueling in the street, I'll find a shotgun."

"Think you could find one if I run afoul of some crazed miners?" Caleb asked.

"Sure. That is, unless there's a good game being held at one of these new saloons you're forcing me to try."

Despite Doc's words, there was no mistaking the look in his eyes. He would back Caleb's play.

"All right, then," Caleb said as an excited fire built up inside of him. "Let's see if I can leave this town as something other than a bouncer."

{4}

The next morning, Caleb was up and eager to start his newest endeavor. Having lost the need to get up at sunrise, he found it more than a little difficult to drag himself out of a perfectly warm bed and into the bitter cold of a Deadwood morning. Dragging Doc from the comfort of his room at the Grand Central Hotel was another matter entirely. Breakfast consisted of warm mush and bacon. He'd barely tasted his first cup of coffee before Caleb spotted the reason for getting up so early in the first place. A few minutes later, Caleb and his guide were in their saddles and putting the mining camp behind them.

Creek Johnson rode a lean mustang and rarely kept to a single trail for very long. Just following Johnson was enough to give Caleb a lesson in riding through rugged country. The horse Caleb had bought was meant as nothing more than an alternative to buying stage or train tickets, and the animal was already starting to wheeze worse than Doc on a bad day.

"How much farther to get to this claim of yours?" Caleb asked.

Johnson looked over his shoulder and shook his head dismissively. "We're almost there."

"You said that a few miles back."

"I was right then and I'm even righter now. You'll catch sight of my spot as soon as we clear these trees."

Before Caleb could gripe any more, his horse carried him through the most recent tangle of sharp branches and into a clearing no more than a dozen square yards in size. When he saw Johnson climb down from his saddle, Caleb asked, "This is it?"

"Sure it is. That river's coughed up more'n enough to be promising."

The river Johnson was so proudly pointing toward was currently a rough stretch of frozen water that was more crooked than some of the roots sticking up from the hardened ground.

"It ain't much in this time of year," Johnson admitted, "but all them kinks and turns make for some mighty fine panning spots. And them rocks over there," he added while walking toward a cluster of boulders about a foot shorter than he was, "is where the real money comes from."

Grudgingly, Caleb climbed down from his horse's nearly broken back. In his mind, he was thanking himself for asking for most of his fee in advance. He was also figuring out a way to describe this scene to Doc so that he didn't come out as an idiot who believed another crazed miner.

"What's so good about those rocks?" Caleb asked. "Is one of them made of gold?"

Johnson was at the largest of the rocks by now and he looked back at Caleb with a gnarled grin on his face. "Not hardly. Come over here and take a look for yerself."

Since he'd already come this far, Caleb went a little farther.

Squatting down and lifting up a thick canopy of branches, Johnson pointed at the rock again. "Go on and have a look."

Caleb thought he'd seen a few bad winters when he'd lived in Texas, but he'd never felt his bones ache or hear his knees creak as badly as they did now. The very notion of squatting down next to Johnson was so unappealing, he considered heading back to town right then and there.

"This'd better be good," Caleb grunted as he hunkered down to look at what was under the branches. The moment he caught sight of what the branches had been covering, Caleb needed to grab onto the rock for support. Only part of the reason for that involved him nearly losing his footing against the frozen soil.

"Holy shit," Caleb muttered. "Is that what it looks like?"

Johnson nodded like a proud poppa. "There's a cave under there that puts the river to shame."

Caleb leaned forward a bit to get a closer look at the cave Johnson was talking about. Although it wasn't much bigger than a small animal's den, there was more than enough gold in the walls to catch the light from outside and reflect it back at him. "How far in does that go?"

"Don't know yet. I've barely been able to wriggle in there and dig some of that gold out to make certain it was the genuine article."

"And?"

Johnson nodded. "It was. But, like I said before, getting in there is the rough part."

Caleb pulled back the canopy a bit more and discovered most of the opening to the small cave had previously been covered by the branches. After hunkering down to get an even closer look, Caleb figured a man might have to crawl on his belly like a snake if he was to get into the rock with enough room to bring a small pickaxe.

"How much gold do you suppose is in there?" Caleb asked.

"Hard to say. The stuff on the walls is the only stuff we can see from here and I think a lot of that's dust. The good news is that the cave goes in quite a ways before heading down."

"You got in there enough to tell all that?"

Johnson winced at the very thought of that. "Hell no, but I got in far enough to pour some water and watch it flow. From what I could hear, this may just be covering a cave that's a hell of a lot bigger than this."

Letting out a low whistle, Caleb listened for an echo. He

heard just enough to lend credence to Johnson's words. Caleb pushed off of the rock with one hand so he could climb back to his feet. As his hand slipped under the canopy, he was able to see the branches hadn't fallen there naturally, but had been woven like a rough kind of quilt and laid there to hide the rock.

Caleb glanced around and didn't see anyone else in the area. He took a step back and let his arm hang just enough to put his pistol within easy reach. "Do your partners know about all of this?"

Johnson nodded. "Yeah. That's what's got me worried. Soon as we found this spot, the others got real quiet and started disappearin' on me. I got an offer to sell my share of the claim and when I refused, they disappeared again. A friend of mine down at the Nuttall Saloon said he saw one of my partners meeting with a gunman by the name of Mayes."

"Mayes? That name sounds familiar." Caleb didn't have to think long before he snapped his fingers and added, "He's supposed to run with Dave Rudabaugh."

"I heard that might be the case, but I wasn't so quick to believe it. You think it's true?"

"Rudabaugh usually sticks close to Texas and New Mexico. I grew up there and owned a saloon in Dallas, so I've heard plenty about him. Seems strange for a man like him to come all the way up here."

"I don't know if Rudabaugh is here or not," Johnson said, "but some of his friends sure are. The man who told me all this ain't got much of a reason to lie."

Still thinking like a saloon owner, Caleb thought about what Johnson had said. The Nuttall Saloon wasn't far from the Bella Union and it wasn't exactly known as being the cultural center of Deadwood. Since the place wasn't even safe enough for Doc to play there on a regular basis, it could have been a second home to anyone who rode with the likes of Arkansas Dave Rudabaugh.

Even with all of those things seeming to hold water, something else was still bothering Caleb. "Why show this to me?" he asked.

Johnson blinked once, but didn't seem surprised by the question. "I thought you should know what you're getting into."

"And you're not worried that I might try to make a move of my own?"

Having presumably kept one hand in his pocket all this time for warmth, Johnson moved that hand just enough to show he was holding his gun and aiming it at Caleb. "I ain't too worried, but I am rethinking my choices as far as gun hands go."

Caleb smirked and nodded at the fact that he'd had a fast one pulled on him for a change. He then showed Johnson a move that was plenty fast enough to earn back some respect. Not only did Caleb draw his pistol, but he had enough time to slap the other man's gun away.

"Well, now," Johnson sputtered in openmouthed surprise. "Seems I was right to come to you after all."

"Maybe. What makes you so certain I won't just put a bullet in you so I can chip this gold out as I please?"

"I already got men gunning for me, remember? If I don't find someone halfway trustworthy to watch my back, I'll be dead before sundown today. If it ain't you that's pulling the trigger, it'll be one of my partners or Lord only knows who else. Besides, us two can get that gold out, but one man won't get so far. If you harm me, you'll just need to bring in more men who'll get ideas of their own."

Caleb stared a hole through Johnson's skull before slowly lowering his gun. "You still willing to cut me in on this as one of your partners?"

"That was if things go wrong and my old partners go through with trying to get rid of me."

"Would you be so worried about hiring someone to cover your back if that wasn't already the case?"

"I suppose not."

"And if your partners truly are siding with known killers," Caleb added, "I doubt they're planning on letting things pan out quietly."

Despite the fact that he was still holding his hands up and

afraid to make a move, Johnson grinned and said, "I was pretty much thinking along those same lines."

"Then why not cut through the bullshit and get to business?" After dropping his gun into its holster, Caleb extended that hand to Johnson. "Make me your partner right now."

Johnson's background as a miner shone through when he straightened up and shook Caleb's hand as if he was signing the Declaration of Independence. His eyes took on a sharp glint and his jaw set into a straight, solid line. "Partners."

"It'll be fifty-fifty, Creek," Caleb warned. "I won't have it any other way."

"We'll split it right down the middle. Hell, that bumps up my percentage anyhow."

Under most other circumstances, Caleb would have asked for something a little more binding. But it was plain to see on Creek Johnson's face that nothing else, legal or otherwise, would have held up as much as that handshake. Once the deal was sealed, Caleb looked toward the small hole in the nearby rocks.

"Now how the hell do you intend on getting that gold out of there?" Caleb asked.

"I'll be picking up a load of dynamite later on today. Should be enough to take out enough of this rock so all's we got to deal with is a hole in the ground."

"What about the gold I can see inside of there?" Caleb asked with a wince.

Creek waved that off like he was shooing away a fly. "I ain't going through all of this to settle for dust. There could be a goddamn mother lode down that hole."

"Or there could just be a family of rabbits."

Although he thought about that for a second, Creek didn't consider it for much more than that. "No man gets rich by settling for the first thing he sees. I been mining long enough to know that dust leading back into rock like that is pointing toward something a whole lot better."

"What if that dynamite buries that cave under a load of rock?" Caleb asked.

"Then at least those asshole partners of mine won't get to it."

"All right, then. Let's go get that dynamite."

Creek stepped away from the rock and pulled the canopy back down over it. Dusting his hands off, he shook his head and said, "We can tend to that once our original business is done. My partners are meeting me here any minute."

"Now I see why you wanted to show me this right away."

"Better to put my cards on the table first than take my chances on you finding out for yourself later on. I also thought you might want to get a better idea of the lay of the land in case you wanted to try and find a better spot."

Glancing at the small clearing, Caleb said, "If I'm going to be any help to you, I'll need to be here. I can't hit much through twenty yards of trees."

As Creek took another look to remind himself of what things looked like away from the river and those rocks, he seemed a little embarrassed. "Guess I ain't exactly an old hand at this sort of thing."

Caleb patted Creek's shoulder. "If it took these other fellas this long to take a stand against one man, they'll probably just scamper off when they see two."

Although Creek started to grin, he twitched at the sound of approaching horses. "Guess we'll find out shortly."

Having heard the rumble of hooves and the snapping of twigs for himself, Caleb backed away from Creek so he could keep the miner in his sight while also watching for whoever else was on their way to the clearing. With all that trampling and rustling, there wasn't any sense in the riders taking their time on their approach. On the contrary, they started emerging from the trees a little sooner than Caleb had expected.

The first one was a man of average build and long hair that hung past his shoulders in a way that made him look somewhat like the recently deceased General Custer. He wore fringed buckskins and gripped his reins with one hand as he surveyed the clearing with narrowed eyes.

Following behind the first man was a fellow who was

almost as wide as his own horse. His thick face was covered by a full beard, which had ensnared more than a few dead leaves. His bulky body and ample gut made it seem like something of a miracle that his horse could carry him without breaking its back.

Even before the second rider could enter the clearing, the first had locked eyes with Caleb and reached for his gun.

The moment Caleb saw that, he slapped his own hand against the grip of his pistol and tensed the muscles in his arm to prepare for a draw.

"Who the hell's that?" the first rider snarled.

Creek held up his hands, but didn't move from his spot. "Take it easy, Albert. This man's here on my invitation."

"Why you sendin' out invitations?" the second rider asked. "This is supposed to be between just us partners."

"Caleb, that big fella's name is Brass," Creek said without taking his eyes off the fat man. "And neither he nor Albert believe in practicing what they preach."

As if to prove Creek's point, a third rider emerged from the trees. He was a slender fellow who wore spectacles perched upon the end of his nose. His bowler hat was dented a bit, but still complemented his gray coat nicely. The attire looked downright fancy in comparison to that of everyone else in the clearing.

"Who's the dandy?" Creek asked.

Brass held out an arm that was thick enough to knock the man in the bowler hat off his horse without much effort. The skinny fellow pulled back on his reins before putting himself through that indignity.

"He's with us," the fat man said. "A new partner."

"We don't have any need for new partners."

Cocking his head at an angle, Albert did his best to stare Caleb down. He lasted for all of three seconds before looking away. "We're striking out a bit," the man with the long hair stated. "Once we dig up what's in that there hole, we're throwing in on some jobs that can land us even more money."

"Ain't the gold gonna make us rich enough?" Creek asked.

Albert narrowed his eyes and put an extra sternness in his tone when he said, "Ain't no such thing as too rich. Besides, no man can retire on gold dust, let alone three men. We can earn a lot more once we invest it."

Caleb looked at Albert and Brass before finally settling his eyes upon the third rider. While the first two were busy staring daggers, the third one sat in his saddle and glared at Creek. Finally, Caleb felt a grin slipping across his face. "You didn't tell him about the cave," he said.

"What cave?" the third rider asked.

"The cave beneath those rocks. That's where the real money is. Any partner worth their salt would've told you that much."

The third rider looked at the fat man. "What is he talking about?"

"The hell if I know," Brass grunted. His eyes searched wildly about until they settled upon the nearby twisting path of ice. "All the gold we got was pulled up from that there river. Well, it wasn't frozen at the time."

"What's going on here?" the third rider asked.

Creek hadn't been pleased when Caleb announced the existence of that cave, but he didn't mind so much when he saw the trouble it had stirred up. "It seems like Albert's doing fine spinning his own yarns," he said. "Why doesn't he do the talking?"

"Fine," Albert snapped. "I will. You're not a partner anymore, Creek, and that's that."

"On what grounds?"

"On the grounds that me and Brass decided, so that's the way it's gonna be."

"You'd rather throw in with Arkansas Dave Rudabaugh?" Creek asked.

"We're not exactly throwing in with him," Albert replied while furiously shaking his head. "We're just giving them some backing, is all. Lending them money. That's all there is to it."

"That backing will be greatly appreciated," the third rider said.

"Greatly appreciated," the skinny man repeated, "and paid back with interest."

Brass nodded as if he'd been asked if he cared for a second piece of cherry pie. "Interest. You hear that, Creek? We can make this gold work for us."

"Smart investing," Albert said proudly. "That's what it is."

Creek allowed his arms to hang at his sides. He then looked over at Caleb before shifting his eyes toward the three men on horseback. Finally, he asked, "Have every last one of you lost your goddamn minds?"

The first two riders squinted in disbelief, while the third merely held his ground and watched what unfolded.

"It's easy money, Creek," Albert said. "We ain't about to go out on any robberies or nothin' like that. We're lending out money to men who can pay it back in kind."

"With interest," Brass added. Looking back at the skinny rider, he asked, "Right?"

The third rider nodded. "Oh, most definitely."

"Where's the rest of them?" Caleb asked.

"Shut your damned mouth, asshole," Albert grunted. "You don't even have a part in this! Just who the fuck are you, anyhow?"

"I'm someone who's starting to understand why Creek would want a new partner," Caleb replied. "Now, I'm sure you men have already taken all the gold you could carry out of here, so keep it and be on your way. You're not going to get the legal deed to this claim."

Albert's head snapped back as if he'd been rapped on the nose. "How'd you . . . ?"

"If one of you already had the documents, you would've set up an ambush instead of a meeting. Hey, Creek, you want to hand over your legal rights to this claim?"

"Hell no," Creek replied.

"Then you got your answer, fellas."

{5}

For the first few seconds after Caleb's statement, none of the other men seemed to know how to respond. Albert looked over at Brass, only to get a perplexed look in return. By the time they looked back at Caleb, they still didn't know quite what to do.

The skinny fellow who'd accompanied the other two didn't seem quite so confused. He drew his pistol and held it high in the air over his head.

While Caleb shifted his aim toward the skinny rider, he wondered what the hell that man was doing. He got his answer when a rifle shot cracked from the other side of the nearby trees to send a round hissing toward Caleb's head.

"Get to cover!" Caleb shouted as he ducked down low. "He's signaling to someone else!"

"Wait a second!" Albert shouted as he gripped his own gun and raised his arm. "Don't shoot Creek!"

"You had your chance to negotiate," the skinny man replied as he lowered his pistol and fired off a shot. "Now's the time for things to be carried out our way."

Caleb's first instinct was to knock that skinny rider from

his saddle with one well-placed shot. Before he could squeeze his trigger, however, another shot was fired from the trees surrounding the clearing. Caleb wasn't hit by the round, but could practically feel the hot lead pass through his hair.

"Back here, Caleb!" Creek shouted.

Hunkering down low, Caleb followed the sound of Creek's voice while firing a few quick shots to cover his movement. The riders had already scattered and were laying down more than enough panicked gunfire to push Caleb back.

Creek was on the other side of the rocks with his back pressed against the rough surface. His gun was drawn and he leaned out to send one of his bullets toward the riders. Seeing Caleb slam into the rock next to him, Creek asked, "You hit?"

"No. How about you?"

"Nah. Them two couldn't hit the broad side of a barn."

"What about whoever's behind that rifle?" Caleb asked.

Gritting his teeth, Creek leaned away from the rocks to get a look toward the trees. When he heard another crack from that rifle, he was just fast enough to pull his head back before a bullet sparked off the rock a few inches from his face. "We may have a problem where that one's concerned. This is the sort of thing I hired you for. Got any ideas?"

"Yeah," Caleb replied as he reached under his coat to pull out a second pistol to match the .44 he was already holding. "It's simple and bound to get real noisy."

"I think I saw sparks from that rifle in those trees, straight ahead and to the left."

Caleb nodded and did his best to picture the clearing in his mind. As he jumped out from behind those rocks, his intention had been to try and flush out that rifleman or at least drive him back far enough to keep from getting picked off. Once he left cover, however, Caleb ran straight into a more pressing concern.

Albert and Brass were off their horses and charging toward the rocks with their guns drawn. They pulled their triggers as quickly as they could, filling the air with more than enough lead to drive Caleb back.

"All right," Caleb said as he slammed his shoulders against the rocks next to Creek. "Maybe I should try a different approach."

Creek let out a frustrated breath and tightened his grip on his own gun. "I hired you to back my play, not catch all the lead for me. On the count of three, we'll both take 'em on."

"Better make it one," Caleb said. "They're headed straight for us."

"All right, then. One and go!"

Without giving themselves enough time to think better about their decision, Caleb and Creek pushed away from the rocks and ran around them from both sides. Even before he had a target in sight, Caleb was firing his pistol. To his right, Creek was firing as well. Suddenly, that little clearing felt more like a battlefield.

Brass was the first man to catch Caleb's eye, simply because he was the biggest and wasn't doing a thing to hide himself. Rather than look for cover, Brass had a .45 in each meaty hand and was pulling both triggers at the same time. He let out a visceral roar, which made the big fellow look more like a wild animal.

In contrast to the big man, Albert had picked his spot and dropped to one knee so he could better defend it. Although he'd been smart enough to present a smaller target, there wasn't anywhere for him to hide and he quickly found himself directly in Creek's sights. Before Johnson could pull his trigger, Albert tossed his empty pistol in favor of something with a little more kick.

"Shotgun!" Creek Johnson shouted as he dove to the right.

Caleb didn't waste a second to look. Instead, he took Creek at his word and jumped to the left a split second before a thunderous blast exploded from less than ten paces in front of him. When he opened his eyes again, Caleb could see Brass grinning down at him. Caleb's ears were ringing from the shotgun's blast, but he didn't need to hear the bigger man's voice in order to get a pretty good idea of what was being said.

Muttering what had to be a victorious taunt, Brass sighted along the top of one pistol and took aim at Caleb's head.

Caleb reacted from pure instinct. His arm snapped up and his finger tightened around his trigger in the space of a heartbeat. His ears were still ringing enough so the bark of his own gun wasn't much more than a muffled thump. Even so, the sight of Brass reeling back from catching one of Caleb's bullets was nothing short of glorious.

"Toss that shotgun, goddammit!" Creek hollered as the gunshots died down enough for his voice to be heard. "This don't have to pan out this way!"

"You had your chance, Creek," Albert replied. "Hand over the deed or I'll cut you in half."

There was no doubt in Caleb's mind that Albert meant what he'd just said. There was plenty of doubt as to whether or not Caleb could do anything before the rifleman in those trees picked them both off.

∞

The rifleman stretched out with his belly on the ground. The dirt was so cold that it felt more like frozen rock beneath him. Gritting his teeth and letting out a slow breath, he gazed through the steam drifting up from his mouth and focused on his target. His finger slowly tightened around his trigger as he prepared to send a round straight through Caleb's head.

"Not a very good day for hunting," said someone from behind the rifleman.

Before the rifleman could turn to get a look at who'd spoken, he felt the cold touch of iron against the back of his head. Hearing the click of a pearl-handled .38 being cocked was just the icing on the cake.

"You wouldn't be taking aim at those fellows over there, would you?" Doc asked as he leaned down to follow the rifleman's line of sight. After a second or two, Doc nodded. "I believe you are. That's not very sporting at all."

"You don't know what you're getting into, mister," the rifleman said. "Now's your chance to walk away."

As the gunshots had rolled through the air and the men in the clearing had shouted back and forth to one another, Doc still looked as if he was out for a leisurely stroll. When he gazed at the rifleman, it was as if he was studying a poorly drawn landscape. "Why is it that men like yourself always feel the need to give ultimatums when you're the ones at the disadvantage?"

The rifleman's jaw hung down as he let out a loud breath.

"I see I've used too many big words," Doc said. "Why don't you just set that rifle down and we can watch things unfold from here?"

"You're gonna shoot me."

"Oh, I doubt there's any need for that. I have confidence that my associate can handle himself just fine so long as he doesn't have someone taking shots at him from hiding."

"If your friend is Creek Johnson, you're in for some bad news."

Doc craned his neck to stare toward the clearing. "Really? The situation doesn't seem so grave from here."

The shooting had died down and the men in the clearing were talking. Doc and the rifleman were too far away to make out exactly what was being said, but Doc looked on as if he was soaking up every last word. The rifleman, on the other hand, wasn't so content to stay in his place.

Slowly stretching out one arm, the rifleman slipped his fingers back around the weapon he'd been forced to relinquish. Before he could close his grip completely, he felt the barrel of Doc's gun press against the back of his head so hard that it drove the rifleman's face into the ground.

"If you're trying to make this bloody," Doc hissed, "that's just the way to go about it."

The rifleman kept his hand where it was as he squirmed to get a look at the man pointing the gun at his head. "You're that lunger cardplayer, aren't you?"

Doc didn't respond to that directly. Instead, he leaned some more of his weight behind his pistol and warned, "Don't make another move or I'll—"

"You'll what? Cough on me?"

Doc's eyes narrowed as he glared down at the rifleman. His face was already pale, but it looked even more chilling as the rage boiled up inside of him. Before he could say another word, he was being shoved aside as the rifleman rolled onto his back and knocked Doc's gun away in the process. The move happened so quickly that Doc didn't get a chance to do more than curse at himself as his gun was swatted from his hand.

The rifleman was still smiling as he got his legs beneath him and balled up his fists. Before he could take a swing at Doc's face, however, the Georgian dentist had pulled a small blade and was lunging at him. When he felt the blade cut through his flesh, the rifleman wasn't smiling any longer.

∽∾

Brass flopped on the ground as he let out a series of pained, sputtering grunts. He'd let one of his guns slip from his grasp so he could press that hand against the bloody wound in his ribs. "You should'a killed me, Injun," the big man grunted.

Caleb only watched Brass long enough to make certain the big man wasn't able to carry out his threat. When he saw the big man was still struggling to stay upright, Caleb was content to point the gun in his left hand at Brass and cover Albert with the gun in his right.

"You men are dead," Albert said in a voice that was as calm as it was calculating. "Both of you."

Caleb grinned and said, "If you're putting all your hopes on that rifleman you got stashed in those trees, then you've got some disappointment headed your way."

For a second, Albert didn't seem too concerned. But, as one second led into another without more than Brass's pained grunts to break the silence, Albert's cool facade started to crack.

"What the hell went wrong with you?" Creek asked. "I thought we was friends."

"We were partners," Albert snapped. "At least we were until you decided to hold out on us."

"I didn't hold out on anything!"

"You wouldn't go along with what we voted and then you wouldn't let us buy you out. What the hell would you call that?"

"It's called keeping away from filth like Dave Rudabaugh and that one there," Creek replied as he waved toward the slender man who'd been content to wait through the previous gunfight at a relatively safe distance.

The moment Caleb saw Creek move his gun hand toward the third rider, his gut clenched. That reflexive twitch proved to be well-founded, since both Albert and Brass took advantage of the opening by trying to bring the argument to a definitive end.

Albert raised his shotgun to aim it at Creek.

Brass propped himself up to sight along the top of his pistol.

When Caleb pulled his triggers, the blood was raging through his head too quickly for him to hear the guns in his hands go off. He could feel them bucking against his palms and could feel the sting of freshly burnt powder in the back of his nose, but the only thing on his mind was surviving the next couple of seconds.

Creek was firing beside him as well and had already dropped to one knee, since Albert was about to unleash the second barrel of his shotgun. Fortunately for Creek, Albert had been hit at least twice already, forcing his aim up just far enough to send his buckshot just over Creek's head and into the trees behind him.

Caleb was still firing the gun in his right hand when he shifted his eyes to the left. He was just in time to see fire erupt from Brass's pistols and feel the sting of hot lead through his hip. As the world tilted and Caleb felt his breath catch in the back of his throat, he swung his arms around so both of them were pointing at Brass. With both of his guns blazing, Caleb cut the larger man down like wheat.

Feeling his backside slam against the ground was enough to jar the fog from Caleb's head. All of his senses came back and he took in the world around him with stark clarity.

Smoke hung heavily in the air and the roar of gunfire rolled away into the distance.

Brass muttered half a curse before spitting out his last breath and giving up the ghost.

Albert was still on his feet, but slumped over and using his shotgun more as a crutch than a weapon.

"Goddamn you, Al!" Creek snarled. "We were partners! Now you force me into a mess like this one?"

"You . . . you're the one who hired a gunman to fight for you," Albert spat.

"If it wasn't for him, I'd be dead."

"We could've all been rich," Albert said. "If you would've just . . ."

"What?" Creek asked. "Signed on with murderers?"

But Albert wasn't able to get another word out. Every ounce of his strength was sapped by simply keeping himself upright. Finally, he let go of his shotgun and propped his hands upon his knees as if the only thing he needed to do was catch his breath.

"Come on, Albert," Creek said with a sigh. "It's too late for Brass, but we can get you to a doctor."

"You mean . . . you and your . . . hired killer? Go to hell."

Creek shook his head and gnawed on his bottom lip as he tried to think of what he should do next. Before he could arrive at a conclusion, Albert made the decision for him.

Having forsaken the shotgun, Albert reached to his boot for a small holdout pistol holstered near his ankle.

Creek did see the holdout pistol, but waited until there was no doubt in his mind concerning Albert's plans for that pistol. Waiting until the holdout gun was almost aimed at him, Creek barked, "Dammit!" and pulled his own trigger.

Albert's entire upper body twisted around as the bullet tore through him. He hit the ground in an awkward heap, squirmed for a bit, and then slumped to a rest.

Pulling in a few deep breaths, Caleb said, "You could have told me those two were that anxious to kill you."

"Aww, hell." Creek sighed. "I would'a told you if I would'a

known for certain. I guess I still had some hope. Where the hell's that other fella?"

Caleb holstered one pistol and reloaded the other as his eyes darted back and forth to search for any trace of the third rider. "Did you see him leave?"

"No, but I was a bit distracted. Maybe we should find whoever was firing that rifle before he decides to finish us off."

After swapping his guns, Caleb reloaded his second pistol as he ran for the trees. Creek was right behind him.

[6]

Doc's face was even paler than normal as he gritted his teeth and leaned against the knife with every bit of strength he could muster. Although he wasn't a picture of good health, it wasn't the exertion that was causing the color to drain from his face. That was being caused by the hand that was currently gripping his throat.

The rifleman had fought to sit upright and was even struggling to his feet after Doc's blade had jabbed into the meat of his upper right arm. As he'd tried to get away from the pallid gambler, he'd only made it easier for Doc to drive his knife all the way down to bone.

"I'll wring your neck, you skinny bastard," the rifleman wheezed.

Despite the fact that his neck was being clamped shut and the air was being squeezed out of him, Doc managed to grin and push out a hacking laugh. "Better than you have . . . tried," he taunted.

For a second, the rifleman couldn't quite believe what he'd just heard. Then, he found another reserve of strength that was put to use in choking Doc even harder.

Doc began to slump and his arm drooped enough to pull the knife a bit out of where it had been lodged. But before the rifleman could feel too much relief, the fire in Doc's eyes was rekindled and he twisted the blade while scraping it against the bone in the rifleman's arm.

The rifleman let out a pained howl. He couldn't let go of Doc's neck fast enough, just because it was the quickest way to put some distance between himself and the other man. Doc kept his grip on the knife's handle and stepped back while pulling the blade free.

Standing in a defensive crouch with his wounded arm farthest from Doc, the rifleman made a quick grab for the gun at his hip.

Doc threw the knife with just enough accuracy to cause the rifleman to pull his head up before getting close to his holster. Before the blade clattered against the frozen dirt, Doc had drawn his second .38 and taken aim.

"You all right, Mayes?" the slender fellow asked from the back of his horse. He already had his own gun in hand and was pointing it at Doc.

Although Doc found himself staring down the barrel of the rider's gun, he seemed to take more of an interest in the fellow's face. "I thought you ran away when the shooting started," Doc said.

The rider was tussled and anxious, but was doing a lot better than Brass and Albert whom he'd left in the clearing by those rocks. Straightening his arm and leaning forward as if to make certain Doc had seen the gun he was holding, the rider immediately began to show signs of panic.

"Go on and shoot this prick," the rifleman said.

"I asked you a question, Mayes," the rider snapped. "Are you all right?"

Mayes nodded. "My arm hurts like a bastard, but I'll live. Now do what I told you and shoot!"

"Pull that trigger and it's the last thing you'll ever do."

Although he didn't glance toward the person who'd just spoken, Doc grinned at the sound of that voice. "Punctual as always, Caleb," Doc said. "Looks like we've got ourselves into a bit of a pickle."

"I told you to fire, Samuel, and that's just what you'll do," Mayes snarled. "I want to see that skinny bastard dead!"

A few beads of sweat emerged from Samuel's forehead and rolled down his cheek. Compared to the picture of calm he'd been when he was flanked by Brass and Albert, Samuel now looked as though he was about to crack. "One wrong move and we'll all die," he muttered.

Caleb planted his feet and squared his shoulders to Samuel. "That's the first sensible thing that's been said in a while."

"So what do we do now?" Doc asked. "Stand around and wait for old age to claim us?"

"You won't be growin' old," Mayes swore.

Doc smirked and replied, "I could have told you that myself. Seems to me like I've got nothing left to lose by speeding up the process."

As if he could feel impending doom rushing in upon him, Samuel quickly said, "We can all walk away from this if we agree to do so like gentlemen."

"Gentlemen?" Creek scoffed from his spot behind Samuel. "That ain't hardly the word I'd use to describe any of you assholes."

"We made our play and it didn't work out," Samuel continued. "Whatever your partners wanted from you, Mr. Johnson, they won't be getting. Whatever payment your partners already made to me and my friend here won't be handed over, either. That means we can just keep what we've got and part ways."

"Just turn around and mosey off?" Doc grumbled. "I'd wager you'd both like that very much."

Mayes bared his teeth as if he was about to bite Doc's arm. "Lower that gun and see what happens, you gutless little—"

"Mayes!" Samuel shouted. "Shut up!"

The sharp tone coming from the smaller man caught everyone off guard. Even Doc took his eyes off Mayes for a fraction of a second to get another look at the slender rider.

Samuel waited until all eyes were on him before he slowly tilted his gun so it was pointing toward the branches over his head. "There. See? We can walk away or we can start shooting. One way we all come out ahead and the other way will end up bad all around."

"Bad for who?" Doc asked.

"He's right, Doc," Caleb said. "That is, if we can hold him to his word."

Doc took those words exactly as they'd been intended and shifted his hawk-like gaze between Samuel and Mayes. Rather than just keep an eye on them or watch for sudden movements, Doc studied those two as he would study an opponent at a high-stakes poker game.

A few seconds later, Doc said, "That little fellow means what he says, but his friend may be a problem."

Even though Samuel obviously didn't like being called the "little fellow," he wasn't quick to dispute Doc's claim. "I'll see to it that he doesn't step out of line," he said.

Slowly, Mayes turned to level a murderous glare at his smaller partner. "What did you just say?" he snarled.

"We can both get out of here alive or we can try to dodge bullets," Samuel said. "It's as simple as that."

"And what'll you tell Dave when he asks?"

"I'll think of something."

After a few seconds, Mayes finally came to the realization that he wasn't one of the ones holding a gun so that meant he didn't really have much say. "All right. I'll call it a draw."

"My, my," Doc said. "How generous of you. Sort of like a dog giving permission to be whipped."

"You said it yourself, Doc," Caleb warned. "He meant what he said and that other one isn't in any position to do anything more than grouse about it."

Doc's eyes shifted over to Johnson. "This is your claim. What would you like to do about it?"

Creek let out a slow sigh. "Those two back there may have turned out to be assholes, but I used to think they were my friends. Now I gotta bury them, so I'd prefer to make that the end of it."

For a moment, Caleb thought that Doc was going to make a play of his own. Then, like a shadow that had been dispelled by a sudden spark, the intensity in Doc's eyes was gone.

"All right," Doc said cheerily. "If we start back now, we should be able to get some proper breakfast." With that, the Georgian holstered his pistol and walked away from the others as if he was simply leaving a church social.

The hairs on the back of Caleb's neck stood up as he waited for Samuel or Mayes to make their move. But neither of those men had much fight left in them. With each second that passed, Mayes grabbed onto the wound in his arm as more blood seeped into his shirt.

Samuel lowered his pistol and backed away. "This has been unfortunate," he said. "We won't be crossing paths this way again."

"We'd better not," Caleb warned. "Because I wouldn't lose a wink of sleep after gunning you down on sight."

Nodding curtly, Samuel backed away and led Mayes to the nearby horses.

Even as he watched the other two ride away, Caleb couldn't quite allow himself to relax. When he slipped his pistol back into its holster, he had a cold feeling in the bottom of his stomach that he was about to get shot.

"Jesus," Creek muttered.

Caleb turned and reached for his gun, confident that his fears had quickly been realized. "What is it?"

"I can't believe they're dead. Both of them."

"Don't forget that it was nearly us taking their places. If it was up to them . . ."

"Yeah, yeah," Creek said warily. "I know." Shifting his eyes toward Doc, he watched as the Georgian bowed his head to cough into a handkerchief before climbing onto the back of a horse tied up nearby. "That a friend of yours?"

Caleb nodded. "Yep."

"Well, after what happened here today, I'd like to call him a friend of mine." Creek started to walk over to Doc's horse, but was stopped when Caleb grabbed his elbow.

"Let him go," Caleb said. "He's not too social when he's like this."

"Like what?"

"He's sick and the sooner he gets to where he needs to be, the better he'll feel."

"Goin' to the doctor, then?"

Shaking his head, Caleb replied, "The Bella Union, more likely. A bottle or two of liquor does as much good for him as any doctor. He just usually winds up talking circles around any physician who tries to do him any good."

Creek watched Doc climb into his saddle, but Doc didn't even look back at him. "I'll have to catch up to him later, then. Right now, there's plenty of work to be done. I need to get these bodies back to town so they can get a proper burial."

Blinking a few times, Caleb glanced back at the clearing as if he expected to find another set of corpses lying there. "If you're talking about those two bastards who tried to stab you in the back and then shoot us both in the front, my vote is to leave them where they are so they can feed some wolves. If you're feeling generous, we can kick some dirt onto them."

"Believe me, friend, generosity ain't got a damn thing to do with it. Albert's second cousin is a good man and he wouldn't like one of his kin to be left out here for the wolves. Considering what I hope to find under them rocks, the least I can do is see to it that those two get buried right."

"You're a good man, Creek. A better man than I am, that's for certain."

"Oh, I don't know about that. You strike me as a decent sort," Creek said with a grin. "At least decent enough to help me haul those two back into town."

Caleb rolled his eyes and let out a haggard sigh, but followed Creek back to the clearing.

⌐⌐⌐

Since the horses were slowed down by the deadweight they were carrying, Caleb and Creek had plenty of time to swap stories as they made their way back to camp. As Caleb rode closer to the middle of the settlement, Deadwood felt more like a proper town rather than just another mining camp. It was always teeming with folks, but what they found waiting for them upon their return gave that phrase a new meaning.

Instead of just teeming with folks, Main Street was positively choked by them. All those eyes shifted toward them and all those lips started flapping. Eventually, most of the crowd moved toward Caleb and Creek as if it meant to stampede directly over them.

"I thought we might attract some attention," Creek whispered, "but this is downright scary."

Since Albert's horse had bolted sometime after the shooting had started, the only other spare animal was the one that had belonged to Brass. Fortunately, that horse had built up one hell of a strong back after hauling the fat man around and didn't seem to mind when Albert's weight was added.

A man walked right up to within a few feet of Brass's horse and reached out to touch one of the bodies slung across the animal's back. Caleb twisted around in his saddle to swat that prying hand away. The morbidly curious local pulled his hand back and looked at the folks gathered behind him.

"It's true!" the man said. "These two are dead!"

Creek glanced back and forth at the faces in the crowd until he spotted one he recognized. "This ain't your affair, Johnny," Creek scolded.

"Murderer!" someone else shouted. Soon, that cry was joined by several others from several other sources.

"Killer!"

"Murderer!"

"Lock him up!"

"Lock, hell! String 'em up!"

Although he chewed on several things he wanted to say, Creek kept his words to himself. Judging by the wild shouting, nothing he said would have done any good.

"There they are!" yet another man shouted. "That's them!"

As he saw more of the crowd close in on him from the

front to cut his horse off from Main Street, Caleb reflexively reached for his pistol. Before he could get to it, someone grabbed his arm and pulled him with almost enough force to take him down from his saddle.

"They're probably the same ones that killed Blue!" another man hollered.

It was only through sheer muscle and force of will that Caleb was able to pull himself free of the other man's grasp. Once he'd pulled his arm back, he balled up his fist and backhanded the man who'd nearly sent him to the ground. Caleb's knuckles struck cleanly and sent the other man stumbling backward.

The fellow who'd grabbed Caleb's arm had a dirty face and a rough beard. After touching the bloody corner of his mouth, he looked up at Caleb and snarled, "He's a goddamn savage!"

"Aw, hell," Caleb muttered.

Even though he rarely told anyone his last name was Wayfinder, Caleb didn't have to say anything to announce his Indian ancestry. The dark hue of his skin and the coal-black tone of his hair was usually more than enough to let folks know where he'd come from.

"Damned savage killed these men!" the fellow with the bloodied mouth shouted. "That's a goddamn hanging offense!"

Turning in his saddle, Caleb looked over to Johnson and said, "You'd best get out of here, Creek."

"The hell I will," Creek replied. "Not after what you done for me today."

Caleb's hand was on his gun, but he had yet to draw. As much as he wanted to get the familiar weight of iron in his hand, he knew that would be the spark to send this whole situation straight to hell. He looked around for the backup plan he'd already put into place, but couldn't find Doc anywhere.

The crowd was getting wilder by the second, forcing Caleb to make the one play he knew would only cause more blood to be spilled. Since he preferred that blood not to be his own, Caleb started to draw his pistol and picked out his first target from all the faces glaring up at him.

"The Injun's got a gun!" an old man shouted from a nearby storefront.

Those words set the entire crowd surging in toward Caleb. They swung their fists along with anything else they could get ahold of. Something solid knocked against Caleb's side, forcing him to let go of his pistol. All Caleb had to do was climb down from his saddle before he was pulled down and then cover his head and face. After that, most of the swinging fists and weapons bounced off of other members of the crowd.

Folks yelled and swore at Caleb while the ones closer to him grabbed his arms and jacket to set him up for a flurry of wild punches. Caleb tried to get to the spot where his gun had landed, but he might as well have been trying to light a match in the middle of a whirlwind.

Suddenly, a voice cut through all the others like a hot iron through frozen soil. "Everyone back the hell away from those men!" it bellowed.

The man who'd spoken was lean yet wide through the shoulders. He strode through the crowd as if it wasn't even there, while also fixing his eyes upon the locals as if daring any of them to get in his way. Even though he didn't need any help in making his way to Caleb's horse, the lean man wasn't alone. There was another, younger fellow with him who had a similar gaze etched into a smoother face.

The older of the two was the one who'd silenced the crowd. He wore a gun on his hip, but didn't make a move toward it. He didn't need to. "Don't you folks got anything better to do than form a mob?" he asked.

The man whose lip Caleb had bloodied shifted anxiously from one foot to another. "We heard there was a killer headed into town, so we decided to meet up with him."

"Well, if you want to hold these men so they can answer to the proper authorities, then that's one thing. If you're just out to act like a pack of wild dogs, then I've got something to say against that."

A few members of the crowd started to regain their composure and inch forward. One of them locked eyes with the younger man standing beside the fellow who'd calmed things down.

Without letting a moment pass after he'd been singled out, the man with the smoother face bowed out his chest and said, "I'll let my brother do the talking, but I'll sure as hell make you wish you hadn't crossed our path."

The man with the steely eyes looked up at Caleb. "What killed those men?"

"Yes," a familiar voice cut in. "Why don't you enlighten all of us?"

When he picked out Samuel's face in the crowd, Caleb wanted to put a bullet through it. He would have done just that if his pistol hadn't been swallowed up by the crowd.

That crowd kept surging forward until a gunshot blasted through the air and drew everyone's eyes toward a man holding his pistol high over his head.

"Everyone stand back," Bullock said. "Give me some room."

Bullock slowly shifted his eyes as if he was glaring at each member of the crowd in turn. That glare was enough to move the crowd back like dust being cleared from the boardwalk by a stiff breeze. "This is official business," Bullock said. "Everyone who ain't a part of it, clear this street so I can sort it out!"

Reluctantly, the locals grumbled and moved away. Now that they weren't clumped together so tightly, the crowd didn't seem nearly as big. In fact, Caleb guessed there may have only been less than two dozen folks clogging up Main Street.

As Bullock approached Caleb, he took notice of the two men who had yet to move from their spots.

"You the law around here?" the steely-eyed man asked.

Bullock shrugged and gave half a nod as a reply. "More or less. I'm acting as sheriff for now, but it won't be official for another month or two. Who are you two men?"

"I'm Wyatt Earp," the steely-eyed man said. Hooking a

thumb toward the man with the smoother face, he added, "This is my brother, Morgan."

Letting out a sigh, Caleb said, "If you two'd like to get acquainted, I can be on my way."

"Can't allow that," Bullock said. "This man here tells me you murdered his friends. And if those two bodies slung over that horse behind you are his friends, then that complicates things even more."

Caleb looked around for a quick way out of the fire and back into the frying pan. Unfortunately, even the two Earp brothers were tipping their hats to Bullock and stepping back.

"Those men are my partners," Creek Johnson said. "Any one of a dozen shopkeepers here in town will tell you that much. You should be one of them, Mr. Bullock."

Bullock glanced at Creek just long enough to nod. "I recall you and that fellow with the long hair buying picks and shovels from my store not too long ago."

"I also bought some dynamite, but that wasn't from your place. I believe it was from a fella by the name of—"

"Never mind that," Bullock cut in. "I believe you. You'll still need to come along with me and cool your heels until I can get this sorted out."

Samuel stepped forward again. "My friends are dead! Do something about it!"

Bullock didn't move. When his eyes shifted to take in the sight of the bodies lying across the fat man's horse, it seemed more like a trick of the light. "Some sort of trouble befall you men out there?"

Creek shrugged and replied, "You might say that, Sheriff. My partners tried to kill me."

"Tried to kill you?"

"Well, tried to kill us both."

Seeing the sheriff's eyes move toward him, Caleb nodded. "I'll vouch for that."

"So this," Bullock said while waving a finger at the two bodies, "was in self-defense?"

"Yes, sir," Creek replied.

"They can't just talk their way out of this," Samuel whined.

When Bullock turned to look at Samuel, it was enough to force the smaller man back a few steps. "This isn't the first time someone's fallen upon a bad end in this camp, so we know how to take care of it. Since I'm the closest thing to a sheriff we have at the moment, I'll take care of it. I sure as hell don't need you nipping at my heels."

"We sure appreciate that," Caleb said. "Creek and I brought these men back to be buried. It's awfully fortunate that you came along to shoo away these folks who got the wrong idea."

"Don't count yourselves as too lucky," Bullock said. "Because you're under arrest."

[7]

What currently passed for Deadwood's jailhouse was actually a shack that must have been one of the sturdier ones in camp. Judging by the dried-up husks in the corner and the scent that had soaked into every plank of the floor, the shack had formerly been used to store corn or possibly smoked ham. Those scents had since mingled with the sweat and puke from Deadwood's drunks and miscreants.

Caleb sat with his back against the farthest wall, which allowed him to watch the shack's only door. When he saw the door move, he jumped to his feet.

Bullock opened the door a crack and leveled a finger at Creek, who sat in a corner. "You're Johnson, right?"

Climbing to his feet, Creek nodded and replied, "That's right."

"And you were part owner of that claim?"

"Right again."

"Some folks down at the Nuttall saw those two partners of yours meeting behind your back. The fat one got drunk and told one of the working girls down there that he was gonna be rich once you were out of the way, so that's more than enough to establish self-defense for me. You're free to go."

Creek looked back at Caleb and smiled, but seemed reluctant to take a step toward the door. "Are you sure?"

Bullock nodded. "This is a mining camp, after all, and folks tend to keep their ears open for talk of jumping claims. There wasn't any shortage of men stepping up to speak on your behalf."

"What about me?" Caleb asked. "Did anyone speak up on my account?"

"A few. One asked to see you before you stand trial."

"Trial, huh? This camp don't even have a proper sheriff, but you've got a courthouse?"

"No courthouse. Justice of the peace will hear you out and decide what's to become of you."

"Why's he to be put on trial?" Creek asked. "He was working with me. If I'm to go free, then so should he!"

Shrugging, Bullock replied, "That's what was decided. There's two dead men who were gunned down by a . . . well . . ."

"An Indian," Caleb muttered. "I suppose it doesn't even matter what sort of blood runs through me or where my family actually came from?"

Bullock shook his head. "Not really. There's been plenty of trouble in these parts that had to do with Indians and the subject's sore for plenty of folks."

"What about the ones who spoke up for me?"

"It was only one and he ain't a local," Bullock replied grudgingly. "He's also not quite as reputable as the bunch who spoke up for Mr. Johnson."

Caleb gritted his teeth and nodded.

Looking Caleb straight in the eyes, Bullock told him, "I'd say your luck's holding up pretty well. A lot worse has happened to folks around here for a lot less. I'll see to it that you get tried for the case at hand just like anyone else would."

"And after that I'll hang?" Caleb asked.

After considering that for a moment, Bullock shook his

head. "Under the circumstances, you might do some jail time. You could go free."

Caleb laughed to himself and sat down on the dirty floor. "Guess I should get used to the smell in here."

"If you're to do jail time, it'll probably be in Yankton."

"Yankton?" Caleb asked. "Where the hell is that?"

"Not too far from here."

Caleb was stunned. A tired laugh from the back of his throat felt more like a punch in the chest. "Great. That's just great. Go on and leave, Creek. There's nothing more for you to do in here."

"You sure about that?"

Caleb nodded.

Slowly, Creek shuffled out of the shack. When he got to Bullock, Creek said, "I wanted to see about burying my partners. Is that all right?"

"Sure. You may want to stay close to camp, though, if you want to speak up for your friend when he gets his hearing."

"Wouldn't miss it for the world," Creek replied with a forced smile. To Caleb, he said, "Keep yer chin up. I won't forget what you done for me."

Although he genuinely appreciated hearing those words, Caleb wasn't able to put much enthusiasm into his voice. "Thanks, Creek."

Bullock stepped aside so Johnson could pass by and then stepped back so he once again filled up the doorway. "For what it's worth, I don't believe you're a murderer."

"Think you could say that at my trial?" Caleb asked.

"Sure."

"Will it do any good?"

"No," Bullock replied.

"Didn't think so."

"You still got a man out here who wants to have a word with you. He says he's a friend of yours. If you want to talk to him, it'll have to be through the window over there."

Caleb looked to where Bullock was pointing and quickly

realized that the man was being very generous when referring to the crooked hole cut in the wall as a window. It was
more of a large crack between two boards and wasn't even
wide enough to slide an arm through. Without saying a word,
Caleb hauled himself over to the window and looked outside.

"Seems like you've gotten yourself into another pickle,"
Doc said with a grin.

Lowering his voice to a harsh whisper, Caleb asked,
"How the hell is it that you're not in here?"

"I made it back to town before the crowd was all riled up.
That, and the fact that I wasn't dragging along two dead bodies might have had something to do with it."

"Well, you need to get me out of here. I don't have much
faith in whatever trial this camp intends on throwing together and I sure as hell know they'd be more than happy to
string up someone who looks like me."

Doc cocked his head to one side. "Isn't ugliness just a
misdemeanor?"

"You're real lucky I can't reach through this window,"
Caleb snarled through gritted teeth.

Glancing to his left, Doc tipped his hat to someone outside
of Caleb's sight. "Sheriff or not, this Bullock person seems
like a good fellow. I doubt he'll let you get strung up before
your duly appointed time."

"What about those two who stepped in for me?" Caleb
asked. "Those brothers?"

"Once the mob dispersed, they went back to minding
their own business. I believe they're selling firewood."

"Selling firewood?"

"Considering the weather, I'd say it's probably a lucrative
business."

"Well, see if you can get them to show up at my trial."

Doc laughed and didn't make any effort to hide it. "Oh,
yes. The trial. That should be a fine display of . . . well . . . it
should be a fine display. If it was anyone but you on the stand,
I might want to buy a ticket."

"But it is gonna be me up there, Doc." Caleb stopped himself before he raised his voice any more. Pressing both hands against the wall and leaning as close to the window as he could, he whispered, "I need to get broke out of here. Fast."

"Both of us have come such a long way," Doc said wistfully. "Only a few short years ago, I was a dentist with real opportunities for advancement and you were the proud owner of a thriving Dallas saloon."

Rather than say another word, Caleb glared at Doc with enough intensity to cut through solid granite. It wasn't long before that stare had its desired effect.

"You shouldn't be in there for more than a few days," Doc said. "It'll take at least that long for them to clear out the store they use for a courthouse and gather the usual bunch of locals who act as judge and jury."

"And executioner?"

"It won't come to that," Doc said without any of the glibness that had been in his voice before.

"You'd better get going now," Bullock said from a few paces away from Doc.

When Caleb craned his neck to get a look past Doc, he saw Bullock walking up to the dentist with his hand resting upon the grip of his holstered gun. He let Doc take his time in moving away from the shack. "Check back later and we should know when the hearing will be," Bullock said.

Doc stepped back. The dim sunlight that seeped through the passing clouds made his face seem even paler. When he raised his hands, he also lifted a familiar walking stick. "I appreciate that, Sheriff," he said with a wheeze.

Bullock winced at the title, but let it pass. Now that he knew the appointment wasn't official just yet, Caleb realized that Bullock had winced that way every time the word "sheriff" had been aimed at him.

As Doc hobbled away, Caleb turned around and leaned back against the wall. He slid down until he was seated upon the floor and surrounded by the echo of his own movements. Since there wasn't anyone else locked up inside the shack,

Caleb guessed he'd have to get used to the thick, malodorous silence within those four dirty walls.

❧

As the sun was dipping below the western horizon, Doc and Creek were on their way back to the claim Johnson had since inherited. Doc was still in a bad way, but didn't need all of his strength since he was riding on a wagon instead of in a saddle. Creek sat beside him and in an easy grip held the reins of the two horses pulling the wagon.

"You sure you're up to this?" Creek asked. "You don't sound too good."

Doc coughed a few times, but soon fell into a series of wheezing, hacking coughs that wracked his entire body. Dabbing at the corner of his mouth with a handkerchief, Doc replied, "I'll be just fine. Better than those two, anyhow."

Creek looked behind him at the rest of the wagon. Apart from its driver and passenger, the only other things in that wagon were the two bodies wrapped in canvas and tied up like parcels awaiting delivery. "Yeah. I suppose so."

"Is it imperative they accompany us?" Doc asked.

"Sure it is! They're the whole reason we're supposed to be out here."

"Since there isn't going to be a hanging today, it doesn't seem as though anyone is too interested in following us."

Creek shook his head and flicked the reins. "There's always someone watching you in that damn camp. And if they ain't watching you, they're gossiping about you behind your damn back. Besides, it turned out that there won't be a proper undertaker around until next week and nobody else was willing to bury these two."

Nodding while pulling his coat around him, Doc hunkered down to keep most of the icy breeze from cutting into his face. His dark, wide-brimmed hat shielded him well enough, but still didn't make the cold any easier to bear. He leaned down upon the stock of a shotgun that propped him up like a crutch.

When they arrived at Johnson's claim, Doc hardly even

recognized it. In fact, he didn't move from his seat until Creek had set the wagon's brake and climbed down.

"I figure on burying them right here," Creek said. "Seems fitting since they died trying to sink their claws into this same patch of land."

Doc scowled at the harsh wind that tore through the clearing like a set of animal claws reaching out from the trees. He made his way down from the wagon and then propped the shotgun against the front wheel. "That's going to be fairly morbid when you continue to work here."

"I'm done with mining," Creek said as he opened the back of the wagon and took one of the picks laying beside the bundled bodies. "At least for the time being. I'm through with mining these hills, that's for damn sure."

"You could always come to Texas. There's plenty of work for stand-up men like you there."

Creek laughed and replied, "I'd better steer clear of that place, too. At least until something bad happens to Dave Rudabaugh."

Much to Creek's surprise, Doc also walked around to the back of the wagon and helped himself to one of the picks. "I'm not sure if Dave Rudabaugh is truly our main concern."

"*Our* concern?" Creek asked.

"Of course," Doc replied sternly. "I nearly got killed right along with you and Caleb earlier, or have you forgotten that already?"

"I didn't forget. I just thought you'd be glad to wash your hands of this mess."

"I most certainly will be. But with Caleb preoccupied for the time being, I'm acting in his stead. It was my understanding that he was to become your partner now that these other two are gone."

"That's the way it sets," Creek replied with a slow nod. "Did Caleb arrange this when you went to speak to him in jail?"

"That's hardly a jail," Doc scoffed as he hefted the pick over his shoulder. "I should know. And yes . . . that's the arrangement."

Creek studied Doc's face as another wintry breeze ripped through the clearing and froze both men right down to the marrow in their bones. Before long, Creek found himself glancing toward the trees where Doc and Mayes had had their scuffle. "All right, then," Creek finally said. "If that's the way it is, I'll go along with it. By all rights, you earned your own cut a hell of a lot more than the two assholes we're about to bury."

Doc's pick dropped first and cracked against the soil with a loud clang. Wincing at the impact that ran all the way up through his arms, Doc said, "That burying business may be a little harder than we thought."

Keeping his pick on his shoulder, Creek grinned and asked, "You say you're from Texas?"

"Georgia, actually."

"Yeah. That'd explain the accent. It'd also explain how ignorant you are in the ways of winters around here."

No matter how much Doc plainly didn't like hearing those words, he couldn't exactly deny them.

Creek didn't let Doc stew for very long before swinging his pick high over his head and then bringing it down. The pick cracked against the soil a bit more solidly than Doc's attempt, but didn't have any more success. Rather than raise the pick again, however, Creek left it there and asked, "Think you can hit that pick with one swing?"

Pulling in a breath, Doc squared himself to the pick that was partially embedded in the near-frozen ground. He kept his eye on his target, hefted his own pick, and then swung down as if he was driving a railroad spike. Doc's swing wasn't perfect, but it struck well enough to send up some sparks as one pick struck against another.

"Try it again," Creek said. "Just a bit more should do it."

Doc went through the same motions a second time and wound up driving the other pick another half inch into the ground.

After testing the handle of his pick, Creek grinned, spat on his palms, and rubbed them together. "All right, then. Fetch that dynamite from the wagon and bring a few sticks over here. Set the rest of it next to them rocks. Preferably not facing us."

Doc took a small wooden case from the wagon and opened it. There were six sticks of dynamite inside, which he divided up as Creek had requested. By the time Doc walked over to Creek, the miner had taken his pick from the ground and was chipping at the hole it had made.

Creek took the two sticks of dynamite, stuck them into the hole, and then covered it up with what little dirt had been chipped away thus far. "You see anyone lurking about?" Creek asked.

Doc was at the rocks already and hunkering down to get a look under the canopy of branches.

"Doc?"

Pulling his attention away from the rocks, Doc walked over to the wagon and removed a lantern that had been hanging from a hook on the driver's side. Once the lantern was lit and the flame was as bright as it was about to get, Doc held it into the small opening.

"Good Lord in heaven," Doc whispered.

When he heard footsteps coming up behind him, Doc turned and reached for his gun. Creek stood there, gazing past him and into the glittering little hollow within the rocks. "Pretty, ain't it?"

"To say the least," Doc replied as he took his hand away from his holster and used it to brace himself against the rocks. "I may be able to get in there and chip away some of that gold. That is . . . if it's real."

"Oh, it's real. It just ain't worth the effort."

"You brought shovels, then?"

Creek blinked once or twice and then looked toward the wagon as if he wasn't quite certain where Doc was headed. "No offense or nothin', but it's too damn cold to dig a proper hole without using dynamite. It is cold enough to kill us both if we stay out here too long after dark, which is right about now anyway. This is my claim and I intend on washing my hands of it. Seems to me that whatever gold is under them rocks probably has some sort of curse on it."

Doc let out a noise that was part cough and part laugh. "Cursed? If I followed that logic, I would have quit after losing my first hand of poker. There's money down there and we need to get whatever we can."

"There's money all through these hills. That don't mean we can just scoop it up, pretty as you please."

"Then what's this batch of dynamite for?" Doc asked while tapping the remaining sticks with his foot.

Creek eyed the dynamite that had been placed next to the rocks. He then looked at Doc carefully. "I was gonna blow these rocks sky high so nobody could get to this hole. The rest of it will make a hole big enough to hold Albert and Brass."

"It's a good thing you're a miner, Creek, because you'd make a terrible poker player."

Knowing better than to push a bad bluff, Creek said, "All right, then. How do I know you won't kill me for this gold the way my other partners tried to do?"

"Because I'm not a miner and I sure don't want to break my back digging in these rocks for however long it'll take to clear it all out. Unlike the fools who'd be happy to waste their lives scratching in the dirt for a few more pretty rocks, I'd like to get as much gold out of there as possible and then move on as quickly as possible. I've got some big plans for that money."

"I may not be able to lie as good as a poker player, but I can spot a lie pretty damn well. That's what saved my bacon from getting fried by those two dead men over there."

"And what's that sixth sense of yours telling you now?" Doc asked.

After a slight hesitation, Creek replied, "That you're good enough with them guns to have killed me by now if that was your intention."

Doc's eyes narrowed a bit as he rasped, "I couldn't exactly be rid of you until you help me with this digging, you know."

Keeping his faith in his initial conclusion, Creek waved off the vague threat and headed back to the little hole that had been picked out of the ground. "Then it'll have to wait until these bodies are buried. That's what I came here to do and that's what's gonna get done."

A minute or so later, there was a muffled thump announcing that the first two sticks of dynamite had gone off. The blast left a good-sized crater in the ground that was just big enough to hold two bodies without leaving more than a slight mound of dirt and a simple marker written upon a plank.

Not long after the marker had been placed, a louder thump rolled through the cold night, followed by the scrapings of picks and shovels against chunks of broken rock.

[8]

Caleb had been to a trial or two in his day. Although he didn't expect a fancy courthouse or even a formal judge, he didn't quite expect to be tossed into a dry-goods store and forced to sit on an overturned crate. Bullock and a younger man stood behind Caleb to make sure he didn't try to escape. Once he saw the official making his way to the proceedings, Caleb didn't want to do anything that would cause him to miss seeing what happened next.

"The Honorable Justice of the Peace E. B. Farnum presiding," announced a gangly man with a bulbous nose and hair that looked like stray bits of brown thread hanging from a faulty seam.

Even more amusing than the sight of the gangly man was the fact that he'd just gone through the trouble of heralding his own arrival.

E. B. Farnum swiped the back of his hand under his bulbous nose and then dug a pair of spectacles from his pocket. After going through the trouble of getting those spectacles situated, Farnum looked at the three men in front of him and asked, "Is this all the witnesses that'll be showing up?"

Following the little man's line of sight, Caleb glanced around and eventually picked out Creek sitting on an old stool, Doc leaning against a table of blankets, and Samuel pacing in front of a shelf full of jarred preserves. Mayes was an even more welcome sight because his arm was in a sling and discolored enough to look like it must have hurt immensely.

"I think this is all there is, E.B.," Bullock said. "Let's get on with it."

"You say these men shot your friends?" Farnum asked Doc.

Before Doc could unleash the comment that was on the tip of his tongue, Samuel spoke up.

"They were my friends, sir!" Samuel snapped. "And I won't be satisfied until justice is served and I get what's rightfully mine!" Just to emphasize his point, Samuel smacked his hand flat against the nearby shelf. That caused the old woman perusing the preserves there to jump and let out a surprised yelp.

"Don't be alarmed, ma'am," Farnum said. "There won't be any more outbursts like that." He then shifted his weight on the stack of flour sacks he was using as a bench and asked, "What's supposed to be rightfully yours?"

"The deed to that claim, of course. Either that or the cash equivalent of whatever gold may have been taken out of there."

"What?" Caleb asked as he jumped to his feet. Before his legs could completely straighten beneath him, he felt Bullock's hand close upon his shoulder and shove him back down again.

"And on what are you basing this claim?" Farnum asked in a tone that seemed wildly out of place for a man perched on a stack of flour sacks.

Placing his hands upon the lapels of his dark blue coat, Samuel replied, "I can produce witnesses that this deal was struck no more than two days ago."

"Now's the time."

Samuel nodded at a few grizzled old-timers whom Caleb had figured were only there for the dry goods. As they stepped forward, the old-timers removed their hats and held them humbly in their hands.

"I was there in the Nuttall," the first old-timer said. "This fellow here and them two that wound up dead the other day, they were all talking about a deal."

"What deal?" Farnum asked.

The old-timer pointed toward Samuel. "That one there gets made into a full partner and that one there," he said while pointing toward Creek, "was out."

"That's a damn lie!" Creek said. "Who the hell is this man, anyway?"

"He's my witness," Samuel replied. "At least I'm not the one keeping company with known murderers."

Farnum leaned forward and wagged his finger. "That's not known just yet."

"Sorry, Your Honor."

Grinning and straightening his posture in hearing that title thrown at him, Farnum said, "Go on. I'll allow it."

Caleb stewed in his spot and let out a sigh that sounded more like a growl.

The second old-timer stepped forward. Although his hair was a bit longer and had a bit less gray, he had the same dirty face and sour expression as the first one. "I heard it, too," he said while shooting a few glances at Samuel. "Fact is, I also heard talk that they were worried something might happen to 'em and if it did, then that fellow there should get everything."

"That would be me, Your Honor," Samuel said victoriously.

"What about you?" Farnum asked as he looked at Caleb. "Do you have anything to say?"

Caleb sat up and cleared his throat, but wasn't able to put on nearly as convincing a display as Samuel. "First of all, I don't know about any deals struck by that man there and the two that were killed," he said while hooking a thumb toward Samuel. "What I do know is that we weren't expecting any trouble when we went out to look at that claim. The next thing I know, we're being attacked. We would have been killed if we hadn't defended ourselves."

"So says the hired gunman," Samuel muttered.

Turning so he could stare directly at Samuel, Caleb asked, "What did you just say?"

Samuel held up his hands and put a look on his face that reminded Caleb of a puppy that was afraid of getting kicked.

"Do you see, Your Honor?" Samuel asked. "He's a violent man."

"Oh, for Christ's sake," Caleb growled.

"And obviously not a churchgoing man, either."

This time, Caleb wasn't able to contain himself. Jumping up and lunging for Samuel was part reflex and part frustration after spending so much time locked up in a stinking old shed. He actually made it half a step this time before Bullock caught his shoulder and shoved him down.

"I am afraid I'll need more than that," Farnum said. "Do you have anything signed in regard to this arrangement?"

Caleb felt his breath catch in the back of his throat. The possibility that he may get a somewhat fair hearing after all suddenly seemed more than possible.

"No," Samuel said. "It was a verbal contract."

Farnum thought that over for a few seconds and nodded. "A contract's a contract. Hand over the deed, Mr. . . ."

"Johnson." Creek sighed.

"If you please, Mr. Johnson."

Following Farnum's order, Creek dug into his pocket for a piece of paper that was folded into fourths. His knuckles grew white as his fingers tightened around the precious document. When he looked over at Bullock, all Creek got was a shrug.

"A man's word around here is his bond," Bullock said. "For something so important, it's usually a good idea to have witnesses on your behalf."

"How could he have witnesses for a deal that was made behind his back?" Doc snapped.

"Yeah!" Caleb said hopefully. "Answer that one."

Samuel rolled his eyes while Farnum cocked his head and scratched his chin.

"I suppose that's a valid point," Farnum said. After deliberating for all of three seconds, Farnum snapped his fingers and said, "Since Mr. Johnson and Mr. . . . ."

"Fletcher," Samuel said.

"Since Mr. Johnson and Mr. Fletcher both have some sort of claim to the deed in question, they're both partners. Sound fair?"

"What about me?" Caleb asked.

Farnum brought his eyes back to Caleb and winced. "Oh, yeah. I almost forgot. This seems to be a dispute between partners and, by all accounts, you were hired on to shoot those two men. If Mr. Fletcher still maintains that—"

"I'll sign over my half of the claim if he drops the charges," Creek interrupted.

"What?" Samuel and Farnum asked simultaneously.

Creek nodded and held out the deed. "If Mr. Fletcher agrees to drop the charges against Caleb, I'll hand over this deed and be done with it."

Doc's eyes had gone wide as saucers. "That's a lot of money, Creek. We can pay for a lawyer to get Caleb out of there. We can pay for a flock of lawyers."

"I couldn't look at myself in the mirror if I knew Caleb was hung on my account," Creek said.

"Fine," Samuel snapped. "I'll drop the charges if you make this official right here and now."

Creek nodded. "It's a deal. Is that good enough?" he asked Farnum.

Sitting atop his flour sacks like a king, Farnum looked around at the small crowd that had gathered to watch the proceedings. Even though most of that crowd had their arms full of dry goods and were still in the middle of their shopping, those folks gawked and waited as if it was their futures on the line.

"As the duly appointed official for this camp of Deadwood," Farnum announced.

Bullock let out a tired sigh and grumbled, "Jesus, E.B. There's other business to be done."

"All right, then," Farnum said with a little less steam behind his voice. "Mr. Fletcher will drop the charges and Mr. Jameson will hand over the deed."

"Johnson," Creek corrected.

"Him, too."

Creek extended his arm and nearly got his hand plucked off in Samuel's rush to get the deed in his possession.

"This is binding, right?" Samuel asked.

Farnum nodded. "You're in possession of that deed and the charges against the Injun are dropped."

Although Caleb normally didn't like to have that word tossed at him, under the circumstances he didn't mind this time.

"The charges in the matter of Brass's death are dropped," Samuel said as he tucked the deed into his pocket.

Having been distracted by one of the old women who'd wandered too close to the front door with her arms full of unpaid merchandise, Farnum looked back at Samuel. "Excuse me?"

"Mr. Brass is one of the men who was killed," Samuel explained. "I'm dropping the charges in that case as agreed. The charges involving the murder of Mr. Albert Hansen, on the other hand, are still pending."

"I . . . suppose so," Farnum said.

This time, it was the man behind Caleb who started to lunge forward. "Now hold up," Bullock said. "That wasn't specified!"

Jabbing a finger toward the official presiding from his sacks of flour, Samuel whined, "But he just said it was! He just said the matter involving Mr. Hansen is still pending."

"I did," Farnum sputtered, "but—"

"But nothing! I want this man to pay for killing my friend! He's a murderer!" Samuel hollered. "I'm sure none of these good people want a murderer turned loose. Or has this camp become a shooting gallery ever since Wild Bill was gunned down in cold blood?"

The matter of Wild Bill Hickok being shot dead in the Number 10 Saloon was still a fresh wound in the side of every Deadwood resident. Folks may have loved Bill or hated him. They may have never met him, but nearly everyone in the camp hated the cowardly son of a bitch who'd pulled that trigger. The fact that Jack McCall had lived more than a few seconds after Bill died didn't set well with anyone. When someone mentioned Bill, folks in Deadwood thought of Jack.

Perhaps that was the way McCall had wanted it.

And the simple fact that McCall got something he wanted was salt poured into the town's shared wound.

"This has nothing to do with . . ." Glancing at the intent stares that had been focused upon him from everyone in that store, Farnum grimaced and struggled to find the proper words. "It has nothing to do with this case."

"It has to do with justice for killers," Samuel insisted. Shifting his attention to the shoppers, he added, "All I want is what's right. That man sitting there is a killer. Everyone in town saw the bodies. Whatever his reasons, he should pay for what he's done."

"I guess I can at least hear from the witnesses who are here on his account," Farnum said.

Samuel turned and glared at Doc. "That one's a killer, too. You want him as a witness?"

Doc didn't even flinch. When he laughed, it might as well have been at a lewd joke. "Sounds like this man isn't entirely of sound mind. I'm here strictly to clear my friend's name."

"And were you there?" Samuel asked. "How else would you know?"

"I was there!" Creek said. "I saw your friends trying to kill us while my partners joined in!"

"To hell with you! At least you're alive!" Samuel said. "And to hell with that skinny prick in the fancy clothes!"

Doc's calm demeanor disappeared quicker than the frozen topsoil when that dynamite had been set off. The anger on his face was so thick, it nearly choked him as he roared and ran toward Samuel. "You cowardly, back-shooting son of a bitch!"

Caleb may not have known Bullock for long, but this was the first time he'd seen the stoic man appear somewhat out of control. Although Bullock did manage to grab hold of Doc's arm, he nearly tripped over himself in the process. Finally, he pulled Doc away with one hand and raised his pistol with the other.

"Don't shoot!" Farnum shouted as he jumped to his feet. "I just had that roof repaired!"

"Regain control of this farce, E.B.," Bullock growled, "or I will."

"The deed's changed hands and belongs to Mr. Farmer."

"Fletcher."

"Fine, fine," Farnum spat. "The charges for one shooting's been dropped and the other will be decided in Yankton."

"What?" Caleb snapped.

"They've got a proper courthouse . . . or uh . . . a higher court. They've also got a proper jail meant to hold a killer, if that's the findings. That's my decision and that's the end of this case!" With that, Farnum grabbed a splintered gavel and knocked it against the top of a crate. "Any more cases to be heard? No? Fine. That's all for today. Now get out of my damn store!"

Caleb had plenty more he wanted to say, but didn't get a chance to air out more than a few syllables before he was hoisted to his feet and shoved toward the front door.

"This is a travesty!" Doc said.

Bullock kept his eyes on everyone else as he pushed Caleb in front of him. Once he was walking across the street, he replied, "It was better than some of the trials I've seen."

"You call this justice?"

"Not hardly." When he spotted a familiar pair of faces at a cart where firewood was being sold, Bullock shook his head and kept walking.

Doc looked in that direction and saw the two steely-eyed brothers. Wyatt looked prepared to walk beside Bullock if the need called for it, and Morgan was just amused by the spectacle working its way from the dry-goods store and into the street.

"You just stay put," Bullock said as he stabbed a finger toward Doc. "I'll come find you when I know what's happening next."

Although Doc may have said something to that, Caleb didn't hear it over the shuffle of his boots against the dirt and the grinding of his teeth. When he was finally able to stop moving, Caleb found himself within four very familiar walls.

The air inside that shack still smelled like someone's regurgitated dinner.

[9]

Caleb figured it had to be well past midnight, but there were still plenty of rowdy voices drifting in from all parts of the camp. Deadwood howled like a living thing all around him, but Caleb wasn't in any spot to enjoy the nightlife. All he wanted at that moment was to curl up in the most comfortable corner of his new home and fall asleep on ground that had probably been pissed on by every drunk in the Black Hills.

He kept his eyes shut when he heard a woman's scream turn into bawdy laughter.

Caleb tried to go to sleep when he heard an entire saloon break out into a horrific rendition of "Camptown Races."

When he heard something rattling within the lock of the door to his shack, Caleb figured it was a dog scraping at the outside of his wall.

The clatter of the lock coming open, however, was unmistakable.

Caleb's head snapped up and he stared at the door. Having been in the dark for several hours, he could easily make out the edges of the door frame outlined in the dim mix of moonlight and torches positioned along the street. He knew better than to check for his gun. Bullock had taken that from Caleb when he was first brought into custody. In fact, Caleb's pockets were turned inside out, leaving him nothing to grab hold of except for the wall itself.

Feeling his blood boil at the prospect of being hauled outside just to be forced to endure a long ride that ended with another bullshit trial, Caleb pressed his hands against the wall and prepared to launch himself at whoever was unfortunate enough to open that door.

The muscles in Caleb's legs tensed, but quickly started to burn with anticipation.

As the door slowly opened, Caleb was already planning where he could run after fighting his way out of Deadwood.

"You in there, Caleb?" asked a shadowy figure who reluctantly stuck his head into the shack. "Goddamn, it's dark."

"Creek?"

Upon hearing that, Creek opened the door a bit more so he could step inside. His face may have been rough and covered with an unruly beard, but it was one of the best sights Caleb could imagine.

"What the hell are you doing here?" Caleb asked.

"I'll explain while we run. Just get out here before someone takes a look this way."

Caleb didn't need to be told twice. He bolted for the door so quickly that he nearly stampeded over Johnson. He didn't stop until he'd reached the darkened window of a nearby storefront and would have kept right on moving if Creek hadn't been fussing with the door of the stinking shack to make sure it looked just the way it had when he'd arrived.

After shutting the door and locking it again, Creek ran back to where Caleb was waiting.

"I didn't figure you as the sort who would break me outta jail," Caleb admitted.

"I didn't break anything," Creek replied. "I had the key."

"And who'd you take that from?"

"The Honorable E. B. Farnum."

Even though he knew he should keep moving, Caleb was

nearly knocked over by that news. Just to make sure, he asked, "You mean the same one who presided over that hearing?"

"One and the same," Creek said as he looked up and down the street.

"The one from *my* hearing?"

Creek laughed and motioned for Caleb to follow him as he headed toward Main Street. "He owns a hotel, also. That's where we've got to drop off this here key."

"Good Lord. Doc didn't do anything to Farnum, did he?"

"Not unless you count making the little weasel rich. Well," Creek added, "at least Farnum's richer than when we found him." Suddenly, Creek cursed under his breath and knocked Caleb toward an alley with nearly enough force to send him straight to the ground. Caleb kept his balance and stayed still just long enough to spot the reason for Creek's outburst.

Caleb didn't recognize the pair of men who strolled along the street, but Creek knew them well enough to tip his hat and greet each of them by name. After those two had moved along, Creek motioned for Caleb to step out from the shadows.

Following Creek onto the boardwalk and down the street, Caleb kept his head down and his eyes peeled. "So, if Farnum's been bribed, why do I need to sneak around like this? Isn't he the duly designated official and all that?"

"Hell, I don't know all the particulars. Doc did most of the talking in that respect. If you really want to know, you can ask Farnum yourself."

Caleb looked at where Creek had stopped and saw the hotel directly in front of him. The front door of that building was already swinging open and Farnum was hustling outside.

"You were supposed to drop the key off alone," Farnum said. "I can't be seen with a fugitive out here in the open."

Although there were plenty of people scattered along the street, none of them seemed particularly interested in what Farnum was doing. The saloons were teeming with life and swarming with willing women, which easily eclipsed the sight of the little man with the bulbous nose.

"After the way things panned out today," Creek said, "you're not in any position to make demands."

Farnum turned his back to the street and pulled his hat down to cover most of his face when he bowed his head. "I did the best I could. Your friend's free, isn't he?"

"Not legally. The deal was for him to be acquitted."

Caleb may not have liked standing by and hearing his fate discussed as if he wasn't there, but it seemed to be leaning in his favor. At the very least, it did him some good to see the little self-important man squirm.

"There was some fast-talking going on in there," Farnum explained. "What was I supposed to do? Make it obvious that I was already leaning one way or another?"

Caleb couldn't resist saying, "Heaven forbid you be-smirch your integrity in this fine community."

Farnum straightened up a bit, took the key from Creek, and gripped the lapel of his coat as if he was posing for a portrait. "I'm respected enough to preside over a trial. A trial, by the way, which wound up perfectly all around. Folks have already forgotten about them two that were killed. There'll be a flap about you escaping from jail, but it wouldn't be the first time it's happened. This camp don't rank high enough with the Federals for any real search to be put into motion."

"And what about Bullock?" Caleb asked.

Farnum ground his teeth together and fretted with the lapels of his coat as if he was waiting for the other two men to forget that question had even come up. When Caleb and Creek only stared at him harder, Farnum grumbled, "You should probably leave town as soon as possible. Actually . . . tonight would be the best. Does Bullock know you went missing yet?"

Caleb choked back the obscenity he wanted to shout and balled his fists. "This is great. Now I'm a fugitive."

Oddly enough, Creek forced back a laugh. "No good deed goes unpunished."

As much as he wanted to hit something or someone, Caleb couldn't help but let out his breath in an exasperated laugh.

When he saw Farnum start to chuckle as well, Caleb lost his sense of humor.

"I take it Doc paid you to see to it I was set loose?" Caleb asked.

"In gold," Creek added.

Farnum nodded quickly. "And I held up my end of the bargain."

"I suppose Doc was guaranteed a smooth hearing and some favorable results. Instead, Creek lost his claim and I'm on the run."

Creek didn't add anything to that, but judging by the look on Farnum's face, he didn't really need to.

"You're gonna get me a new horse," Caleb said. "Plus, some supplies for the ride I've gotta take."

"What? This is preposterous!"

"Then maybe I should just see about taking some kind of refund out of your hide." Even though Caleb didn't have a gun at his side, the intensity in his voice was more than enough to back him up. All he needed to do was take half a step forward to bring about some immediate results.

"All right, all right," Farnum said. "You're right. Things didn't work out exactly as I thought they would, but that's only because that other fellow talked right over me. I can get you a horse, but supplies?"

"You've got a whole store," Creek pointed out.

"Yeah," Caleb added. "I was in your store for that disgrace of a hearing."

"Fine, fine. Follow me and I'll take you there myself. But you'll have to be quick and you can only have a few necessities for that ride you're taking. Once you get that horse, you'd best hop onto it and get out of here as quickly as you can."

Caleb let out a short, humorless laugh. "Believe me. The sooner I put this place behind me, the better."

True to his word, Farnum led Caleb and Creek around to the back entrance of his dry-goods store and let them stock up. Creek only took a small helping of coffee and some jerked beef, but Caleb stuffed his pockets a bit more. By the time he left that store, Caleb had managed to snag everything from the supplies he actually needed to a new hat, a shiny pocketknife, and a few expensive-looking trinkets he didn't need. Before he made his way to the coats and suits in the back of the store, Caleb felt an insistent tugging on his sleeve.

."Time to go," Creek said. "There's a couple horses around back. Pick one and put it to work."

"All right," Caleb replied as he placed his new hat on his head. "Nice doing business with you."

Creek managed to wait until he was out of the store before busting out into laughter. "Now that was funny. I thought for sure you were gonna get a new set of clothes out of that deal."

"If I didn't think his merchandise was infested by fleas, I might have done that." Stepping up to a stall in a small lot behind the store, Caleb asked, "Are those the horses Farnum was talking about?"

"Yep," Creek replied. "Brass sold them to Farnum a few weeks ago."

Caleb wasted no time in selecting one of the two animals and taking its reins. "Well, this one's mine now. Let's get the hell out of this godforsaken camp."

"Not so fast," Creek said. "And we can't go that way."

Craning his neck to look down the alley he was about to use, Caleb asked, "Why not?"

"Because we're set to meet up with Doc in an hour and we can't get to the spot from that direction. Besides, we need to take a quick ride past the Bella Union and let Doc know we're on track. He may just need a little backing right about now."

～～～

"Three's full," Doc announced as he laid his cards down for everyone at the table to see.

Vasily squinted and leaned forward to examine the cards more closely. Seated directly across from Doc, Alice Ivers shook her head and pitched her hand. The man next to Doc let out a sigh and slapped his cards down as if he meant to punish them.

"Easy now, Bullock," Doc said. "Those cards didn't do anything wrong."

"The hell they didn't," Bullock replied. "They just cost me my third hand of the night. Maybe I should pack it in."

"You think like that and you won't ever come out ahead," Alice said.

Vasily knocked on the table as if he was knocking on a door. "Then deal. No more talk."

"Where's Randal?" Doc asked as he shuffled the deck and looked around. "I thought he was going to show up here tonight, as well."

"I don't know," Bullock said as he checked his pocket watch. "But if I see him, I'll let him know you're looking for him. Right now, I should get going."

"Too late to leave now," Doc said. "You've already got your hand in front of you."

Bullock looked down and saw a neat pile of five cards lying facedown in front of him. They'd been dealt so quickly and so quietly that he didn't even realize they were headed his way.

Alice took the unlit cigar from her mouth and rolled it between her fingers. "Rules are rules, Sheriff. It wouldn't be proper to let perfectly good cards be pitched without being played."

While Bullock may have seemed somewhat annoyed at first, Alice's soothing tone and sweet glance seemed to have dulled his edge. "All right. But this is the last hand. I've got rounds to make."

"Not even officially in office and already adhering to your duties," Doc said. "How civic-minded of you."

"Sometimes I don't know when you're pulling my leg or not, Doc," Bullock replied in a somewhat warning tone.

Doc shrugged and fanned his cards. "Sometimes, neither do I. What say you, Vasily?"

"I say raise. One hundred dollars."

Alice studied the Russian, but not for very long. "That does it for me," she said as she tossed in her cards.

Bullock got his cards situated and then promptly tossed

them onto the same stack as Alice's. "Me, too. Good night to you all."

"I'm in," Doc announced. As he counted up the money needed to cover the raise, Doc looked at the saloon's front window. The glance was quick and went unnoticed simply because he'd been doing it throughout the entire game. In fact, the excellent view of that window was why he'd chosen his seat in the first place. Doc spotted two familiar men approaching the saloon. Creek gave a quick wave into the Bella Union and Caleb rode alongside him with his hat pulled down and his head hanging low to obscure his face.

Unfortunately, it seemed that Bullock was also about to catch sight of Caleb and Creek riding down Main Street.

Vasily asked for two cards and Doc flipped them to him. Then Doc dealt himself the two he'd needed to fill in what he'd discarded. Only a few seconds had passed, but that was long enough for Bullock to say his good-byes to a few of the locals in the place and head for the door.

Creek and Caleb were just now passing in front of the saloon.

"What the hell is that?" Doc asked in a loud, offended tone.

Vasily was still in the process of gathering his cards. "What?"

"That extra card under your arm," Doc replied with angrily narrowed eyes.

At first, Vasily was grinning. But when he moved his arm and found the card that had been wedged under there, his smile quickly disappeared. "I don't know where that came from."

Doc pounded the table with his fist and got up quickly enough to knock his chair over. "The only two places it could have come from is your sleeve or your palm. Either way, you're in for some trouble."

Still holding his arms up, Vasily looked around like a drowning man searching for a low-hanging branch. "You were sitting there, Alice. What did you see?"

Alice gnawed on her cigar for what felt like an eternity. It didn't take a particularly keen observer to figure Vasily was genuinely upset. Her powers of observation had been put to the test, however, when she'd barely caught sight of Doc flipping that extra card under Vasily's arm during the deal. The only reason she hadn't said anything before was out of pure curiosity to see where such a reckless and peculiar maneuver could be leading.

When she caught Doc glancing at Bullock, Alice figured out at least a piece of Doc's plan. "I didn't see anything," she finally replied. "Just leave me out of this one."

Doc didn't waste any more time before leveling an arm at Bullock and saying, "As the closest thing to the law in this camp, you should settle this, Bullock!"

Even though Bullock had been watching Doc's table since the commotion had started, he seemed just as confused as everyone else in the room. Grudgingly, he walked back to the table and asked, "What the hell's going on here? This was a friendly game when I left it."

"And I thought it still was," Doc replied. "That is, until this one started palming aces."

Vasily still hadn't touched the card that had been found under his elbow. "I never even saw that card until Doc pointed it out. This is some sort of mistake."

Reaching down to the table, Bullock picked up the card and flipped it over. It was the ace of clubs.

"How'd you know it was an ace, Doc?" Bullock asked.

Without missing a beat, Doc shrugged and asked, "What other card would someone want to palm?"

After mulling that over, Bullock snapped the card back onto the table. "I've had enough of this already and I sure as hell am not going through another official hearing. There's already a man in my jail bound for the courthouse in Yankton and I'm too damn tired to haul another one in. You two men want to settle this like civil folks or do I have to keep talking?"

There was a moment of heavy silence as everyone in the room seemed to hold their breath. All eyes were drifting from Bullock to Doc and to Vasily, just waiting to find out whose blood would get spilled first.

As always, Doc was the first to break the silence.

"I'll be the bigger man," Doc said. "Consider the matter settled."

Bullock blinked and relaxed his posture, but kept his hand by his gun. "You sure about that?"

Looking at the Russian, Doc asked, "What'd you have before the draw?"

Vasily showed his cards. "Three nines."

"You've got me beat," Doc replied as he showed a pair of tens and the ace of hearts. "Take the pot. Now, if you'll excuse me, I'll be on my way."

Bullock nodded and let out the breath he'd been holding.

"Wait a second," Vasily growled. "You cannot accuse me of cheating and walk away. Where did that card come from?"

"Oh, I'm sure it was an honest mistake," Doc replied in a voice that was laced with just enough sarcasm to ruffle Vasily's feathers.

"Admit what you did, Holliday," Vasily snapped.

Doc held up his hands as he walked toward the door. "I admitted a mistake and settled the score fairly. Does anyone dispute that?"

Nobody spoke, although Alice did let out a giggle, which she covered up with her hand.

"You're a picture of decorum, Vasily," Doc said. "Keep up the fine display."

If Vasily had intended on letting the matter drop, his mind was quickly changed when he saw the grin on Doc's face and the subtle wink Doc gave as he turned his back to the rest of the room.

"Don't turn your back to me, Holliday!" Vasily shouted.

And then the Russian made the worst move he could make. He went for his gun and called down a chaotic torrent as everyone from Bullock, the bartender, and every man responsible for keeping the peace within the Bella Union armed themselves in kind.

The saloon erupted with the stomping of boots against floorboards, the overturning of chairs, and so many shouting voices that they all blended into one.

Doc walked outside, checked his watch, and then nodded

to Caleb and Creek who were waiting farther down the street at the edge of Chinatown. Before taking another step, Doc turned and eased the door open so he could reach inside the Bella Union. After taking his coat from the stand near the door, Doc pulled it on and walked quickly down the street.

As more and more people were drawn to the sounds coming from the Bella Union, Doc untied his horse from a nearby post, climbed into the saddle, and rode away. By the time he got to Caleb and Creek, Doc was laughing hard enough to dredge up some nasty coughs from the back of his throat.

"What the hell was that about?" Caleb asked.

Doc appeared to be truly offended. "That's a fine way to thank me for a perfectly good distraction. Or would you have preferred it if Bullock stepped outside just in time to watch you moseying along, pretty as you please?"

"If you two wanna bicker, how about we do it once we're a few miles away from camp," Creek suggested. "Between the jailbreak and looting Farnum's store, Caleb isn't exactly welcome around here no more."

Doc grinned and nodded as he extended a hand. "Well done, my friend. I hope you soaked that little weasel for all he's worth."

Perhaps it was the smell of fresh air or the prospect of leaving Deadwood, but Caleb smiled and shook Doc's hand. "I did my best, Doc. All the same, Creek's right. We should put this camp behind us and maybe even find a spot to lay low for a bit."

"What do you say, Creek?" Doc asked. "Care to join us?"

Creek Johnson seemed amused by the other two, but winced as he saw the commotion now spilling out of the Bella Union and onto Main Street. "Seems like I don't have a lot of choice."

{10}

It wasn't an easy ride through the Black Hills. After parting ways with Creek Johnson a few miles outside of Deadwood, Doc and Caleb rode south with the hopes of catching a train bound for Laclede, Kansas. It would have been a tedious process under any circumstances, but the harsh winter only made things worse. Piles of snow made it difficult to tell the difference between a patch of rugged trail and a cluster of rocks. Bitter cold made their horses want to move slower, while the thought of crossing paths with anyone looking to drag them back into jail made the riders want to go faster. No matter what pace they kept, the winding paths snaking through the Black Hills made it hard to tell if they were truly making any progress at all.

Despite the fact that they weren't native to the Dakotas, both men knew plenty of more direct routes to get where they were going. Unfortunately, those routes would only bring them closer to anyone out searching for the fugitives escaping local justice. Caleb wasn't certain he could get all the way to Kansas without anyone seeing him, but he thought it was a good idea to try to get as far from Deadwood as possible without running the risk of his whereabouts being reported back to Bullock. That, combined with the ever-present cold, made the entire next day more of a trial than the farce held in E. B. Farnum's store.

For all the trouble Caleb had in adjusting to the northern climate, Doc found it progressively difficult to keep upright for more than a few hours at a stretch. Although he would insist he was fine after a bout of coughing, Doc kept spitting bloody wads onto the snowy ground. Caleb kept his eye on the Georgian, but knew it was useless to suggest anything other than moving forward along their chosen path.

"Where's Laclede, anyway?" Caleb asked as he shifted to try to get more comfortable in the frozen leather of his saddle.

Doc cleared his throat and spoke in a voice that was strained from the effort of holding back a cough. "Kansas," he said.

"I know that much, but what's there?"

"I have family there."

"No offense, but why do I want to pay your family a visit?"

"My aunt Anna lives in Laclede. She'll be happy to see us and she's a fine cook. When's the last time you've had a proper home-cooked supper?"

"As tempting as that sounds," Caleb said, "there's better ways to spend our time. Didn't you say Farnum would see to it that nobody bothered to come looking for us?"

Doc grinned as he recalled his last days in Deadwood. "Oh, yes. But do you honestly think he can back that up?"

Reluctantly, Caleb shrugged. "Probably not. He may not even bother trying if that proves to be too much work."

"Oh, he'll hold it up. It's either that or risk letting folks know about the gold we gave him. Something tells me the Honorable Mr. Farnum isn't one to be parted with his gold. Speaking of which," Doc added as he dug into one of his saddlebags. "Here's your cut."

For a moment, Caleb didn't realize what Doc was talking about. His memory was jogged quickly enough when Doc handed him a small pouch that was a whole lot heavier than it looked.

"Is this . . . from Creek?" Caleb asked.

"That's right. You look perplexed, Caleb. If I've made a mistake, you can most certainly hand it back."

"I don't think so," Caleb snapped. He then opened the pouch and took a quick look inside. When he saw the rough chunks of gold sitting amid a generous helping of glittering dust, he cinched the pouch shut and tucked it away.

Doc leaned his head back and glanced at the snow-covered trees rising up to his left like the walls of a fort. "If you'd like to invest in my current run of good luck, I could always use a bigger stake. I can't guarantee your return, but it could prove to be a hell of an investment."

Glancing around to make sure nobody was paying too much attention to him, Caleb said, "I've learned firsthand how luck can change, remember?"

"Oh, yes," Doc replied sleepily. "You really should adopt a more optimistic outlook where that's concerned."

"My outlook's just fine. Actually, from that same outlook, I saw Creek hand over the deed to his claim."

Doc stared at Caleb with a furrowed brow. "From your outlook? I was under the impression you'd been properly educated. That sounds like one of those miners talking."

"My grammar may not be perfect, but my eyesight is just fine and I sure as hell saw Creek hand over that deed during my hearing."

Settling back into his saddle, Doc let a smile take up residence beneath the thick mustache on his upper lip. "Indeed, you did."

"Then where'd this gold come from?"

"Did you hear the explosions that night Creek and I went to put those two partners of his into the ground?"

"Yeah."

"Only one of those was for a grave."

Caleb leaned forward and lowered his voice as if he was worried some of the animals tucked away in their holes might be listening in. "The rest was to blow up those rocks?"

Doc nodded. "Creek wasn't lying about the gold that was under there. We could have gotten more if we had the time or a few extra sets of hands, but I'd say we made out pretty well."

"How much did you get?"

"I'm not a miner, but it seemed like a lot to me. Creek was happy and the illustrious Mr. Farnum could barely contain himself with what we gave him. Creek had his doubts about whether or not Farnum would be swayed when it came to his capacities as a judge, but I knew better than to underestimate the depths of a small man's depravity."

Even though Caleb nodded, it wasn't entirely due to what Doc was saying. "And I assume you got a cut of that gold?"

"Of course. I daresay I earned every bit of it."

"I'm not arguing, Doc. I'm just saying we all made out pretty well. Creek included."

Doc shrugged and folded his arms across his chest. "He could have gotten a lot more if he wasn't so quick to hand over that deed. Then again, he didn't seem as happy as I would have expected when we were scooping away those blasted rocks. Maybe it wasn't as big of a strike as he'd thought."

"Or maybe he's smarter than most folks and knows when to pull up stakes and cash in for a profit."

"Either way, I know whoever's the legal owner of that claim now is going to have to go through plenty of trouble to find any more gold," Doc said. "We were there well into the next morning and picked up all the gold that was loosed in that explosion. Creek loaded up a wagon with rocks I thought were useless, but he probably knew what he was doing."

"Was there a cave?" Caleb asked.

Doc opened one eye halfway and looked at Caleb with a puzzled expression. "Pardon?"

"Under the rocks. Was there a cave under there?"

"There was a hole with some frozen water in it, but I'd hardly call it a cave."

Caleb let out a breath that drifted from his mouth like

steam from a kettle. It was the closest he'd been to relaxed since he'd left Deadwood. "Then maybe Creek's even smarter than I thought. He was banking on a cave being under those rocks that was supposed to be lined with gold."

Doc let out a short snort of a laugh. "That'd explain why he was so quick to hand over that deed. And here I thought I deserved an award for my talents as an actor back at that hearing."

Both men sat back and enjoyed the ride for a few moments before Caleb spoke up.

"Where are we supposed to board this train again?"

After a moment to think it over, Doc replied, "I don't recall the name of the town, but it's not far from here. We should be able to get a ticket to Kansas City from there and then on to Laclede."

"Maybe I'll buy a ticket to St. Louis."

"St. Louis, huh? I might join you. There's supposed to be some fine games being held there over the summer."

"Not over the summer, Doc. I think I may head there now. I can buy my ticket when we get to Kansas City. There's gotta be a line that runs from there to—"

"You'll miss out on my aunt's cooking," Doc warned.

"Maybe I'll stop by her place on my way back. That is, if you leave word for her to expect me."

Doc shrugged. "You can go where you want. I'm not your keeper. I just think you may want to keep your head down for a little while and the best way to accomplish that doesn't involve starting up a game in St. Louis."

"Actually, I was kicking around the idea of starting up a gambling hall. I wouldn't run the place," Caleb explained. "But this gold should be enough to put together a decent establishment and with all the things I've picked up these last few years, it'd be a whole lot easier running card games than a saloon. Once things get rolling, I'm sure I could scrape up another investor who might be interested in having a place they can call home away from home."

"You'd better not be looking at me when you say that. I prefer to clean out card games, not run them for a living."

"Consider it, Doc. I know I'm not cut out for running a business and nobody in their right mind would say you were."

"I agree wholeheartedly with that," Doc said.

"But there's something to be said in having something real to your name. Something more than fancy clothes or whatever can fit into a saddlebag."

"Some of us don't have the luxury of thinking that far into the future."

"It doesn't need to be a big commitment," Caleb explained as he shifted his eyes toward the horizon. "More of an investment. I'd have some respectable sort running the place and I'd keep my head down until I'm not wanted by some lawman or another. You could just be a silent partner. We would come and go when we please, keep a room for when one of us is in town, sit in on the good games, maybe even see a profit for those times when I don't have bags of gold falling into my hands."

Doc made a rumbling sound under his breath. "I don't know about you, but I plan on having as much gold fall into my hands as possible."

"You know what I mean, Doc."

"And if you had this place of yours, I suppose you'd go there in the tough times," Doc pointed out. "Times like these right now."

"Well . . . sure."

"And when you got there, anyone who knew you had a stake in that place would know exactly where to find you?"

"Well . . . yeah."

Settling back into his saddle as if he was about to doze off, Doc muttered, "That plan sounds like a real daisy."

Caleb wanted to tell Doc that it was a hell of a plan, that it was a plan worth the price of a ticket to St. Louis. Seeing the self-satisfied look on Doc's face, Caleb thought about plenty of things he wanted to say to him. There was only one thing preventing Caleb from saying them: He knew Doc was right.

Letting out a sigh, Caleb stared down at his boots.

"Here," Doc said as he reached over to hand his flask to Caleb. "This'll help."

The whiskey was a cheap variety that had been purchased in Deadwood when quantity was more of a concern than quality. It burned Caleb's throat and ran down his gullet like a flame following a trail of kerosene.

Once again, Doc was right.

The whiskey did help.

{11}

Even as Doc swung down from his saddle after his long ride, he still didn't know the name of the town where he'd wound up. One thing he knew for certain was that there was no train coming through that place, since there were no tracks in sight. There was, however, a platform used for loading stagecoaches next to a wooden board advertising rides to a station where trains could be boarded. Pulling in a shallow breath, Doc straightened his coat and set his priorities in order.

"I believe that's a saloon over there," he said. "I wonder if they're still serving lunch."

Caleb dismounted as well, tied his horse to a hitching post, and rubbed his backside until he regained some feeling back there. "Go from one seat to another? No thanks."

"Whether we catch a train, a stagecoach, or ride our horses even farther into the ground, this may be our last chance to eat something that's less than a week old."

"I'd rather stretch my legs," Caleb replied. Without another word, he hobbled to the small building that sold tickets for the stagecoach.

It was still cold, but not nearly as bad as it had been the

previous few days. Then again, just having some buildings around them to shield them from the wind could have made most of the difference. Keeping his coat over his shoulders, Doc took hold of his walking stick and made his way across the platform. He kept his back straight and his chin held high. He also kept his arm stiff and the muscles in his shoulder tensed to disguise the fact that he was supporting most of his weight upon the cane.

As Doc stepped over to the board where the stagecoach's schedule was displayed, he nodded to everyone who met his gaze. The folks who took in the sight of his lean, pale face with a hint of pity were disregarded as if they'd suddenly blinked from existence. Doc found what he wanted on the schedule fairly quickly. What he saw left him in a good enough mood to whistle a lively tune as he crossed the street and headed for the saloon he'd spotted before. Like most saloons catering to travelers, this one was small and sure to be overpriced. From Doc's experience, it would also be fairly well packed with gamblers who were more concerned with killing time than protecting their money.

"'Scuse me," someone asked from behind Doc and to his right. "You know where I can find a man named Holliday?"

As he turned around, Doc was prepared for plenty of things. His hand tightened around the top of his walking stick and he shifted his arms to double-check that both of his guns were where they should be. Even as he prepared himself for the worst, Doc wore a friendly, relaxed smile.

"That's my name," Doc said. "Who's asking?"

The man who approached Doc was in his early thirties with tussled red hair that made him look more like a big kid. His eyes were somewhat close set but warm. "I've heard plenty about you, Holliday. Or should I call you Doc?"

"If you call me doctor, I can check your teeth for free."

Just then, a set of heavy steps moved in toward Doc from behind. They swooped toward him and stopped just short of running him over. When they came to a stop, the sound of those steps gave way to a low, scratchy voice. "I ain't callin' you a doctor, but I will call you a gravedigger. You're sure as hell gonna need one."

Doc felt a rough hand shove him between the shoulder blades toward a narrow building next to the ticket office. Rather than allow himself to be shoved any further, Doc turned so he could get a look at the man behind him. Although the man's face was easy enough to see, it was the gun in his hand that caught Doc's attention.

"What's the meaning of this?" Doc asked.

"Oh, you didn't like my joke?" the gunman asked. "After the shit you pulled in Deadwood, I would'a thought you'd like a good joke."

The gunman had a lean, muscular build and a slightly stooped posture that was common among cowboys. His hair was the color of sun-bleached dirt and several scars of varying freshness crossed his cheeks and neck. Cold, twitchy eyes glared defiantly at Doc. They were killer's eyes and they practically begged Doc to make a move. When that move didn't come, the gunman nodded toward the redhead and motioned for Doc to follow him into the narrow building.

Before the door was open all the way, the smell that drifted from the building let Doc know it was an outhouse built to accommodate several people at once. One man wearing spectacles was on his way out and was hurried along as the redhead practically tossed him into the street. The gunman who'd stepped up behind Doc spun the Georgian around like a rag doll and shoved him into the outhouse. While Doc couldn't help but wince at the overpowering stench inside the well-used building, the gunman barely seemed to notice.

"You know who I am?" the gunman asked.

"No, but I suppose you're about to tell me."

"I'm Arkansas Dave Rudabaugh. When you thought you were cheating Sammy in Deadwood, you were cheating me. What've you got to say about that?"

Doc was well versed in how to read a man across a poker table, but a blind man wouldn't have had trouble deciphering the murderous glint in Rudabaugh's eyes. For that reason, Doc made a choice he seldom favored and kept his mouth shut.

Rudabaugh nodded slowly. "That's what I thought. I ought to kill you right now for cheating me outta what's rightfully mine."

"And what might that be?" Doc asked.

"My gold!" Rudabaugh snapped as he grabbed Doc by the lapel. Even as he slammed Doc against a wall, Rudabaugh kept his gun wedged up under Doc's ribs. "Sammy checked out that claim hisself before he got his hands on the deed. He knew there was gold there. When he got a look after that trial, all he found was a pile of rocks."

Gritting his teeth and choking back the anger welling up in the back of his throat, Doc hissed, "That's ridiculous. He should have also found the bodies of two men buried there. I believe you may have known them."

Rudabaugh wouldn't have looked more stunned if Doc had grown a tail and wagged it. That quickly gave way to a more intense version of the sneer that had been on his face before. "You want me to shoot you?" he asked. "Because I will."

Staring Rudabaugh dead in the eyes, Doc replied, "Then go ahead and do it. You came all the way up here to shoot someone, then either get it over with or stop wasting my time. The only thing that smells worse than the inside of this shithouse is the air coming out of your mouth."

In the space of a second, Rudabaugh went from shocked to enraged. He took a step back so he could raise his pistol to face level, giving Doc a fraction of a second in which to act.

Doc only needed half that time.

Slapping Rudabaugh's hand away, Doc didn't even flinch when the gun went off inside the confines of that outhouse. Even though the redhead was in there to back Rudabaugh's play, he didn't have enough room to maneuver well enough to be of any real help. Doc was able to toss his cane to his left hand while pulling one of his guns from under his coat before Rudabaugh knew what was happening.

Despite being surprised by the changing situation, Rudabaugh only needed to bring his arm back and pull his trigger. His shot was quick and didn't draw any blood, but it did come close enough to throw off Doc's aim. Both men's shots punched holes through the outhouse and put a gritty haze into the foul air.

Doc snapped his left arm forward to bury the cane's handle into Rudabaugh's stomach. The sharp impact knocked Rudabaugh back a few steps while driving a good portion of the wind from his lungs. Still pulling in a haggard breath, Rudabaugh lowered his shoulder and charged Doc like a bull.

Holding out his arm so he could sight properly along the top of his pistol, the redhead aimed over Rudabaugh's lowered head and picked his target. He was so focused on taking his shot that he missed the sound of the door opening behind him.

A hand slapped down upon the redhead's shoulder and clamped shut in a powerful grip. Before the redhead could get a look behind him, he was being hauled from the outhouse like a cat being picked up by the scruff of its neck.

"What the hell do you think you're doing?" Caleb snarled as he spun the redhead around and shoved him up against the side of the outhouse.

Gritting his teeth, the redhead twitched his head back and forth to get a look at what he was facing. There were a few people nearby, but they stayed close to the stagecoach platform and watched from a fairly safe distance. None of them were interested in joining the fray.

Keeping his grip on the redhead's shoulder, Caleb pointed his gun at the man's face and thumbed the trigger back. "Nobody there's gonna help you," he growled. "Who the hell are you?"

Since all he got in response to that question was a silent glare, Caleb asked, "Where's Doc?"

The redhead didn't need to say a thing. Instead, Caleb got the answer to one of his questions when the back end of the outhouse cracked open like a rotten egg. Caleb may not have been able to see the wall break, but he could hear the splintering wood and scuffling boots just fine.

Suddenly, Doc staggered into Caleb's sight. His boots skidded against the frozen dirt, tripping Doc up as he stumbled far enough to knock the backs of his legs against the side of the stagecoach platform. But even as he was falling backward, Doc took a swipe at Rudabaugh with his cane.

Rudabaugh lunged forward to fire a point-blank shot at Doc when he caught the end of the cane on his forearm. The impact made a loud crack and put a pained wince upon Rudabaugh's face. "You skinny son of a bitch," he snapped as he drove a boot into Doc's ribs.

Although most of the wind was knocked out of him from that kick, Doc still managed to roll to one side as Rudabaugh followed up with a powerful stomp. Rudabaugh's heel pounded against the edge of the platform, bringing a few loud obscenities to his lips.

Like most of the other folks nearby, Caleb had been unable to look away from the brutal spectacle. He knew he'd taken his eyes away from the redhead for a bit too long when he felt the other man wriggle out of his grasp. Thinking he might already be too late to correct his mistake, Caleb turned to face the redhead and was just in time to see the gunman point his pistol directly at his head.

Caleb let his reflexes take over and dropped to one knee. The redhead pulled his trigger and sent a round hissing through the spot where Caleb's head had been. When Caleb pulled his own trigger, it was quick but somewhat accurate.

The redhead let out a pained shriek as hot lead ripped through his hip and glanced off bone. It wasn't a fatal shot, but had enough kick behind it to spin the redhead like a top before he fell over.

"Hand over that gold and this can end right now," Rudabaugh said.

Caleb glanced quickly over to Doc and Rudabaugh, but was more concerned with the redhead on the ground in front of him. Keeping his gun aimed at the redhead, Caleb stepped forward so he could disarm the other man. Before he could get close enough to take the redhead's gun, Caleb saw the man roll onto his back and raise his pistol.

Caleb aimed and prepared to fire, but stopped short when he realized any muscle twitch would probably cause the redhead's gun to go off. Since the redhead seemed to have come to the same conclusion regarding Caleb, both men found themselves in a standoff.

For the moment, Doc and Rudabaugh were in a similar situation.

The silence that followed Rudabaugh's ultimatum was soon broken by dry, hacking laughter.

"You must need spectacles, Dave," Doc said through his laughter. "This doesn't exactly strike me as a moment where you have the upper hand."

"It don't, huh?" Leaning forward a bit so he loomed over the fallen dentist, Rudabaugh practically touched the end of his gun's barrel against Doc's forehead. "What about now?"

"Right about now," Doc replied, "you should be praying that I don't get a twitch in my finger."

Rudabaugh's eyes snapped downward just long enough to see the gun in Doc's hand. Not only was the pearl-handled .38 aimed at Rudabaugh's chest, but the trigger was already halfway pulled.

Slowly, a filthy grin crept onto Rudabaugh's face. "You don't wanna shoot me."

"Oh, I'm inclined to disagree," Doc said.

"You shoot me, and you might as well be shooting that pretty little Alice, too."

Doc furrowed his brow and looked over at Caleb as if he hoped to find something a bit more encouraging. Finding nothing of the sort, Doc shifted his eyes back to Rudabaugh and asked, "What are you talking about?"

"That pretty lady you played cards with in Deadwood," Rudabaugh said. "The one who chews on a cigar while tossing one crooked deal after another. I believe her name's Poker Alice."

Seeing that he now had Doc's undivided attention, Rudabaugh started to relax. He shifted back upon one foot before he saw Doc's gun arm tense. Remaining fixed in his spot, Rudabaugh ran his tongue along his teeth and spoke in a quick, rasping voice. "I heard you got a sweet spot for that

Alice. You and her played in the Bella Union just like two peas in a pod."

"So?" Doc asked.

"So, if I don't get outta this place alive, the man I got holding on to Alice for safekeeping will put a bullet through her pretty face."

The lines etched into Doc's face deepened into a disgusted scowl. "Using a woman to cover your own hide? That's pathetic."

"Call it what you will, but at least I ain't a liar and a card cheat."

"Fine, then," Doc said. "Run away from here with your tail between your legs."

"To hell with that!" Caleb shouted. "He's bluffing about Alice!"

When Doc smiled, it was a humorless expression that seemed more chilling than anything else. "That makes him even more pathetic. Either way, he's not worth wasting another bullet."

Despite the posturing from Doc and Caleb, Rudabaugh didn't lose his grin. Even hearing the pained whimpers coming from the wounded redhead wasn't enough to put the slightest bit of concern upon Rudabaugh's face.

"You think I'm bluffing?" Rudabaugh asked. "Then you must not give a shit about Alice, after all. That may not be so bad. She's pretty enough to earn her keep one way or another. Since your friend seems to have put a hurting on Brad over there, I'll be able to ride that bitch myself all night long."

"Caleb's right," Doc said evenly. "You're bluffing."

Rudabaugh rolled his eyes up slightly and pulled in a deep breath as if he was fondly remembering a summer day from his youth. "My partner told me she was sitting at one of the back tables in the Bella Union. It was hard to get her out of her chair because she had her hooks deep into some skinny fella with a strange accent. I believe his name was Vastly or somethin' like that."

Doc's eyes narrowed and the muscles in his jaw tensed.

"There was another fella there, too," Rudabaugh continued. "Some asshole who ran an opera house. Alice was cleaning both of them out when my boys snatched her up and dragged her behind the Union. They meant to fuck her right then and there, but I told 'em to hold off until I got here. Now that you sidetracked me for this long, I can't wait to get back to her. I hear she's got a fine, tight little—"

"I can kill you and be back in Deadwood before any of your boys know you're gone," Doc snapped.

Shrugging, Rudabaugh said, "Maybe . . . maybe not. There's an easier way to get her cut loose, though."

Doc shifted his weight, but was unwilling to lower his gun or drop his cane.

Since the man in front of him was wounded and on the ground, Caleb was better able to do what Doc couldn't. Reaching into his pocket, Caleb found the pouch of gold Doc had given him. "Here," he said while tossing the pouch to Rudabaugh. "Take your damn gold."

Although he twitched at the sudden movement of the pouch flying toward him, Rudabaugh was still able to reach out with his free hand and snatch the pouch from the air. He weighed the pouch in his hand and then fumbled with it until he was able to take a quick look inside.

"This can't be all there is," Rudabaugh said as he clamped his hand around the pouch and stuffed it into his jacket pocket. "Sammy told me there was a hell of a lot more than could be stuffed into a pouch this size. Even ten pouches this size wouldn't cover it."

"The man who owned that claim didn't even know for certain what was there," Caleb said. "Nobody could know until they blasted those rocks away."

But Rudabaugh was shaking his head defiantly. "I ain't stupid and I ain't about to listen to your lies. You best collect that gold and bring it to that claim by sundown tomorrow or pretty little Alice will be cut up and left for the coyotes."

As he slowly lowered his gun arm, Rudabaugh eased away from Doc like a snake slithering back into its hole. The more time that passed without Doc making a move, the more Rudabaugh grinned. "You know I ain't bluffing," he said. "Bring me my goddamn gold or that bitch's blood will be on your hands."

Rudabaugh chuckled once under his breath as he turned away from Doc and walked around the outhouse. When he got within arm's reach of Caleb, he stared Caleb straight in the eyes and asked, "What're you gonna do, Injun? You wanna scalp my friend like the savage you are?"

As much as Caleb wanted to jam his gun barrel into a very unpleasant place on Rudabaugh's person, he kept himself from doing so.

"That's what I thought, red man," Rudabaugh sneered. Resting his gun casually upon his shoulder, Rudabaugh pulled in a breath and spat in Caleb's face. "That's for shooting my friend," he grunted.

While offering his free hand to the redhead, Rudabaugh said, "Come on, Brad. Let's go see how that pretty lady's doing."

Brad hissed in pain as he took the hand Rudabaugh offered and was hauled to his feet. The wound in the redhead's hip was slick with blood, but looked more like a deep scratch than anything else. After a few assisted steps, Brad was practically shoved to one of the horses tied up next to the stagecoach platform.

Rudabaugh kept his gun moving between Caleb and Doc. Once he was in the saddle, he took the reins and got his horse moving to the nearby trail. "Hope you folks enjoyed the show," Rudabaugh said to the petrified onlookers huddled upon the platform. With that, he rode away. Brad had lost most of the color in his face and had broken into a cold sweat after climbing into his own saddle, but managed to follow close behind Rudabaugh.

Before the thunder of those hooves could fade, Caleb had holstered his gun and rushed over to help Doc. By the time he got to where Doc had stumbled, Caleb found the Georgian was already on his feet.

"Do you really think he's got Alice?" Caleb asked.

Doc dusted himself off and looked around at the others standing nearby as if praying he could shoot one of them. By the time he looked back at Caleb, the rage in Doc's eyes hadn't even begun to fade. "I don't care if he got his hands on Alice or is just spouting off. I want that animal dead. You hear me, Caleb? Dead."

[12]

Caleb and Doc circled back toward Deadwood using a trail they'd found when they'd rushed out the last time. Actually, they'd found something only similar to a trail. It was a stretch of land that cut through the trees and led toward Deadwood—barely wide enough to accommodate a horse and only widened out in a few spots here and there. But Doc didn't much care how treacherous the trail was. It led toward Deadwood by way of Creek's relinquished claim, and that was all he cared about.

The night was cold enough to freeze the sweat in a man's boots. Although there was a half-moon visible in the starry sky, the darkness was thick enough to keep most prudent folks in their homes or close to a crackling fire. Since prudence was the farthest thing from their minds, Doc and Caleb rode slowly and never took their eyes from the trail.

After finding the river that snaked toward the claim, the two men tied off their horses and struck out on foot. They kept their feet moving just slow enough to feel the irregularities in the ground that they couldn't see. Dressed in battered riding clothes and an old jacket, Doc was nothing like the finely dressed gentleman that had left Deadwood. His eyes were narrowed and filled with purpose. His guns were worn in plain sight so he could get to them at the first hint of trouble.

Caleb was too focused to be so angry. Whenever he thought about Dave Rudabaugh, he could feel the blood boiling in his veins. Since he was given the task of keeping them both on track and not getting lost in the Black Hills, Caleb did his level best to try not to think about the outlaw. Considering the company he kept, that wasn't such an easy task.

"If that son of a bitch is foolish enough to show his face, I'll be more than happy to put a bullet through it," Doc snarled.

"He'll be there," Caleb replied. "Dave wanted that gold too badly for him not to show up. I just didn't know you cared for Alice so much."

Doc didn't even flinch. "She's a hell of a gambler and knows how to look out for her partners. She may have pulled a few trick plays, but she's never done anything to deserve being handled by the likes of that pig."

"Trick plays, huh?" Caleb asked. "Is that the new word for cheating?"

It took a moment, but the grin eventually found its way onto Doc's face. The gesture only managed to curl one end of his brushy mustache. "Tricks of the trade, my friend. Every professional has them."

"I guess card shears are less imposing than those tooth extractors you used to wave around."

"And they extract a hell of a lot more money, too."

The partners took a few more steps along the stream before both of them instinctively slowed down and stopped.

"This isn't far from where I found that rifleman," Doc said.

Caleb nodded. "And that means the claim is just ahead. I don't think anyone else is here yet. You think Creek is anywhere about?"

After pushing aside some of the bushes, Doc dropped to one knee and drew the .38 that hung under his left arm. "No," he said while checking the rounds inside the .38's cylinder. "Even if we did know where he went, there's no need to bother him."

Caleb watched Doc for a few more seconds before furrowing his brow and fixing a hard glare upon Doc. "How much gold did you and Creek get?"

"Why ask that now?"

"Because Rudabaugh's under the impression there was a ton of it and so was Creek. In fact, Creek was pretty convincing when he told me there had to have been more under those rocks than what could be split into a few pouches."

Doc smirked, holstered his first .38, and drew the second one. "That's funny," he said while checking the rounds in that pistol. "After all the jobs we've done together, you still get worried about being cheated out of your share."

"What about that time in Cheyenne?"

"An honest mistake," Doc quickly replied.

"All right, then. If you only have as much gold as I already handed over, how do you think Rudabaugh is going to react when that's all he gets? He's expecting one hell of a big strike."

"Oh, he'll be stricken all right," Doc said as he hefted one .38 in each hand. "At least ten or twelve times."

Even though the sunlight had been fading, Caleb saw Doc as if he was looking at him under a clear, afternoon sky. "You're not planning on handing anything over."

"Never was," Doc said. "And don't worry about the gold you gave away. I'm certain that horse's ass will have it on him when he comes to meet us here. We can take it off whatever's left of him."

Just then, the sounds of branches snapping and hooves crunching against the cold ground announced the presence of several approaching riders. Doc and Caleb crouched down behind the thick tangle of branches and studied the clearing. In the nearby spot that had once been Creek Johnson's legal property, a trickle of water ran beneath cracked layers of ice. The pile of rocks had been disassembled and scattered around to reveal a shallow, empty hole.

"So you just want us to go in with guns blazing?" Caleb asked.

"What else would you suggest?"

After taking a moment to think, Caleb replied, "I don't know. After all the talk I heard from Creek, I thought he'd stashed more of that gold around here and told you about it while I was locked up."

Doc chuckled under his breath and peeked through the tangled branches in front of him. "Seems like you have a bigger optimistic streak in you than I'd thought. Either that, or you've spent too much time around these miners."

The approaching horses were getting close enough for a few of the riders' hushed voices to be heard. Caleb's hand went to the pistol at his side and drew it. He didn't need to check the gun to know if it was loaded. The .44 was as much a part of him as the fingers wrapped around its grip.

"So is there a plan?" Caleb asked.

Cocking his head slightly, Doc pondered that question for almost a full second before answering, "We let that smug jackass think he's got the upper hand until the first opportunity comes along for us to prove him wrong."

"Since you're so riled up, why don't you lead the way and I'll stay back to cover you?"

Doc's entire body was coiled like a spring and his eyes were fixed upon the clearing, waiting for the first sight of Rudabaugh or his men. "Fine," he said.

"What about Alice?"

"She's a smart woman," Doc hissed. "She'll know when to duck."

Caleb held his gun at the ready and listened to the approaching horses. The hooves sounded so close that he knew he should be able to see the gunmen at any moment. Before the first horse's nose emerged from the shadows cast by the trees across the clearing, Doc stepped out from his cover.

The Georgia-born dentist shrugged his shoulders to loosen his coat from around him. Flexing his fingers and arms, Doc let out a slow breath to prepare himself for what was to come.

Despite what he'd agreed to before, Caleb didn't like the way the horses had slowed down to mill about within those shadows. Knowing better than to think Doc would back down or retreat into some better cover, Caleb stepped out from his own spot to stand at Doc's side.

Shooting a quick look at Caleb, Doc nodded and then squared off with the trees.

"What's the matter, Dave?" Doc said under his breath. "Are you stupid enough to think we hadn't spotted you yet?"

At first, Caleb was certain it would only be a few more seconds before Rudabaugh either charged into the clearing or took a shot at them. Since there wasn't any gold in sight, his money was on the former.

But the longer it took for Rudabaugh to show himself, the more nervous Caleb got. That nervousness grew when he heard more horses stomping through the bushes around to his left.

"There's a lot more than two of them," Caleb whispered.

Doc nodded. "I know. And they're flanking us."

The shapes they'd already spotted stayed in the shadows. Since the other horses were closing in like a noose around him and Doc, Caleb raised his pistol and aimed at what he thought was the closest of the shadows.

"Come on out where we can see you," Caleb demanded. "And do it quick."

One dark figure rode forward, but it wasn't Dave Rudabaugh. It wasn't even the redhead who'd been called Brad. The man was familiar to both Caleb and Doc, but was the last one they'd expected to lead the others into the clearing.

"You both came," Samuel said in his shrill, twanging voice. "How convenient." Shifting in his saddle, Samuel looked back at the other riders and shouted, "I found them!"

As Caleb watched, more horses drew closer. It wasn't until then that he realized the rest of those horses had been circling the clearing rather than closing in on it directly. Although Caleb had been mistaken to think the horses were coming at him before, they were now all most definitely approaching the clearing.

"Where'd you go, Sam?" asked one of the riders.

"Over here! There's a clearing. I think it's that Injun who escaped."

"You heard the man," Bullock shouted from just beyond the clearing. "Let's bring that prisoner back to where he belongs!"

Caleb was frozen to his spot.

Doc swore under his breath as he backed away from the trees. "That son of a bitch double-crossed us," he snarled.

At least half a dozen horses were coming into the clearing near the pile of charred rocks. When they tried to retrace their steps, Caleb and Doc made another unsettling discovery.

"They're closing in from behind us," Caleb said.

Doc gritted his teeth and added, "From this side, too."

And as he frantically searched for a way out of that clearing that didn't involve charging through an armed posse who had something to prove, all Caleb could see was the slender figure sitting in his saddle, looking on with a smug grin on his face.

Waiting until Bullock and the other men were coming up next to him, Samuel announced, "I told you they'd be back here, Mr. Bullock. Maybe you should shoot them before they try to get away with my gold."

"First thing's first," Bullock said. "Round 'em up, boys!"

Those words brought the rest of the posse closing in on the clearing from every side that a horse could navigate. When he looked at Doc, Caleb knew the gambler was one bad decision away from ending his days of coughing up blood in a blaze of glory.

Since he didn't want to take his chances on another Deadwood trial or spend another night in that stinking shack, Caleb only had one choice.

"Come on, Doc! Follow me!" Caleb said as he turned and bolted toward the frozen stream.

Doc watched for a moment, right along with the rest of the men invading that clearing. The sight of Caleb running at full speed toward a sheet of half-frozen, half-cracked ice was more than enough to bring a smile to Doc's face.

"Oh, this ought to be fun," Doc muttered as he ran toward the stream as fast as his legs could carry him.

The clearing erupted with gunfire of all makes and models. Pistols of different calibers barked and spat hot lead at the two men fleeing toward the river. Shotguns sent waves of thunder through the air and tore apart tree trunks while chipping away at fallen rock. Fortunately, most of those shots were taken in a hurry before the men pulling the triggers could get a good look at their targets.

As he ran, Caleb ignored the panic gripping him like a cold, iron fist clamped around his stomach. He tried not to think about the bullets hissing past him or the pain that sparked in his ankles, knees, legs, and arms as he charged onto the fragile ice. The truth of the matter was that he hadn't actually planned on making it to the river before getting caught or killed.

Although Doc had followed Caleb to the edge of the stream, he stopped and turned so he could draw his second pistol. Caleb's voice was swallowed up by the roar of gunfire as Doc pulled his triggers and fired into the nearby clearing.

The stream was only four or five yards across, but that didn't mean it was easy going. Every one of Caleb's steps was a struggle to keep from skidding too far ahead and falling on his ass or stomping down too hard and punching his leg through the ice. No matter how hard he tried, Caleb still knocked several holes into the frozen crust. As luck would have it, he was able to pull his boots out of the holes he'd created and launch himself onto the opposite bank before finally losing his balance.

Caleb twisted around to land on his side. As he hit the cold, hard-packed ground, he was firing his gun into the trees.

Doc, on the other hand, was a sight to see.

Even as he fired both guns at once, Doc still wasn't making enough noise to cover his raucous laughter and almost maniacal hollering.

"Come on across!" Caleb yelled. "I'll cover you!"

At first, it seemed as if Doc hadn't heard what Caleb said.

Before Caleb drew enough breath to repeat himself, he saw Doc turn around to face the stream.

As soon as Doc stopped firing, Bullock and the others rushed toward him like a wave of thundering hooves intent on crushing him into dust. Still hesitant to kill Bullock or any of his men, Caleb fired over their heads. He still kept his aim low enough to let the posse know he meant business.

Judging by the look on Doc's face, he may have been running through an open field on his way to a picnic. A wide smile was plastered underneath his mustache, and he raced toward the already cracked ice without any fear of what might happen if he took one misstep.

Caleb winced as he saw Doc rush onto the ice. Then again, it wasn't the time to take things slow. Letting Doc do his best to get across the stream, Caleb kept firing until the hammers of both of his pistols slapped against the backs of spent rounds.

There was a moment of deathly calm as the posse realized Caleb's firing had stopped. In that short space of time, Caleb heard Doc's voice as he scrambled past.

"Come on," Doc wheezed. "What the hell are you waiting for?"

Keeping his comments to himself, Caleb got to his feet and backed away from the stream. His hands were already going through the motions of reloading his pistols and his eyes were fixed upon the approaching posse. What he couldn't believe was that Bullock and the rest of those men had come to a stop.

"Goddammit!" Bullock shouted. "We need to get across!"

Caleb looked down at the water and saw that most of the ice had been shattered by the two sets of boots that had stomped over it. Although one more man could have possibly inched his way across, there was no way in hell a single horse could take a step onto what remained of the frozen surface. Since the horses had already come to a stop, they couldn't exactly jump across from where they were standing.

Still surprised that he was alive, Caleb backed away until there was suitable cover between him and that stream. After that, he swallowed his pride, turned tail, and ran. Even though he never liked to run from a fight, it felt pretty good this time around. Judging by the smile that was still on Doc's face when Caleb caught up to him, the Georgian was thinking along those same lines.

Despite getting tripped up at the stream, Bullock and his posse didn't give Caleb and Doc much of a head start before getting back on their trail. Unfortunately for the riders, Caleb and Doc didn't need to get too far into a thick mass of shadow-enshrouded trees before they were out of sight. And once they were out of sight, they might as well have been picked up and swept away by the hand of God.

The darkness was an inky curtain that only got thicker as the minutes turned into hours.

The ground was frozen too solid to hold any tracks.

What little noise Caleb and Doc made before finding a good spot to hide was covered up by the wind whistling through bare branches and the rumble of anxious hooves against the earth.

Before too long, it was just too cold for men to be out fumbling in the dark so far away from camp. Once he and his men started to lose feeling in various extremities, Bullock signaled for them to head back to Deadwood.

The lawmen grumbled among themselves and a few even wanted to continue the search. One of the most vocal of that particular group was the man who'd pointed the finger at Caleb in the first place.

"We can't just let them go!" Samuel said. "After all they did, you're just going to let them go?"

Bullock's voice was a distinctive snarl that was easy enough to distinguish from the rest. "I didn't let anyone do anything," he said. "I did the best I could, but the fact remains that we don't have any jurisdiction much farther outside of camp."

"So that's all a man needs to do to get away with a crime? Just run far enough away and the law will throw up its hands?"

"There won't be any real law in Deadwood until my appointment becomes official," Bullock snapped. "Besides that, I've got reason to believe there was more than enough money passed around to muck up the whole process anyway. I intend on doing the best I can, so cool your goddamn heels and give my men some peace and quiet. It's been a long night and I won't freeze to death on your say-so."

Silence fell upon the men that cut deeper than any chill in the air. Even though he couldn't quite make out the faces of all the men involved, Caleb was still grinning from ear to ear. He remained on his belly amid some dead bushes for a few more seconds, even though the naked branches were digging into his back and several cold rocks were grinding against his ribs.

"Fine," Samuel muttered.

"It certainly is," Bullock replied before Samuel could get another word in. "And I'm damn glad you approve."

That exchange, followed by Samuel's pointless muttering as the rest of the men rode away, made all of Caleb's discomfort worth his while. Dark shapes moved away, leaving Samuel by himself on the edge of the clearing.

Caleb was about to move back, but stayed where he was when he saw Samuel urge his horse a few more paces into the clearing. Narrowing his eyes, Caleb held his breath to protect against the off chance that steam from his nose or mouth might be spotted drifting through the air.

Samuel was a small figure perched atop his horse, huddled against the cold. His eyes caught a few stray beams of moonlight as they slowly took in the clearing. The promising patch of land that he'd acquired from Creek Johnson was now in shambles. Rocks were strewn everywhere after having been picked through and kicked in all directions. The river was cracked and shattered.

Most important, there wasn't a trace of gold to be found.

Even though nobody would expect to find such a treasure in plain sight, there was also a feeling a man got when standing upon that claim. It was a sense most miners had that ran all the way down to an instinctual level.

That land was picked bare.

Caleb knew it.

Samuel knew it.

Whatever gold that may still be there was buried so deep under rock or was so far at the bottom of the river that it made the clearing just as valuable as any other random chunk of land in the Black Hills.

After muttering something under his breath, Samuel turned his horse around and followed in Bullock's tracks.

Waiting until he could no longer hear the stomping of hooves in the distance, Caleb backed out of the bushes that had kept him hidden just across the frozen stream. Doc was waiting right where he'd left him. The pale man slouched in his saddle as if nothing more than good balance and the lack of a breeze was keeping him from falling.

"They're gone," Caleb announced as he climbed onto the back of his own horse.

Doc coughed into his hand, started to speak, and then was cut short by a fit of hacking that shook his shoulders.

Even though Doc was doing his best to keep from making too much noise, Caleb looked around nervously for any sign that someone else may have heard. "You all right?" he asked.

Once his breath tapered off to a wheeze, Doc filled his lungs as best he could and lowered the hand from his mouth. "They might have circled back. One of them's got to know another way to cross this stream. Any one of those men could know this land a lot better than we do."

"Yeah, but I don't think any of them were interested."

"How can you be certain?"

"Because Bullock was talking to that shifty fellow like he was a kid," Caleb replied with a smirk. "I also heard mention that there's no official law in that camp just yet."

Doc nodded, but that simple motion seemed to have dislodged something in his throat. He lowered his head and fished out a handkerchief from his pocket so he could clear the mess that had been kicked up. "Folks were talking about that at one of the games I attended," Doc explained. "Quite amusing, really, to hear the same locals complain about having no law while also grousing about there being too much of it."

"Yeah," Caleb said as he studied Doc's face. "Are you sure you're all right?"

Doc pulled himself up so he could sit regally in his saddle. With blood trickling from the corner of one mouth, he declared, "Don't I look all right to you?"

With that, Doc promptly let out a breath and slumped forward.

As Caleb lunged forward to try to get ahold of the Georgian's arm or anything else that could be used as a handle, he thought about all the warnings Doc had been given from one physician or another regarding his condition. No matter how vehemently a doctor insisted that consumption be treated diligently and held off by plenty of rest and any of a dozen special diets, Doc would always continue doing whatever the hell he wanted.

Whether that meant gambling for days on end without sleep or scrambling across frozen streams at all hours of the night, Doc did what he pleased. No matter how pale his skin became or how sunken his cheeks may get, Doc had a tongue that was quick enough to convince most anyone that he was just as capable as anyone else on God's green earth.

Strangely enough, there were times when Caleb forgot Doc was sick. There were plenty of times when it seemed that Doc had enough of a spark in his eye to let him outlive damn near anyone. Considering everything they'd been through, it was hard for Caleb to believe a cough could do someone like Doc much harm at all.

All of that flooded through Caleb's mind in the time it took for him to get within arm's reach of Doc and extend his hand. The instant Caleb's fingers closed around Doc's elbow, the slender dentist shook free of his grasp.

"Don't bother," Doc snapped. "I'm fine."

"You nearly fell from your horse."

"But I didn't," Doc said as he straightened up and pulled in a haggard breath. "As you can plainly see."

Caleb studied the other man and had to admit that Doc was doing just fine without his help. Somehow, Doc always managed to stay upright and keep riding while also looking like death warmed over. Then again, considering the nasty bite in the air, not much of anything could stay warmed over for very long.

"Let's get out of here," Caleb said. "No matter what Bullock wants to do, I think that skinny fellow intended on finding us."

"Let him come. He can bring as many outlaws from Texas as he pleases. That little bastard probably doesn't even know Dave Rudabaugh."

"But . . . we saw them both at . . ." Rather than finish his observation, Caleb took a closer look at Doc's face. He'd seen the dentist drunk plenty of times, but there was usually more life in his eyes than there was right now. "Come on," he said while refraining from laying a hand on Doc or his horse. "I know a place we can go that's not too far from here."

"You mean that place where we found Rudabaugh?" Doc asked.

"Not hardly. It's a trading post that has a few rooms to rent. Shouldn't be more than a mile or so from here."

"What about this spot?" Doc asked as he warily looked around. "I'm always being told the mountain air will do me good."

"We can't afford to build a fire and we'll freeze to death without one, so your idea is out of the question."

"Then by all means, lead on."

Caleb led on.

Fortunately, the terrain required them to take their time and ride slowly from one patch of rocks to another. Even if they'd both been in their prime, Caleb and Doc would have had to slow down to navigate from the hills and back onto a more accommodating trail.

Once they got some level ground beneath their horses' hooves, they pointed their noses east and snapped the reins. On some level, Caleb wanted to see Doc fall from his saddle just to prove that he needed to accept a bit of help every now and then. He kept a close eye on the slender figure beside him throughout the next several hours, waiting to see if that hard lesson would be taught that night.

It was close to morning by the time they reached the trading post. Doc's eyes brightened when they arrived, but dimmed once he was staggering through the door to his room. There was little wonder as to why all the rooms were available. Instead of being over the trading post as Caleb had thought, they were tacked onto the back of it. The rates were cheap, but still seemed expensive for a closet with a cot propped against one wall. The air stank of its previous tenants and offered next to no protection from the cold night air. Fortunately, the paper-thin walls made it easier for Caleb to keep track of Doc's well-being.

He could hear Doc in the room next to his. The Georgian coughed every couple of seconds as he shuffled heavily across the floor and dropped onto his cot. Once he was down, the coughing stopped for the amount of time required for Doc to take a pull from his flask. As always, the whiskey eased his coughing just enough for him to fall asleep.

Despite the fact that a posse could be nipping at his heels, that a known killer was probably out looking for him, and that his own partner may be knocking on death's door, Caleb curled up on his rented cot and closed his eyes.

It wasn't the best night's sleep he'd ever had, but any little taste of unconsciousness was a welcome change of pace.

[14]

When Caleb woke up the next morning, he threw on some clothes and staggered out of his room. The trading post was even shoddier than it had seemed the night before. In fact, there were no boards beneath his feet and no real walls around him. Instead, large wooden slats were laid over canvas-covered ground. The walls were made of similar slats that weren't even tall enough to reach the top of the tent that had looked vaguely like a building to wearier eyes.

There were doors within frames, but those could have been knocked over by any shoulder with more than fifty pounds behind it. Caleb rubbed his eyes and looked at the next room to find that door partially open. He knocked a few times to announce himself, but knew that wouldn't do much good. He realized just how true that was when he stuck his head into the room and took a look inside.

Doc was gone.

Even though Caleb had braced himself to find the dentist curled up in a heap or splayed upon the floor, he hadn't been prepared to find an empty room. Doc was really gone and

Caleb couldn't even hazard a guess as to how a man in Doc's condition had so easily given him the slip. As soon as he spotted someone who looked like they worked at the trading post, Caleb walked over to them and asked, "Where's the man who rented this room?"

The person Caleb had spotted was a small woman who had her arms loaded with folded blankets and towels that were more likely meant to be sold up front rather than distributed to the rental rooms. Her eyes widened at the sight of him and she reflexively took a step back. "I don't know who you mean," she said. "I just got here."

Caleb forced a friendlier expression onto his face and took a step back so his holstered pistol wasn't so prominently displayed. "He's a friend of mine," he explained. "He's also sick."

"Oh, you mean the man with the horrible cough?"

"That's the one."

She nodded toward the front of the tent. "He stepped outside after breakfast."

"He's already eaten?"

"Yes," she replied. "You can help yourself to whatever's left, since you're a paying customer and all. Just go next door to Bud's place."

"All right. Thanks."

The woman was all too eager to move away from Caleb and she did so as quickly as her feet could carry her. As he walked to the front of the trading post, Caleb glanced around as if it was the first time he'd seen it. Considering he'd only passed by the trading post once before over a month ago, Caleb wasn't too shocked to discover the place wasn't exactly as he'd remembered it.

Now that there was more than the occasional sputtering lantern for light, he could see the canvas walls fluttering against the wooden frame supporting them. The trading post was large for a tent, but it was still most definitely a tent. To the right of the front door, there was a flap held open by a hook and eye, leading to another smaller tent where breakfast was being served. Caleb could smell coffee and biscuits coming from that direction, but wanted to tend to another matter before filling his stomach.

Stepping outside was akin to being shoved into a tub of cold water. The moment he made it through the crooked doorway, Caleb was enveloped in an icy wind that lanced straight through his chest and put such a grip upon his lungs that it became impossible to take a breath.

Doc stood a few paces out with his arms crossed and his chin raised to the unrelenting cold.

"You trying to freeze to death, Doc?" Caleb asked as he stepped up beside the dentist. "Mountain air's one thing. This is about to snap my fingers off one at a time."

When he looked over at Caleb, Doc showed the usual spark in his eye. His skin hung off his face in much the same way that the canvas hung off the wooden frames of the tent behind him. "It's bracing, Caleb. Makes a man feel happy to be alive."

Taking a moment to try to see what the fuss was about, Caleb closed his eyes and pulled in as much of a breath as he could. When he opened his eyes again, he saw wide-open terrain littered with boulders and trees that had been stripped of everything other than their bark.

Even though he felt like he was being stabbed by icicles, Caleb smiled. "You know what makes me feel happy?" he asked. "Not seeing anyone pointing a gun at us."

"And do you know what will make you feel even better?" Doc asked.

"What?"

"Some of those biscuits. I can't say much about the presentation, but Bud is one hell of a fine cook."

Caleb looked over at the dentist to see if Doc was kidding. Not only was Doc serious, but he seemed to be in better spirits than Caleb himself.

"Maybe I will have some breakfast," Caleb said. "Just as long as the coffee's hot, it'll be better than standing out here."

"I believe I'll join you."

Both men stepped into the smaller tent situated beside the trading post and found a few empty chairs around a lopsided table. After waiting by themselves for a minute or two, the woman who'd been carrying the sheets earlier rushed inside and placed some dented tin cups in front of them.

"Back for more, I see," she said with a cheerful smile. That smile became a bit more forced when she aimed it at Caleb. "And you, as well."

"I recommend the biscuits and gravy," Doc said.

"That and the coffee should be fine," Caleb said. "That is, unless you've got something else cooking?"

"That's all we got," the woman replied. Before long, she returned with a kettle of coffee to fill the cups. "I'll just leave this here so you can help yourselves."

Doc stirred his coffee and fished out the bigger clumps of grounds with his spoon. Although he seemed completely focused upon his task, he also seemed to know the exact moment when the woman had gone far enough away from him to speak without being heard. "As much as I hate to be forced away from a place as delightful as that mining camp, we should probably put some more distance between ourselves and Deadwood."

"I agree wholeheartedly. You still set on Laclede?"

"There are a few other towns in Kansas I'd like to visit along the way."

After sipping his coffee, Caleb winced and grumbled, "Alice gave you the talk about Dodge City, huh?"

"We must go where the winds of fortune guide us," Doc said as he spiked his coffee with some whiskey from his flask.

"After what happened so far, I'm surprised the winds of fortune haven't blown us both straight to hell."

"Give them time, my friend."

The coffee was as strong as it was gritty. Every sip Caleb took, he could feel the brew pulling his eyelids open from the inside and the wet grounds gathering on the back of his throat. "We may not have much time before Bullock and the rest come hunting for us."

Doc shrugged his shoulders and then shook his head. "I don't think they got much of a look at us."

"What?" Caleb asked as he nearly dropped his cup. "How the hell could you think something like that? Were all those men blind?"

"No, but they couldn't see in the dark, either. Most of them barely made it out of those trees before we had our backs to them, and it sounds like Samuel's word doesn't hold much water with Bullock."

"We were close enough to spit on that posse, Doc."

"We were also trying to keep our heads down while running for our lives. Judging by how wild their shots were, I'd say that posse was doing the same. Can you honestly tell me you remember the faces of all those men that were in that clearing?"

After a bit of consideration, Caleb had to shake his head. "No, but I knew Bullock and Samuel were there."

"That's because you knew Samuel might be there and you recognized Bullock's voice."

"If that asshole told Bullock what he needed to hear to get him to that clearing with all his men, then those men must have known we'd be there, too."

"Yes," Doc said with a smirk. "But we are not bound to the letter of the law. We can use our instincts a lot more than your average posse. They need to justify what they did and prove they were right."

Caleb let out a short, humorless laugh. "Sounds to me like you think awfully highly of peacekeepers."

"It's all just a game, my friend. If you want to come out ahead, you've got to know what's going on across the table from you. Once you've got the other players figured out, everything becomes a whole lot easier."

"Sure. You're having the time of your life while we both become wanted men."

Caleb heard a clipped sigh behind him. When he turned around, he saw the woman who'd brought him his coffee carrying his breakfast on a few loaded plates. She set the plates onto the table before asking, "Those wanted men are around here?"

"Pardon?" Doc asked with surprisingly convincing ignorance written upon his face.

Leaning forward, she whispered, "I thought I heard you say something about wanted men. There was some sort of shooting outside of Deadwood last night, you know."

Doc recoiled a bit and placed a hand to his heart. "Dear Lord. Are you joking?"

While Caleb shot a warning glance to Doc, it seemed that the dramatics weren't being laid on thick enough to do any damage just yet.

The woman nodded at Doc and said, "I heard it just this morning. Someone broke out of jail and was chased from Deadwood by a whole posse of armed men."

Caleb felt the bottom of his stomach drop as a chill went up his back that had nothing to do with the weather.

Doc scowled a bit and asked, "Do you think they caught those men?"

She scowled as well before shrugging her shoulders. "I don't know, but there was an awfully big ruckus outside of Deadwood and I think those wanted men got away." After she'd said that, the woman turned away from Doc and took a hard look at the gun hanging from Caleb's hip.

"Well," Doc said quickly, "it's a good thing we're careful when traveling."

"Yes," she said slowly. "I suppose it is."

Before the silence could get much thicker, Doc pulled in a breath and let it out with a series of convulsive coughs. He dabbed at his mouth with his handkerchief, picked up his coffee, and sipped the murky brew.

"Thanks for the breakfast," Caleb said. "How much do we owe you?"

The change in the woman's face was subtle but noticeable. Instead of eyeing Caleb suspiciously, she now seemed slightly ashamed for wanting to put some distance between herself and the pale, wheezing man in front of her.

"A dollar for the both of you seeing as how you're guests," she said quickly. "I'll add it to your bill."

Despite the fact that Doc eased up on his cough once his audience was gone, it was obviously still a chore for him to draw an unimpeded breath. "You see?" he said with a smirk. "The rumors are already flying. If anyone with any real authority knew for certain who we were, they would have spread our names far and wide by now."

"She's one lady who serves biscuits in a tent, Doc. Don't get too proud of yourself just yet."

"This is also one of the closest settlements to Deadwood," Doc pointed out. "This should be the first place any pursuers would look."

"True, but I still don't want to stay here any longer than we have to." When he took a bite of his biscuits, Caleb found his spirits brightening. He dug his fork into another piece, sopped up some of the thick gravy, and then smiled as he chewed it up. "I think these biscuits made everything else worth the trouble."

"That and the gold."

"Yeah. Whatever's left of it."

"We've got enough to travel on," Doc said. "And enough to get us both rolling once we find a good game."

"That game had better be far away from the Black Hills."

Doc scowled and shook his head. "Why, Caleb, I thought you'd be the last person frightened by a bit of bluster and wild gunfire."

"Not frightened," Caleb said simply. "Just practicing what you preach. I don't think Bullock is a man to be trifled with and I sure as hell don't think he's happy about me leaving his jail so far ahead of schedule."

The scowl on Doc's face shifted a bit. Some folks might have mistaken the look as something more sinister, but Caleb knew he was being watched like a hawk for a reason that should be revealed when Doc opened his mouth next.

"And what," Doc asked carefully, "would you do if Bullock did come after you? I doubt you'd get such civil treatment as before."

Caleb didn't think too long about that one. "I'd gun him down where he stood," he replied before taking another bite of his breakfast. He barely got through chewing those biscuits before cracking a smile. "Hell, I don't know what I'd do. For a moment, you really looked like you believed I was cold enough to kill him."

A wide grin appeared on Doc's face that shaved ten years off of his haggard facade. "Just checking to see if you've changed very much since we left Texas. I've heard some stories about what you do when you're on your own and not all of them are complimentary."

"You're the last man to knock someone for having rumors circulating about them, Doc. From what I've heard about you, I'm lucky to be alive after being in the same room with you for more than an hour."

"You are lucky," Doc said as he tapped the table. "After what you stirred up in Deadwood, I should be rid of you right here and now."

"I'd say I pulled my weight more than enough to earn back some of what Rudabaugh stole from me. Nothing too unreasonable. Just enough to get me started again once we get away from here."

"Reasonable, huh?" Doc muttered. "I would have thought you'd forgotten the meaning of that word right before you let me charge up to that posse with guns blazing like a damned madman."

Caleb chuckled and shook his head as he kept shoveling more biscuits and gravy into his mouth.

Taking the pouch from his pocket, Doc tossed it to Caleb. "How's that for reasonable?"

Keeping his fork in one hand, Caleb picked up the pouch and hefted it for a second. "It's light," he said.

Doc nodded. "I already split it up. Take a look and if you disagree with my division . . ."

"Nah," Caleb replied as he tucked the pouch into a jacket pocket. "Feels about right since you already split it up."

"Good. Now I was thinking we could surely throw anyone off our tracks if we head west. We may skirt past Deadwood again, but I doubt Bullock will be looking for us in that neck of the woods."

"You really are crazy," Caleb grumbled.

"Not crazy, but not afraid of someone pretending to be a sheriff and a few prospectors who decide to play at being a posse."

"And you think I am afraid of them?"

"I don't know," Doc said evenly. "Why don't you tell me?"

What followed was a few tense moments that might have gone unnoticed until one of the two partners decided to take a shot at the other. Caleb's gaze became as cold as the air that ripped through the tent, while Doc stared back at him as if daring Caleb to make a move.

Finally, Caleb asked, "What about Rudabaugh? After the way he slapped you around, I'd think you wouldn't be so quick to step where he might be watching."

Where some men might have gladly jumped at the invitation to take a swing at Caleb, Doc grinned. "He's made his play," Doc replied. "He meant to get us killed and he failed. As for the rest of it . . . you're right. He did manage to catch me at a disadvantage. You can be certain it won't happen again. By the way," he added, "I may have done some over-stepping of my own. Of all the things someone could call you, a coward isn't one of them."

Caleb accepted the apology with a nod and then went back to the posture he'd had before things had gotten tense. "You think Alice is being held somewhere?"

"That was just a way to get me to jump," Doc admitted. "I'm ashamed at how well it worked. If he really did have Alice, he wouldn't have bothered having his man tip off Bullock. Dave's probably scampered back to Texas by now, but we can check on Alice when we pass through."

"I'm through running in circles around here," Caleb said as he waved his fork in the air to illustrate his point amid a few threads of loose gravy. "I say we steer clear of the Dakotas and head back to somewhere we had some better luck."

"It's not as if the rest of the continent knows what goes on in mining camps and every saloon. We need to go where the money is and that's west."

"That's a gambler talking. I'd say the only sort of gambler I've proven myself to be is one who'll starve to death without a penny to his name."

Doc fought to hold back a smirk at his partner's expense. "There's always medical school."

Shaking his head, Caleb did his best to keep from laughing at Doc's jab. He held out for about two seconds. Before too long, his eye was drawn to the tailored vest beneath Doc's coat. More specifically, he caught sight of the diamond stickpin that was the one constant piece of finery he wore. "Your father gave that to you, didn't he?" Caleb asked.

Doc's hand reflexively went to the stickpin as if he was guarding it from attack. "That's right. He gave it to me before I left home. You know that."

"When's the last time you saw your family?"

All of the humor drained from Doc's face, leaving him more like a ghost than the jovial man he'd been moments ago. "What business is that of yours?"

"You suggested we go visit your aunt," Caleb replied as he raised his hands. "All I'm saying is that you do that rather than head off to gamble some more. The cards will still be there when you're feeling better."

Doc sat motionless for a few seconds, but then he blinked and nodded. After pouring some more coffee from the kettle left in the middle of the table, he added a splash of whiskey and said, "Perhaps I will, perhaps I won't. What about your family?"

"They're in Texas. I have an uncle who's not far from Dallas."

"And when's the last time you checked in on them?"

"It's been a while," Caleb replied.

"Then why don't you bring your whole life to a halt so you can go swap childhood remembrances? Some of us don't have that kind of time to pass around."

"And you'll have even less if you keep things up the way you have."

Doc shook his head and drank half of his coffee in one sip. Gritting his teeth as the whiskey worked its way through his system, he said, "You're my partner, Caleb. Not my nursemaid. If you insist on being the latter, I'll just have to dismiss you from service. I'd prefer someone who fills out a nursemaid's dress a hell of a lot better than you, anyway."

"Point taken." Caleb sighed. "Just trying to—"

Before Caleb could finish that sentence, the sound of hooves thumping against the frozen ground rumbled through the air. Thanks to the canvas walls of the tent, the sounds of horses and their riders could be heard as clearly as if they were galloping straight up to Caleb's table.

"Take a look inside each of those tents," one of the men outside said. "We'll be right here if you flush one of them out."

Caleb jumped to his feet. "Aww, hell. Is that Bullock?"

Doc grinned and replied, "Maybe paying a visit to the family isn't such a bad idea, after all."

[15]

The woman who'd served them breakfast was heading toward the table when Doc and Caleb bolted past her. She started to ask them where they were going, but didn't get the chance before they were gone. When she looked at the table where they'd been sitting, she saw some money lying there beneath the plate of mostly eaten biscuits. Since there was enough money to cover the price of what they'd ordered, she shrugged and walked outside to see what all the commotion was about.

Caleb led the way through the little room that serviced as a kitchen. Sure enough, there was a flap next to a pile of crates that was held up by a hook. "You don't think they got a good look at you, huh?" Caleb asked.

After checking to make sure his guns were fully loaded, Doc nodded. "I think there's a good chance that—"

"Fine. See if you've got enough steam to get the horses before we're caught."

"A challenge?"

"Sure."

"Perfect." Doc stepped through the flap, but paused before going too far. "Care to make it interesting?"

"What?"

"If I make it back with the horses without stirring up too much of a fuss, I win your portion of the gold."

Caleb could hear footsteps drawing closer. In fact, the longer he listened, the more it seemed the footsteps were closing in on him from all sides. "Jesus, you truly are crazy."

Waving his hand impatiently, Doc said, "I'm Georgia born, Caleb. I thrive in the heat."

"Fine, fine. It's a bet."

Doc nodded and started to walk away. This time, he was stopped when Caleb reached out to grab his elbow.

"Wait," Caleb snapped. "What if I win?"

"If you win, I think we'll have bigger problems than this wager."

"It's not a wager if I've got nothing to win."

Shaking his head in a mix of admiration and disbelief, Doc said, "If I draw too much attention, you can have all the gold and I won't ask about it again."

"Deal," Caleb said with a grin.

As he hurried away from the restaurant, Doc grumbled, "And he says I'm the crazy one!"

Caleb listened carefully for what was going on around the other side of the tent. The horses weren't moving. The men weren't talking. Everything was fairly quiet. That was more than enough to get Caleb worried.

As soon as he heard the woman in the restaurant greeting her new guests, Caleb knew it was time to get moving.

"Good day, Mr. Bullock," she said. "What brings you out here?"

"Looking for some men who might be dangerous," Bullock replied. "I don't suppose you've . . ."

Caleb didn't stick around to hear any more. Instead, he left through the flap and made his way toward the back of the neighboring trading post. Doc was nowhere to be found, which wasn't too big of a surprise since the horses were kept in another tent.

Silently cursing every crunch made by his boots against the frozen ground, Caleb kept moving until he spotted some-one else poking around the back of the trading post. The other man was leaning forward and trying to get a look through a rip in the canvas wall of what had been Doc's room. His back was to Caleb, making him unable to turn around fast enough to stop what was about to happen.

One of Caleb's hands clamped over the man's mouth and the other hand reached around to pluck the gun from the man's holster. In one powerful movement, Caleb pulled the man away from the side of the tent and spun him around. When he got a look at the man's face, Caleb was too sur-prised to keep quiet.

"What the hell are you doing here?" Caleb snarled.

Since he couldn't speak at the moment, Brad delivered an elbow to Caleb's ribs that loosened his grip on him. "Dave still wants his gold, asshole," Brad grunted.

"You're riding with Bullock?"

"I don't explain myself to dead men." With that, Brad reached across his belly to draw the knife that hung from his belt. He pulled it from its sheath and slashed at Caleb's face in one quick motion.

Caleb batted the knife away and snapped a quick punch into Brad's gut, then pulled back his arm and sent his fist for-ward a second time. "Tell Rudabaugh his chickenshit trap didn't work," Caleb said as he ducked beneath another quick slash from Brad's knife. When he came up again, Caleb lifted his knee to slam it into the other man's gut.

All those blows were more than enough to rob Brad of his breath. He staggered back while swiping at the air with his knife.

"I'll bet Bullock would love to know you ride with the likes of Rudabaugh," Caleb said.

Despite the effort it took to fill his lungs, Brad hacked up a laugh and smiled. "Why don't you tell him yourself? He's dying to get his hands on you."

"What's going on back there?" Bullock shouted from somewhere nearby. "Did you find someone?"

Caleb watched Brad closely. He wondered if the outlaw was going to risk continuing the fight or gamble with whatever partnership had been struck with Bullock. Caleb got his answer even quicker than he'd expected.

"I found him!" Brad shouted. "He's right back here!"

Caleb thought about shooting Brad right then and there. He also thought about how quickly the sound of a gunshot would bring Bullock to the spot where Caleb was standing and how bad it would look to have killed a man when he was already wanted on suspicion of murder. Whether Bullock knew about Brad's ties to Rudabaugh or not, shooting a member of a posse never worked to a man's favor.

All of that flashed through Caleb's mind in the time it took for him to draw his gun and slam the pistol across Brad's face. Before Brad could drop to the ground, Caleb was running around the back of the trading post.

As he rounded the corner of the larger tent, Caleb heard more horses coming around to cut him off. He swore under his breath and tightened his grip on his gun, hoping he would be given more choices than shooting Bullock or catching a few bullets for himself.

Waving to Caleb as he rode into Caleb's sight, Doc said, "I thought you'd be happy to see me."

Caleb didn't let out the breath he'd been holding until he saw that Doc was holding on to the reins of two horses as opposed to just his own. Scrambling into his saddle, Caleb wheezed, "We need to get the hell out of here."

"Is that Brad?"

"Yeah, I'll explain later," Caleb snapped. The next thing he snapped was his reins as he dug his heels into his horse's sides for good measure. The animal let out a whinny and bolted away from the settlement.

Doc rode directly behind him and leaned forward while holding his hat in place with his free hand. Turning to look back at the camp, Doc calmly reported, "They've seen us."

When Caleb took a look back for himself, he saw several horses clustered in front of the trading post. Already, the men riding those horses were motioning to one another and pointing toward Caleb and Doc.

Caleb needed to shout to be heard over the thunder of the horses' hooves and the rush of blood through his own veins. "What the hell do we do now?"

"We can make a stand if you want," Doc shouted back. "But even I was planning on living past today."

"Then we run?"

"We've already got a head start on them and there's plenty of trails winding through these hills."

"Yeah, and Bullock probably knows all of them," Caleb shouted.

One gunshot cracked through the air behind them. That was followed by more shots as the posse's horses gained momentum.

"As much as I love our debates," Doc hollered, "we don't have the time."

Nodding once, Caleb looked over at Doc and said, "Then we go with our first plan and pay our families a visit."

It took Doc a moment, but another gunshot from his pursuers seemed to jog his memory. "You mean split up?"

"I doubt those men will want to let either one of us go. If they do all gang up on one of us, the other can circle around to draw some off."

"Since you're the one with the run of bad luck, that sounds fine to me," Doc replied. "There's just one more thing to settle."

"What?"

"The bet. I wasn't the one to stir up this commotion, so I won the bet."

"Jesus," Caleb grunted as he dug into his jacket pocket to retrieve his bag of gold. He tossed the pouch to Doc and shouted, "Take it! I don't care if I see that damned gold again."

Doc grabbed the pouch from the air and used that same hand to tip his hat. "Off to the families, then. I'll send word to you once things settle down around here."

"You're coming back?"

"Not for long," Doc said with a shrug. "I need to check on Alice and then I'll just have to see how my luck holds up from there." And before Caleb could say a word to talk him out of it, Doc snapped his reins and steered off to the right.

Even though the gunshots were being fired at shorter intervals, Caleb took a moment to glance over his shoulder and watch Doc ride away. Part of him was checking to see if the posse would split up. Another part wondered if it would be the last time he'd ever see Doc alive. Rather than dwell on such a gloomy matter, Caleb tapped his heels against his horse's sides and pulled his reins to the left.

The animal had already been running close to its limit and the sudden incentive combined with the gunshots was enough to put a fright into it. Sensing the panic churning in the animal's belly, Caleb hung on and let the horse bolt. As long as it bolted in the proper direction, he wasn't about to complain.

Before too long, Caleb's horse settled into a gallop and worked off some of the steam it had built up in its initial panic. The gunshots weren't having much of an effect any longer, since they were already fading away.

Caleb shifted once more in his saddle to get a look behind him. Rather than check on Doc, he searched for the men that were pursuing him. Sure enough, the posse had split up and only a few of them were chasing him. Since Doc was nowhere to be found, the rest of the posse members had more or less disappeared. The terrain was fairly open for the moment, but there was a mess of rocks and trees straight ahead.

In fact, those trees were a little closer than Caleb had expected. When he faced forward once more, he sucked in a quick breath and pulled sharply on his reins in hopes of avoiding the rocks that were only a few paces in front of him. His horse wasn't quite ready to break its legs just yet, because it jumped a heartbeat before Caleb could give the command.

Letting out a bellowing breath, Caleb's horse leapt over the rocks and landed upon the cold ground. Almost immediately, its hooves skidded against the frozen dirt and the horse scrambled to right itself.

This time, Caleb was prepared. He shifted his weight in the opposite direction to the horse's momentum and tugged on the reins in short, strong pulls. That was enough to get the animal's attention and guide it back around so it could regain its footing. For a moment, the horse and rider were a mass of flailing limbs. Once that moment passed, both were upright and moving forward.

Caleb didn't waste time in checking behind him again. Instead, he picked the spot he wanted to go and snapped his reins. After rounding a bend, he pulled back hard and fought to convince the horse to come to a stop. Caleb jumped from the saddle as soon as he could do so without breaking his neck. The instant his boots hit the ground, he ducked low and pulled his horse with him to a thick bunch of dead bushes clustered around some rocks.

It took plenty of muscle and a good amount of sweet-talking to get the horse to follow him, but Caleb eventually got the animal behind those bushes. Unfortunately, the animal wasn't so keen on hunkering down.

The posse members were getting closer. Caleb could hear the rumble of those hooves getting louder by the second.

His horse was more nervous than ever. Not only did it fight against the reins, but it seemed close to biting at his hand.

Fearing that he may already be too late, Caleb dropped himself straight down while pulling on the reins hard enough to strain most of the muscles in his back, shoulders, and arms. Whether he'd imposed his will upon the horse or some divinity had stepped in to do the job, Caleb somehow got the horse to lie with its side upon the ground.

As the posse closed in on him, Caleb pressed himself flat against the rocks and held his breath. He also clenched his eyes shut. If that posse was truly on Rudabaugh's side, Caleb just didn't want to see what was coming before it got there.

The hooves thumped against the ground to send a rumble through every one of Caleb's bones.

The ground shook. Even the rocks and bushes trembled with their approach.

The posse came at him like a storm.

It snapped branches and kicked up plenty of cold gravel that rained back down to pelt upon Caleb's face. And then the storm was gone.

Even as the sound of those hooves faded, Caleb was slow to open his eyes. When he did, it was like peeling his eyelids away from where they'd been glued to his face.

But he wasn't greeted by the sight of angry faces looking down at him. There were no gun barrels aimed in his direction. There was just the swirling dust several yards away to mark where the storm had passed him by.

Although he'd become unfamiliar with good luck, Caleb knew better than to question it. He got to his feet and urged his horse to do the same. From there, he rode west simply because the posse had been moving south. As long as he was headed that way, he kicked around the notion of racing through Deadwood to check on Alice.

And after that, it was onward to Texas.

～～～

The other half of the posse broke through a thin row of trees and thundered ahead. A few of them fired shots at the horse in the distance in front of them, but they knew they were well outside of pistol range. Bullock was at the head of the group and he reached around to draw the rifle from the boot hanging from his saddle without taking his eyes from his target.

Having ridden onto a relatively flat stretch of trail, Bullock adjusted himself to his horse's movements and brought his rifle to his shoulder. He narrowed his eyes to fix upon the horse ahead of him, but paused before squeezing the trigger.

"Goddamn," Bullock muttered as his aim bobbled uncontrollably with the horse's motions. Lowering the rifle, he leaned forward and stared even harder at the horse in the distance. "Goddamn!"

"What is it?" one of the other men asked.

"There's nobody on that horse!"

"Then we hit him already?"

Rather than answer that question, Bullock signaled for

the others to come to a stop. His men gathered around him, but not all of them were too happy about it.

"What the hell are we stopping for?" another member of the posse groused. "He's getting away!"

"He already got away!" Bullock snapped. "Or he's already dead. Spread out and start looking for a body. I'll head back to see if that bastard circled around the other way."

Even though his men scattered as they were supposed to, Bullock kept swearing under his breath. The profanities he let fly only got more colorful before he finally made it back to the group of tents where the chase had begun. Spotting Brad propped up against a barrel, Bullock looked around at the locals who'd stepped outside.

"Has anyone seen the men who did this?" Bullock asked as he pointed down to Brad.

The merchants as well as a few folks who'd just arrived that morning all looked at each other and shook their heads.

"What about the men who rode out of here?" Bullock asked. "The ones we were chasing. Anyone seen them?"

More blank stares.

Bullock looked around, but there wasn't much to see. The collection of wood-framed tents creaked in the breeze. Although he could hear folks talking or coughing inside those tents, Bullock didn't find any hint that Doc or Caleb had made it back to that spot. In fact, the longer he thought about it, the madder he got for wasting the time it had taken to ride back there.

"Shit," Bullock muttered as he brought his horse around and rode back toward his men.

Once Bullock was out of sight, the other folks went right back to their own business. One of the folks who'd poked a head from inside a tent was an old woman who ran the trading post.

"Whatever they wanted, I guess they didn't find it," she grumbled as she pulled her head back into the store. "You sure you don't need a doctor?"

The man she was addressing had stumbled into the tent less than a minute before Bullock had arrived. His face was chalky white and coated in sweat. He was dressed like a dandy, but those clothes were rumpled, filthy, and torn. As ragged as he looked, he still had a smile that was just friendly enough to charm the old woman. He showed that smile to her now and shook his head.

"No, thank you, ma'am," Doc replied in his warm Southern drawl. "I'm just a bit winded."

"Would you like some water?"

"You are a godsend."

She scooped up some water from a barrel and handed the dented ladle over to Doc. After taking a few sips, he coughed and wiped his mouth with the back of his hand.

"Aren't you one of those fellows who rented a room from my husband?" she asked.

"Yes, ma'am."

Wincing a bit, she added, "He told me you sounded kind of sick."

"I'm sure I did."

Since Doc's appearance pretty much spoke for him on that subject, the woman found another one. "What happened to you?" she asked.

"My horse threw me when those gunmen raced out of here," Doc lied.

"You mean those boys that Mr. Bullock is after?"

"That posse might have spooked my horse even more than the outlaws. Either way, I had to walk back here."

Even though Doc had only walked a short distance from where he'd jumped off his horse, his appearance was more than enough to sell his story.

The old woman nodded and showed him a motherly smile.

"My horse also made off with my belongings," Doc said. "I'll need to buy a few things."

"I can help you there."

Doc smiled and nodded slowly. "How fortunate."

[16]

Alice turned out to be just fine.

After sneaking into Deadwood just long enough to spot her inside the Bella Union, Caleb rode south in as much of a straight line as he could manage. Since he barely had more than a few dollars to scrape together, his plan was to get to a good-sized town, sell his horse, and use that money to buy a train ticket to Texas.

More than once in the next few days, he was forced to bolt from one camp or another on account of a stranger looking at him for too long or a group of horses riding at him in too straight of a line. He wasn't certain if any of those men had been Bullock or associates of Dave Rudabaugh, but Caleb wasn't about to take that chance. Since his intention was to keep moving, that's precisely what he did.

He kept riding and kept pushing that horse until he thought the animal would keel over from sheer exhaustion. But the horse kept going. If Caleb needed to get up from a dead sleep and run because of a strange noise he'd heard, that horse would carry him. That horse outran the posse that had chased him out of the Dakotas. It had gotten him through a few close scrapes in Indian country and it didn't even fuss when it was forced to eat dead grass sprouting up from frozen ground.

That horse carried him deep into Nebraska without breaking stride. Once he got within a day's ride of the Colorado border, Caleb thought he might be forced to eat that old horse. The weather turned even worse and nearly buried him in a storm that pounced on him quicker than a mountain lion. After a few days, the winds blew away enough of the snow for him to get moving again. Caleb led his horse a ways and then finally rode to clearer ground.

When he made it to Denver, Caleb's plan was still to sell the horse and catch a train. But that just wasn't going to happen. Instead, he took what little money he had left and bought the horse a warm stall in a good stable. Not only did that horse eat better than he did that night, it also got a name.

"What do you think?" Caleb asked as he patted the horse's nose. "What name suits you best? Lucky?"

Caleb might have been tired, but he wasn't too tired to find the humor in that.

"What about Snowball? Both of us nearly wound up as one of those before we got here."

The stable's owner walked up to Caleb and cleared his throat. "Looks like that left shoe is about to go. I can repair it if you like."

Leaning into the stall, Caleb took a look at the horse's hind leg. He couldn't see exactly what was wrong with the shoe, but he knew all too well that the old girl had been favoring that leg for plenty of miles.

"Yeah," Caleb said as he failed to think of one time the horse had fussed or slowed down. "How much to fix it up?"

"Depends on how bad it is," the man replied with a shrug.

Caleb dug into his pockets and fished out the few remaining coins he had. It wasn't much. "This is about all I've got," he said as he extended his hand to display the pathetic amount he'd managed to scrape together.

The man winced and let out a slow hiss through his teeth. "I hate to say it, but I doubt that'll be enough."

Feeling around in his other pocket, Caleb dug one last penny from the bottom and held it out proudly. "What about now?" he asked with a smile.

The man shook his head, but laughed. "I'll see what I can do. You must really care for that horse."

"She's done all right by me."

"What's her name?"

Caleb blinked, looked at the horse, and got a blink from the animal in return. Suddenly, he flipped that last coin he'd found into the air so it could land in his other hand with a clink. "Penny," he announced. "Her name's Penny."

"Well, I've got a few old nags that should'a been traded long ago, so I know what it's like to be partial to one like her," the man said. "I can't do anything too fancy, but I'll see to it that she walks straight and don't hurt herself."

"I appreciate that."

"Where you stayin'?"

"What?" Caleb asked.

"You staying at a hotel or do you know anyone around here?" the man asked. "I need to know where to find you to let you know when Penny's ready to run."

Caleb sighed and said, "I haven't quite figured that one out yet. I'll just check with you after a while."

"Well, my wife has been trying for years to make me into a good Christian, so I suppose a good place to start would be to give you a place to stay."

"I couldn't accept that," Caleb said.

"You wouldn't be acceptin' nothin'," the man grunted. "You'd be working for it. Clean out these stalls and stack them bales of hay over there and you'll have your room."

"I'd need to do more work than that, wouldn't I?"

"Not if you're sleeping up there," the man replied as he pointed to the stable's loft. "There's some old blankets up there and no holes in the roof, so it should do you just fine. If not, that's—"

"It'll be fine," Caleb said quickly. "Where's your broom?"

"Good. I suppose the both of us should get to work. What's yer name, anyway?"

Considering the circumstances of his departure from Deadwood and the possibility that there could still be men out to hunt him down, Caleb knew he should be keeping his head down and staying hidden whenever possible. The last time Doc had been in Denver, he'd gone by the name Tom Mackey. Unfortunately, Caleb was too damn tired to come up with anything so original.

"Mack . . . Smith."

"Good to meet ya, Mack," the stable's owner said. "I'm Bob. The broom's right over there."

It wasn't long before Caleb started to think his luck actually had taken a turn for the better. Not only did he have a place to sleep for the night, but Bob kept a mighty clean stable. Caleb was done with his chores in time for a bowl of hot soup and some freshly baked bread compliments of Bob's wife.

The next day, Caleb called in a few favors he'd earned the last time he was in Denver and managed to pull together a line on some cardplayers that were having worse luck than he was. He borrowed some money and spent the next several weeks working to pay off the loans. Of course, his definition of work wasn't exactly the same as everyone else's.

His first few games were sloppy. Although he'd won a couple hands thanks to an old rancher's facial tic, Caleb knew he wasn't going to make any progress that way. The stakes weren't high enough and his luck was still shaky at best. Since he couldn't get decent cards dealt to him, he palmed a few good ones and saved them for later.

If any of his opponents were professionals, they would have picked up on the move right away. Fortunately, they were too drunk to make out how he was winning more than his share. At night, Caleb practiced his card handling and perfected his technique for palming chips. He started making his rounds to some of the old spots, plucking loose chips whenever he could. Thanks to the big games being held in New Mexico and California, there weren't many familiar players to catch him scraping at the saloon's scraps.

After another month or so, Caleb regained some of his edge at the actual game of poker and was able to hold his own in a real game. His streak was quick to end and after that, most of his victories weren't of the honest variety. Still, they repaid his loans and filled his pockets with more than dust.

When spring arrived, he and Penny caught a train to Dallas only to discover his family had moved on and hadn't seen fit to leave anything more than an empty house. Caleb wasn't too surprised, since the last words he'd shared with any of his relatives had been anything but civil.

The Wayfinders weren't exactly feuding, but they weren't the warmest family under the sun. They were mainly a collection of loners who'd been forced to live together through no fault of their own. Blood ties had kept them together for as long as was required, but once they were cut they stayed that way.

After all this time away from them, Caleb doubted he could have thought of much to say if there had been a reunion.

The Busted Flush was still in business. Even though Caleb had helped build that saloon, he didn't want to do more than pass it by to make sure it hadn't burned down. In fact, the longer he stayed in Dallas, the more he felt like he was walking backward.

For the moment, forward seemed to be east. That was the direction Caleb picked once he put Dallas behind him again. Actually, Penny was the one who chose that direction, since the horse decided to walk that way the moment Caleb eased up on the reins.

"Looks just as good as any other direction," Caleb said. "You seem to have better luck than I do anyhow."

Caleb made it to Louisiana in May of 1877. The air was heating up and gave him a welcome change from the frozen misery he'd gotten in the Dakotas. No matter what he'd been told about the swamplands, he still wasn't prepared for the first time the ground sank beneath his feet. The warm sucking sound he heard when he'd pulled his leg back out had sent the fear of God through his heart. There was just something about the ground grabbing hold and not wanting to let go that didn't set well with him.

That fear lasted until he woke up on the first morning and saw the sunlight slicing through the loblolly pines as birds sang songs around him that he'd never heard before. There was also something about the way the local girls rolled their tongues around their words that made him want to stay awhile. A few more crooked card games against a bunch of drunks who didn't know any better, and Caleb pulled together enough money to buy his own little shack on a patch of land a stone's throw from a swamp.

Not long after that, he got a cold feeling in the pit of his stomach. The joy of walking forward was curling up like a caterpillar under too much sun. In its place was the suspicion that he was becoming just as stagnant as the groundwater beneath him.

The pittance of money he could dredge up was still coming in a steady trickle, but there was no joy in stealing from men who were too stupid to put up a fight. If he'd wanted that, he could have stayed in Dallas and poured drinks for a living. Even Penny was getting anxious to stretch her legs again.

Around this time, Caleb wondered what had happened to Doc.

There hadn't been any letters waiting for him in Dallas, which was the spot where Doc knew Caleb would be heading. Now that he was well out of Dallas, Caleb couldn't really expect Doc to track him down. It wasn't that he didn't care about what happened to his partner. Caleb was mostly reluctant to get any sort of confirmation regarding the inevitable fate of John Holliday.

Even now, Caleb had to grin and shake his head when he thought about Doc. The man was crazy, but he was also too stubborn to just sip his medicine and fade away. Instead, Doc preferred to swig his medicine from a flask and raise some hell.

Suddenly, Caleb realized he was thinking about Doc as

if the man was already dead. For all he knew, that could be completely true. The odds were certainly stacked in that direction. Then again, Doc was awfully good at stacking the odds in his favor.

Wherever Doc was, Caleb wished him the best.

[17]

◈ Six months earlier ◈

Doc crept into Deadwood less than a day after Caleb had slipped through the camp. He kept to himself and did everything he could so that he wouldn't be noticed. The scent of whiskey on his breath was so strong, it seemed the liquor flowed through Doc's veins in greater quantities than blood. His sunken eyes were hooded and his head was perpetually bowed. The wide-brimmed hat he wore covered up enough of his face to keep himself hidden while he was inside Bullock's jurisdiction.

Even if he was directly in front of that posse, Doc figured he had a good chance of going unnoticed. For the time being, he was just another frail figure propped up by a cane. It stuck in his craw to even think such a thing, but Doc played that role well enough to get into the back entrance of the Bella Union and have a word with Alice Ivers.

Doc didn't get a chance to say much of anything to her. Neither Bullock nor anyone resembling a posse member was in sight, but Doc wasn't about to gamble everything on him being able to pick one of those men from a crowd. He made do with seeing Alice's face, giving her a curt nod, and leaving the saloon.

From there, Doc rode to the stagecoach platform in the nameless town where he'd first crossed paths with Dave Rudabaugh and purchased a ticket to Kansas. As much as he would have liked to meet up with the outlaw again, Doc didn't find any familiar faces there either.

On the train to Kansas City, Doc refused to lean back and rest his head upon the window or anything else. He sat up as straight as he could and used his cane to remain that way. When he slept, he let his head nod forward and closed his eyes. There would be plenty of time later for being stretched out on his back. For now, he sat up like a living person.

Every breath Doc took was a trial.

Every inhale was a set of claws raking against wet meat.

Every exhale was a wheezing gasp or shuddering cough.

His condition had affected him since he was a boy. Even as a baby, Doc had been sick enough to stay in bed more often than he was on his hands and knees. There had always been times when he had to sit back and let his condition have its way with him. Although Doc may have admitted that to himself when the quiet times came, he didn't have to like it.

When he caught himself thinking too hard about what his condition had in store for him in the years to come, Doc reached for his flask and took a drink.

The whiskey burned a bit, but that was just enough to remind him of where he was. As it passed through him, the liquor dulled his thoughts and senses the way fire dulled jagged iron so it could be molded into something else.

When he inhaled again, it was easier.

When he exhaled, it was to let out a slow, relieved sigh.

Doc's head bowed and his arms pressed in against his holstered guns. Only then was he able to get some rest.

～～～

When he arrived in Kansas City, Doc knew he had to stay for a while. It wasn't because of an inviting saloon he'd spotted or any particular whim. He simply wasn't feeling up to the task of moving on.

His condition was getting worse.

As that thought passed through his head, Doc had to chuckle. Making that observation was similar to predicting the sun was going to move from the east to the west. His condition was always going to get worse, simply because it had nowhere else to go.

Lately, however, it had been bad.

Rather than cash in the gold he'd won from Caleb, Doc made his way to a saloon and started playing. His luck wasn't great, but he found his skills were normally sharp enough to make up for that deficit. He played until he had enough to rent a room for a good amount of time and then got up to leave.

"Where the hell d'you think yer going?" asked the tall man who'd been sitting directly across from Doc.

"I'm tired," Doc replied. "And I intend on getting some sleep."

"Really? Right now, you got to go to sleep?"

"That usually is the remedy for my particular ailment."

Scowling beneath a long mustache, the tall man looked Doc up and down. His eyes were sharp and focused. With hair that flowed past his shoulders in a wild mane, he looked like one of the many men trying to invoke the spirit of the recently departed Bill Hickok. "Looks to me like your ailment ain't something that sleep's gonna cure. Why don't you sit back down and play while you still got the breath?"

Doc gritted his teeth and coughed once in the back of his throat. "Your concern is heartwarming. If it's all the same to you, I'll be on my way."

"Sit down, I says."

This time, there was no attempt at humor in the tall man's voice. His eyes were fixed upon Doc and his hand rested upon the pistol strapped across his belly. "No man wins a pot that big and then just gets up to leave," he warned. "A man should get a chance to win some of his money back. It's only sporting."

"Watch your tone, sir," Doc warned. "I just returned from the Dakotas and I learned that men who gussy themselves up like you don't fare too well."

If there was any doubt the tall man was paying his own tribute to Wild Bill, it was dispelled when he flinched at the merest mention of Hickok's unfortunate demise. "You talk about someone gussying themselves up and you're dressed like that?" he growled. "I should—"

"You should what?"

Doc hardly moved when he asked that question.

He didn't reach for his gun.

The look in Doc's eyes was more than enough to get the job done.

Although the tall man looked worried at first, he hastily tried to cover it up by chuckling uncomfortably. When he shifted in his seat, it looked more like he was squirming.

"Do whatever the hell you like," the tall man grunted. "I came here to play cards, not squabble like a couple of . . . well . . . I came here to play cards."

Doc nodded and slowly moved his eyes away from the man across from him. When he walked away from the table, he fought with every bit of strength he had to keep from coughing. The itch that had started in the back of his throat now felt like a set of jagged fingernails scraping against the inside of his neck. His mouth was dry, and when he pulled in a breath through his nose, it got even drier.

Although Doc walked with a slow stride, he gripped the handle of his cane hard enough to whiten his knuckles. Even after he left the saloon, Doc waited until he was farther down the street before giving in to the itch that had all but overpowered him. The coughs were relief and torture at the same time. Once he'd gotten them out of his system, he took a drink from his flask and let out an easier breath.

The hotel he'd spotted upon entering town was just ahead. Doc didn't pay attention to street names, storefronts, or anything else around him. All he wanted was to get to a room and stay there for a while. Anything beyond that seemed too far away to worry about.

He checked in, paid for a week in advance, and arranged for a bath.

A tub was brought to his room by a boy in his early teens. After that, some buckets of hot water were carried in by a young woman who looked to be just shy of her twentieth birthday. When she stepped into his room, Doc couldn't help but notice the way her cotton blouse clung to her chest. The smile on her face told him that she'd been expecting scrutiny the moment she'd heard that she was delivering the water to a man traveling alone.

"Hello," she said as she pushed open the door with her hip. "I brought you your . . ." As soon as she got a look at Doc's face, her expression lost its sheen and her smile became forced.

Accustomed to seeing that reaction from folks when he was having one of his bad spells, Doc waved toward the tub and said, "Over there will be fine."

"Are you feeling all right?" she asked.

Lifting his chin to aim his sunken eyes in her direction, he replied, "Fine and dandy, why do you ask?"

"You don't look so good. Should I get a doctor?"

"Check on me after I've had my bath. I'll be a new man."

"Sure," she said as she set the buckets down next to the tub. "I'll do that."

It didn't take an experienced cardplayer to know she was lying. In fact, she barely tried to hide her disdain as she turned her back on him and headed for the door. "There's a few more buckets outside. You want me to bring them?"

"Yes."

She brought them to the room and set them just inside the door. When she smiled at him again, she must have thought she was doing him a favor.

Doc filled the tub and chuckled under his breath as he settled into the hot water. He knew plenty of folks didn't know the real differences between his consumption and the Black Plague, but he was still amazed at how vastly their reactions differed. Some looked at him with pity in their eyes and others couldn't get themselves to look in his direction. Doc didn't concern himself with all of that, since neither of those two reactions set well with him.

That was the good thing about spending so much time in a saloon. Folks there were more accustomed to unusual sights. Gamblers didn't worry about much more than their odds of winning a hand. Bartenders only wanted to sell whiskey. Whores only wanted to sell themselves. The dancing girls only wanted applause, and Doc was willing to accommodate every one of those groups in one way or another. Most everyone else in a saloon was too drunk to know he was there.

For the moment, Doc was enjoying the next best thing to a saloon: solitude.

He kept on enjoying it until the water started to cool and he drifted off to sleep with his arms draped along the sides of the tub.

⌒⌒⌒

Doc didn't cash in the rest of his gold until it was absolutely necessary. His streak at the poker tables wasn't exactly dying, but he simply wasn't able to get out of his room every night of the week. There were also no big games happening at the moment, so he sustained himself for as long as he could and spent a bit of his winnings to lease a storefront where he could hang his shingle.

An advertisement went in the newspaper and Doc eventually saw his first few customers. While he may have been a little rusty where his skills as a dentist were concerned, a little bit of practice went a long way. Soon, his hands were going through the motions that he'd learned in the Pennsylvania College of Dental Surgery as if he'd only been on an extended sabbatical.

As winter's grip loosened and spring made its presence known, Doc was feeling more like his usual self. He'd taken to riding the train to nearby towns in search of a good game, but his condition only worsened the more he tried to maintain his preferred habits. More and more, it seemed he needed to move on whether or not he had the strength to do so. He sure as hell didn't want to be buried in Kansas City.

Dodge City was supposed to be a great town for gambling and there was always plenty going on in Colorado. The gambler's circuit had some interesting stops in California, Arizona, and New Mexico—all of which were more promising than where he was now.

But to make a dent in the circuit, Doc needed more money than he had. Without a stake, no gambler could get a start unless he wanted to claw his way up from the little games and into the big ones. Since he was starting to be recognized in certain sections of the circuit, Doc didn't like the prospect of being seen taking silver dollars from drunks. He'd worked too hard to gain his reputation. It may not be the most sterling one around, but he'd earned every bit of it.

There were other ways to build up a bankroll. One of them was to put nose to grindstone and earn enough to have some left over once the essentials were covered. Doc knew he could build up his practice to a respectable level, but he could never become too rich by pulling teeth. Although folks came to his practice, they winced whenever Doc had to put down his instruments so he could hack into a handkerchief.

In April of 1877, Doc found himself leaving his office earlier and earlier before finally taking down his shingle altogether. As soon as he realized he still cared enough to pay close attention to street names or his neighbors' faces, the urge to move on became close to unbearable.

Doc sold what he could, collected his money, and made arrangements to spend some time with family in Laclede, Kansas. His aunt hadn't gotten any letters or received any word from Caleb, which hadn't come as a big surprise. That man was an enterprising sort, who liked to take the occasional stab at respectability. Doc figured it was only a matter of time before Caleb came back around.

In May, Doc was feeling well enough to make the long train ride back to Texas. He didn't need his cane to sit upright any longer and some of the color had returned to his cheeks. He even sparked up some conversations with a few other passengers that trumped the ones he'd had with folks he'd seen every day outside his practice.

While he may have been making small talk here and there, Doc was thinking about the same thing he'd been thinking about when he'd left Kansas City. He needed more money to build up steam on the gambler's circuit.

He arrived in Dennison, Texas, and cashed in the last of the gold he'd carried out of the Black Hills. The man who worked the scales was a grizzled old-timer with a full head of perfectly combed white hair. He was either an honest buyer or a horrible cheat, because he nodded in approval the moment he saw Doc's gold. He kept on nodding as he meticulously balanced the scale.

"You'd be amazed how rare it is that I see the real thing anymore," the old man said.

"Pardon me?"

"This gold. It's the real thing."

"It damn well better be," Doc replied with just enough of a smirk to take the edge from his words.

The old man made a note on the scrap of paper he kept next to the scales and said, "It's just that so many men come in here with a handful of fool's gold and expect to walk out as rich men. Some might say it's funny that men who make it their business to dig for gold don't even know one sparkling rock from another."

"And would you be one of those people?"

After glancing at Doc to find him smiling back at him, the old man nodded. "Yeah. I know the difference real good."

"Will I be walking out of here a rich man?"

"Not quite, but you should be wearing a smile on your face." Holding up the paper and tapping a number written on the bottom of it, he asked, "How's that grab you?"

Doc nodded and reflexively kept himself from doing much more. Years of playing poker had given him the reflex of hiding his reaction to such beautiful sights. "Looks pretty good. Would I have gotten a better price somewhere else?"

That question cut below the quick and the man furrowed

his brow while snapping the paper back. "You calling me a cheat?"

"Not at all. Just making certain that you wouldn't be the sort who might look at a man dressed as I am and assume he doesn't know how much this gold should be worth."

The old man shrugged and muttered, "I can add another ten percent."

Doc extended his arm and shook the old man's hand in a powerful grip. "A pleasure doing business with you, sir. I'll be certain to steer anyone I know in this direction."

After counting his money and stashing it in several different pockets, Doc walked outside and onto the streets of Dennison. The last time he'd been there was when he'd first arrived in Texas after leaving Georgia. It felt like a lifetime ago, and he looked upon the place now with a new set of eyes. Rather than looking to eke out a few more years as if he was wringing the last few drops from a wet rag, Doc sized up the place to see what he might be able to wring out of it. His eyes snapped from one spot to another as his mind sifted through limitless possibilities that would get him to where he wanted to go.

He wanted to go back onto the gambler's circuit.

Doc could hear the cards calling to him like a siren song. Every moment he spent away from a poker table felt like a year wasted.

Rather than charge into the first game he could find, Doc kept thinking about everything he needed to get back into the life he'd been forced to leave behind while he was too sick to leave his room. There was more to life than just gathering money and then spending it. For a gambler's life, those other things tended to be a bit more colorful. In that regard, Doc had to sharpen the necessary skills the way he would need to prepare his tools before operating on a set of rotten teeth.

Doc's knowledge of Dennison was good enough for him to pick out a good stretch of open land not too far out of town. He rented a horse and rode out to that lonely stretch of road until he found a spot that suited his needs. It wasn't anything elaborate; it was just a patch of open ground bordered by some trees and a few mossy stumps.

It felt good for Doc to roll up his sleeves and walk among the tall grass until he found a few rocks and some junk scattered near the road. Throughout his most recent bad spells, Doc hadn't been well enough to leave his hotel rooms. When he'd visited his family, that situation hadn't changed. Now that he was fending for himself and breathing the fresh air, Doc swore he could feel years being tacked onto his life.

Having found a few bottles in the grass, Doc set those up on the stumps at various heights. He then took rocks of various sizes along with a few clumps of dirt and scattered them about where he could see them. Once that was done, he whistled to himself and walked a few paces back.

Doc closed his eyes and kept whistling. When he opened them, he turned around to get a fresh look at the display he'd set up. His hand flashed to the pearl-handled .38 under his left shoulder and cleared leather fairly smoothly.

That wasn't good enough.

After holstering the gun, Doc lowered his head and let his arms hang at his sides. He then looked up, drew the gun without a hitch, and fired a shot at the farthest stump. Some splinters flew, but not much else. The second shot caused one of the bottles to jump and the third made it pop like a soap bubble.

Doc pulled in a breath and forced his eyes open wide so the sunlight could drive away some of the whiskey haze in his head. Shifting his aim, Doc fired another pair of shots that sparked against one of his target rocks and clumps of dirt, respectively. As he pulled his trigger the sixth time, Doc was already drawing his second gun with his left hand. That bullet clipped the neck off of the second bottle, sending glass through the air in a fine spray.

With another set of practiced motions, Doc holstered his first gun and transferred the second into his right hand. He emptied that one a bit quicker and managed to shatter the rest of the second bottle and hit another pair of rocks in the process. He kept his eyes on his targets as he reloaded both guns without looking down to see what his hands were doing.

This time, he raised both guns at the same time and fired at one of the nearby trees. He couldn't help but grin like a kid when he heard all the thunder coming from his combined guns. Although he hit fewer targets, he got close enough to put a dent into one of the trees that was roughly equivalent to a shotgun blast.

Doc's perfectly trimmed mustache curled up as he held on to his grin for a bit longer. He flipped one of the pistols around his trigger finger before dropping it into its holster. He did the same to the other one, but added a few flourishes that spun the gun around quickly enough to turn it into a gleaming blur.

After reloading a second time, Doc drew the pistols and aimed at one of the remaining targets. There was no need for a flourish this time, since he'd already proved his point to the only person that mattered.

He was ready.

Breckenridge, Texas

∞ July 1877 ∞

At first glance, Breckenridge barely even looked like a town. That wasn't exactly a fair criticism, considering the place wasn't much more than a year old, but Doc had seen trading posts that felt more permanent. Then again, at least Breckenridge's buildings weren't sheets of canvas propped up by wooden frames. One thing Doc certainly couldn't fault the place for was its saloons.

He didn't take the time to count them all, but those saloons seemed to match the stores and other businesses one to one. Breckenridge had plenty of room to grow, but Doc wasn't there to speculate about the town's future. He was in Breckenridge to gamble and there was plenty of that to be done.

The gambler's circuit wasn't exactly a formal thing. There were no maps to follow or books to read regarding what places were hosting the best games. In fact, it wasn't much more than the right words being passed around by the right mouths. Once Doc had started playing again over the last few months, he'd bought his way into some bigger games. Some of those players pointed him toward another game being held a few miles down the road and some of those players had pointed him toward Breckenridge. The moment Doc arrived to find all those saloons and all those gambling parlors, he felt like he'd truly come home.

By the end of his second day there, Doc had settled upon the Reading as his unofficial residence. It was a clean place with a well-stocked bar that never made him wait for a drink. The Reading was a saloon, but had more gamblers than drunks, which made for higher stakes at the tables. Most important, the Reading never closed. Different faces showed up behind the bar and different ladies would bring the drinks, but the gamblers could play for hours or days on end. At the moment, Doc was putting that policy to the test.

The game had started just over thirty hours ago. When Doc had first approached the table, he'd needed to push in between two of the existing six players. Now he was one of only four remaining. The pots, on the other hand, had only been getting bigger.

"Raise," Doc announced after glancing at his cards. He tossed a few clay chips onto the pile in the middle of the table and cleared his throat.

The man to Doc's left was a slender fellow in his mid-thirties. He had the build of a cowboy and a permanent scowl etched onto his face. His light red hair was cut close to the scalp, making his face seem even more lean. Despite appearances, Marc Abel was a friendly fellow who took his losses graciously and fought like the devil for every win. It was that tenacity that saw him through several near busts and built his stack of chips to a respectable height.

"Sounds good to me," Abel said with a sly grin. "Why not raise it some more? How's another hundred grab ya?"

Although he had to wait a bit before responding, Doc locked eyes with Abel and studied him. Abel stared right back, ignoring the next man in the betting order who was a Mexican landowner in his late forties named Armando.

Armando never gave a last name and nobody asked for one. He didn't mention what sort of land he owned and nobody asked about it. Armando let his cards do his talking. This time, he let his chips say a few words as he tossed in enough to cover both raises, plus another two hundred to boot.

Doc slowly shifted his eyes toward the man to his right, who was also the next person to act. "I suppose you'll fold, Henry."

Henry Kahn was a burly fellow with clothes that looked as if they'd just been stitched together that morning. Despite the fine quality of the material, he was sweating through it enough to darken the spots under his arms as well as larger patches on his back and chest.

"What the hell do you know, Holliday?" Kahn replied. Pitching a bundle of money onto the pot, he flicked his eyebrows up and asked, "What do you think of that?"

Coughing as he cocked his head to one side, Doc threw his cards toward the dealer. That man also happened to be Henry Kahn. "I think you're about to lose a good amount of money."

Armando and Abel chuckled, but Kahn didn't think it was so funny.

"A man should keep his mouth shut if he don't intend on playing a hand," Kahn snapped.

"Is that a rule now?" Doc asked with exaggerated confusion. "I must have missed that lesson."

Kahn chuckled nervously and said, "You want some more lessons, you just keep watching me play. That is, if you stay alive long enough."

Doc coughed a few more times, which Kahn found amusing, but otherwise didn't reply.

Shaking his head, Abel eyed his stack of chips. He wound up eyeing the chips in the pot even more. "I suppose it's too late to back out now," he said as he tossed in enough to cover the raise. "What've you got there, Armando?"

The Mexican smirked and nodded slowly as he laid down his hand to display a queen-high straight.

Since Kahn seemed more interested in chewing his lip than doing anything, Abel filled the silence by letting out a short string of profanities.

"You beat my three wise men," Abel said as he showed his triple kings. "Nice hand."

Armando nodded to acknowledge the compliment while choosing to ignore the profanities that had preceded it. By the time he looked over at Kahn, Armando's shade of a smile was gone. "What have you got?"

Kahn's cheeks had flushed red and the muscles in his jaw were flinching beneath his skin. After grabbing his cards, he looked over at Doc and found the pale Georgian eyeing him intently. Finally, Kahn nudged his cards facedown onto the ones Doc had discarded. "You win," Kahn muttered.

"What did you have?" Doc asked.

"Never you mind, Holliday. You didn't pay to see 'em."

"I did," Abel said.

"So did I," Armando added.

Kahn looked around at the table like a dog that was about to bite someone's hand. When he snapped his mouth open, it was only to say, "You got your money, Armando. Don't push it."

The Mexican shrugged and lost interest in the matter. He was kept busy enough raking in the pot.

Abel looked as though he was going to say something, but backed off when he saw the spark in Kahn's eyes. "Just trying to keep things friendly," he said.

The cards were collected and passed over to Doc, who shuffled and dealt them to each man. "Don't fret too much, Henry," Doc said. "I'm sure your father can give you some money so you can keep playing with us."

"That supposed to be funny?"

After dealing the last of the cards, Doc raised his eyebrows and replied, "Why, not at all. Wasn't that your father who gave you all that money before the game started? I thought there was a resemblance."

"I don't need no help from my father or anyone else."

"I wouldn't dare to imply otherwise."

Kahn was leaning toward Doc as if he was in the middle of a fight. What made the scene look so odd was that Doc reclined in his chair and calmly arranged his hand as though he was playing at someone's kitchen table.

While Kahn glared at Doc, Abel started moving a few dollars into the pot. "You ever been to Dallas, Doc?" he asked.

Doc nodded. "Sure. That's a fine town."

"You know someone named Mike?"

"Why, no." Doc chuckled. "If I'd crossed paths with someone who had such a distinct name as that, I'm sure I'd remember."

Marc nodded and added, "Mike Abel. He was shot dead in a place called the Busted Flush over in Dallas."

"You mean Loco Mike Abel?"

"That's the one!" Marc replied.

But Doc shook his head and continued arranging his cards. "Never heard of him."

"He was my cousin and I heard you were in town when he died."

Lifting his eyes so he could look directly at Marc, Doc said, "There was plenty going on in Dallas while I was there and there's been plenty going on since. I've been to the Busted Flush and I may have seen your cousin once or twice. I did not, however, kill the man."

Suddenly losing the intensity in his eyes, Marc said, "Just asking a question, is all. Mike was an asshole, but it'd be nice to know how he met his Maker. After what I heard about you I thought . . ." Apparently, Marc also gave a thought about what his next words should be. Finally, he shrugged and said, "I thought you might have known something."

Doc shook his head. "All I know about Mike is what you've already mentioned."

Since Marc wasn't quite sure how to take that, he finished making his bet and let the matter drop.

The bet was small, but Armando still didn't seem interested in bumping it up. He tossed in enough to match it and waved to the bartender for another beer to be brought over.

"All right, Holliday," Kahn muttered as he quickly looked at his cards. "If we're done swapping stories about Dallas, I'll raise it another fifty."

"Lady Luck's never been particularly fond of me," Doc answered in a voice that had just enough of a wheeze in it to get his point across. "But make it another twenty, anyhow."

Abel flipped his cards to Doc and said, "I think I'll join Armando for another beer."

Doc nodded as if he'd seen that one coming a mile away and kept nodding when Armando separated the pittance from his stack of chips required to cover the bet. "Your move, Henry," Doc said. "Or would you rather have someone fetch your daddy?"

"Fuck you, Holliday." Grinning as if he'd just delivered the Gettysburg Address, Kahn called the raise and threw one of his cards toward Doc.

Ignoring the discard that had come out of turn, Doc looked across the table at Armando. "How many, sir?" he asked in his stately Southern manner.

Armando held up two fingers and then slid that many of his cards to Doc.

After replacing those cards with fresh ones from the deck, Doc gradually shifted his eyes to Kahn.

"I already told you what I need," Kahn snapped.

Doc took his time in dealing one card to fill up Kahn's hand. "And the dealer takes two," Doc announced.

Knowing it was his turn to act, Armando looked up at Doc and then over at Kahn. He didn't need a second glance at his own cards before he folded them.

"Smart move," Kahn boasted. When he glanced down at his newly re-formed hand, Kahn blinked and pulled in a quick breath the way a dog would test the air for a scent. "I'll bet fifty."

Doc had yet to look at his own two replacement cards. Instead, his eyes were more focused upon the dwindling pile of money in front of Kahn. "How much do you have left there, Henry?"

"Two hundred."

"Looks more like one eighty-eight to me."

"Close enough, goddammit."

Doc smirked and forced a straight expression onto his face. "All right, then. I'll see your fifty and raise another two hundred."

Kahn's knuckles whitened as he tightened his grip around his cards. "Trying to buy this pot, Holliday?"

"Can't you call?" Doc asked innocently. "Or don't you trust your own prowess at mathematics?"

Letting out a snorting breath, Kahn fumbled through his chips. When he was done, he looked at the dents around his chubby fingers. The rings that had been there a few days ago were now resting among Doc's chips. Thinking back to how Doc had purposely held that jewelry back after winning it made Kahn's jaw clamp shut even tighter.

"Tell you what," Doc replied smoothly. "I'd lower my bet to one eighty-eight, but you would only call. It might be better if you—"

"I do call," Kahn said quickly as he pushed in his chips. He smiled and nodded as if he was receiving a round of applause for his actions. Looking around at Abel and Armando in turn, he said, "The cocky prick hasn't even looked at his cards yet. Looks like your mouth's flapping too quick for your brain to catch up. What's the matter, Holliday?" Kahn asked when he didn't get an immediate response from Doc. "Didn't you think we all saw you drinking that whiskey like it was water? I knew it'd catch up to you sooner rather than later."

"Call with what?" Doc asked. "You're out of money."

"I'm good for it."

Doc didn't move from his spot. When he spoke, his lips barely moved to form his words. "Daddy's not here, Henry. Match the bet or fold."

Kahn's eyes kept darting around the table. "This is bullshit. This ain't a way to run a game! Don't you two have anything to say?"

Abel started to mutter something, but cut himself short before he could make a sound. Instead, he simply held up his hands and leaned back from the table. The only words he eventually got out were, "I'm out of this hand."

"What about you, Armando?" Kahn asked.

The Mexican shrugged and looked at Doc with an

unmistakably scolding tilt of his head. "This has been a friendly game and a man should be given a chance to cover his bet."

Despite the surprise on his face upon hearing that response, Kahn pounced on it. "There! You see?"

"What can you put up to cover your bet?" Doc asked.

"It's only sporting to bet something I can cover."

"Now you're pushing it."

"Armando could have bought every pot for the last hour," Kahn pointed out as he waved a hand toward the Mexican. "But he didn't. Marc slipped up and bet more than he had a while ago," he said with another wave toward the redhead. "We let it go. This is a friendly game."

Doc coughed and ran the edge of his finger along the bottom of his mustache. "There's a big difference between you and them, Henry. I don't particularly like you."

Kahn shot up from his chair and slammed both hands down upon the table. Upon seeing that, Doc leaned back and shrugged just enough to free the handles of his guns from beneath his coat. Armando protected his chips and Marc Abel scooted his chair back so he could slap one hand against the gun at his side.

"I got connections to half the business owners in this town," Kahn growled. "I can put this whole damn saloon up for a bet if I wanted to."

Watching Kahn's display got Doc laughing so hard that he almost had a hard time forming his words. "Now, that would be impressive! Too bad you didn't put so much effort into learning how to count."

Most everyone else in the saloon stopped what they were doing so they could put some distance between themselves and Doc's table.

"Take a look, everybody!" Kahn shouted to the entire saloon. "This skinny little asshole is too chickenshit to play like a man!"

"Is this how all of your games turn out?" Doc asked. "Because then it's no wonder you can't earn enough to leave this trading post."

"What's going on there, Henry?" the bartender shouted.

"This prick is . . . he's . . ."

"What?"

"Yes, Henry," Doc said smoothly. "What am I doing that's worth all this fuss?"

Letting out a breath, Kahn lowered himself into his chair. Rather than slam his hands against the table again, he patted them onto the chipped wood and straightened some of the mess he'd made.

Once everyone at the table took their spots again, the rest of the saloon lost interest in them.

"Fine," Kahn said. "If that's how we want to play, that's how we play."

"No more of this shit again, though," Armando said. "Agreed?"

"Hell, yes, I agree." Abel chuckled. "I don't want to be raised out of every game."

Doc nodded. "That's reasonable. As a matter of fact, I'm willing to shake hands and chop the pot right now."

Kahn shook his head. "No need for that. Let's keep the bet the way it is and show our cards. Winner takes it."

"How very civil of you," Doc replied. "Unfortunately, as you can see, your outburst has upset this table beyond repair."

Glancing down at the tussled cards, Kahn started to shake his head. "I didn't do that. You messed up those cards."

"I certainly didn't pound on the table."

The longer Kahn glared at Doc, the more his eye twitched. "You know I had a good hand."

"I think everyone knows by now."

"You messed up those cards so you wouldn't have to show. That's also why you wanted to chop the pot rather than play the hand through." Kahn shook his head some more and waved off the rest of the table. "You're a cowardly little prick who's too drunk to play a straight game of poker."

Although it wasn't as big of a scene as what had transpired before, Doc could feel the eyes of everyone in that saloon turning his way. "What did you say?" he asked.

"You heard me, Holliday."

Breckenridge may have been a small excuse for a town, but it had caught the attention of plenty of gamblers. Many of those gamblers were in town at that moment and enough were in the Reading to be able to spread the word of what they saw to towns much bigger than Breckenridge.

Doc already had to fight twice as hard to be considered strong enough to run his own faro games or hold his own at a table. Being seen as weak enough to be pushed around by the likes of Henry Kahn could not be tolerated.

"No," Doc said coldly. "I think you should repeat yourself just so we're clear."

"You want to make this into a fight? Is that what you want?"

Doc moved his hand away from his gun and reached for the cane that he'd propped against the table. Gripping the cane's handle, he used it to haul himself up from his chair. "You insist on making a spectacle of yourself, Henry. All I ask is that you make certain nobody misunderstands what you said."

Kahn got to his feet as well and stepped forward so he was close enough to make himself an awkward target if Doc decided to draw. Just for good measure, he rested his own hand upon the holstered Smith & Wesson on his hip. Speaking in a mocking tone, he pronounced every word as if he was trying to explain a steam engine to a slow child. "I said you are a cowardly . . . little . . . prick . . . who is too drunk . . . to—"

Without taking his eyes off Khan, Doc brought up his cane to drive the handle straight into the other man's gut. Not only did the chopping blow cut Kahn off in midsentence but it drove a gasping breath out of him as well.

Marc Abel let out a surprised holler and even Armando was caught off his guard enough to reflexively back away from the table and his chips.

Kahn's first reaction was to draw his gun. He didn't even clear leather before Doc hit him again with his cane. The polished wooden stick cracked against Kahn's gun arm and caused the man to grunt in pain. Doc sent the cane straight up to catch Kahn squarely on the chin and snap his head backward.

"Cowardly?" Doc asked as he kicked away his chair. From there, he took a step back from the table and gave himself some room to bring back his cane again. "Who's the coward now?"

Kahn was too busy covering his head with both arms to respond.

Doc swung the cane at a downward angle to connect with Kahn's knee. The moment Kahn dropped, Doc set upon him like a lion that had just separated the weakest antelope from its herd.

The cane chopped through the air again and again, landing upon Kahn's ribs and shoulders with one solid thump after another. When Kahn looked up to speak, he caught the cane's handle across his face. Kahn might have lost all of his teeth if he hadn't been quick enough to bring up his arm to shield his jaw from the next blow.

Gritting his teeth, Doc tightened his grip around the cane and brought it down hard enough on Kahn's shoulder to drop him to his belly. Doc stood over him with the cane raised, but paused before dropping it again. His breathing was forced and sweat poured down his face. Behind him, the saloon's front door swung open and several men rushed inside.

Loosening his grip on the cane so it could slide through his fingers, Doc caught it at the handle and propped it against the floor the way it was meant to be used. He then reached down and flipped over Kahn's cards.

"I'll be damned," Doc said between rasping breaths. "Looks like you won."

The men who'd charged into the saloon were directed to the back by several sets of waving fingers. Only a blind man would have missed the sight of Doc standing over the bloody mess named Henry Kahn.

One of the men who'd stormed into the Reading was a stocky Texan with a round face and an unkempt mustache. "What the hell's going on here?" he asked.

"Just a friendly game," Doc replied. "Who are you?"

"We're the law around here, mister. And you're under arrest."

[19]

Thanks to accounts given by both Armando and Marc Abel, both Doc and Henry Kahn were arrested. The stories given by the other two players at that table weren't as colorful or exaggerated as the ones given by some of the other folks in the saloon, but they all pointed to the fact that both men involved in the scuffle played their parts in bringing it to its conclusion.

Despite the fact that Doc reeked of whiskey, he was more than willing to explain himself to the lawmen after being dragged away from the Reading. The sheriff's office had a few cells in the back, but they weren't occupied just yet.

"Mr. Kahn accused me of cheating," Doc told the man with the unkempt mustache. "A gentleman of my upbringing does not take kindly to such words."

"So you nearly beat him to death with a cane?" the lawman asked.

Glancing down at the empty holsters strapped around his shoulders, Doc replied, "I thought it would be better than the alternative."

One of the younger lawmen took Kahn to the back of the

sheriff's office so they could speak a little less formally. The man who talked to him had a thin beard that was almost light enough to blend in with his skin.

The deputy leaned against the back wall of the office and asked, "What the hell happened, Henry?"

"You've known me for a few years, Cal. I'm not the sort to spill blood every time a hand doesn't go my way."

"What did you say to that sick fella?"

"Nothing that called for what he done!"

Cal winced a bit and stared at Kahn. It was true that he was familiar with the gambler, which was why he was giving him a chance to keep talking.

"Fine," Kahn eventually grunted. "I locked horns with him, but the pecker was cheating."

"Do you know that for certain?"

Once more, Kahn paused before speaking. Letting out a breath that was part sigh and part growl, he said, "No."

"What exactly did he do?"

"He . . . aw, forget it."

Glancing back toward the office where Doc was being held, Cal said, "Everyone in the Reading is talking about how that skinny fella beat you down. If that's true, we at least got him for—"

"It wasn't like that!" Kahn snapped. "They didn't see everything. He got the drop on me, is all. No sick little pecker like that can whip me like a damned dog!"

Although he nodded to what Kahn was saying, Cal couldn't keep quiet for long. "Maybe you should have a word with some of them drunks down at the Reading before they spread that story too far."

"Don't you worry. I will. What about the diseased asshole who swung that cane at me? What's gonna happen to him?"

"You're the one that would pursue that further," Cal replied. "If you don't show just cause for us to hold him, then you'll both be turned loose."

"Has he said anything about me?" Kahn asked.

All Cal had to do was lean into the back door of the office and see the exasperated shake of the sheriff's head. When he looked back at Kahn, he said, "Looks like he ain't saying much that's useful."

"Then I'll settle it my way."

"There's gonna be a fine."

"What?"

"For the both of you," Cal added. "For the disturbance and damage and such."

"For Christ's sake, I nearly lost all I got in that damn game!"

"What about your father?"

Kahn's face darkened and he gritted his teeth. "What if I don't pay the fine?"

"Then you'll spend the night in jail. I'll see to it that it won't be much longer than that."

When he looked into the office to find Doc handing over enough money to cover his own fine, Kahn gritted his teeth and snarled, "Fine. Where's my goddamn cot?"

Less than an hour later, Kahn was released. When he saw Cal pull open the door of his cell, Kahn sat up from his cot and asked, "What's the meaning of this?"

"Your fine's been paid. Get on out of here."

"Is my father around?"

The deputy shook his head. "He's not the one who paid. It was some skinny fellow in a dark suit."

Kahn jumped from his cot and pulled his coat on as he stormed out of the cell. "That son of a bitch! He's got some damn nerve if he thinks he can buy me off after what he did."

"Not that skinny fellow," Cal added. "Another one. He's waiting outside."

Glancing suspiciously out the front door, Kahn asked, "You know who it is?"

Cal shook his head.

"And I'm free to go?"

Cal nodded. "Try to stay out of trouble."

"And for God's sake," the sheriff hollered from behind his desk across from the two cells built into the back of his office, "stay the hell away from that lunger."

The quick mention of Holliday was enough to put a dark scowl upon Kahn's face. He didn't say a word to any of the lawmen as he started to walk out the door. Before he could get more than a step outside, he stopped and turned to look at the sheriff. "Can I have my gun back?"

The lawman with the unruly mustache let out a sigh and stood up. Keeping both hands upon the top of his desk, he locked eyes with Kahn and asked, "You gonna do anything stupid?"

Kahn had to force himself to wait and slip into his poker face before he replied, "No. I've had enough of that for a while."

Although he didn't seem overly happy about it, the sheriff tossed him his gun belt and then his gun. "I'll be keeping my eye on you," he said as he settled back into his chair.

Kahn buckled his holster around his waist and resisted the temptation to reload his pistol right there. Instead, he walked outside and found the skinny man Cal had told him about.

"You the one that paid my fine?" Kahn asked.

The skinny man nodded. "I am. You seemed to need a little help. Samuel Fletcher is the name."

After shaking the hand Samuel offered, Kahn walked down the street toward the Reading. "I appreciate it, but I didn't need any help. I would've been out of that cell after my nap was done."

"I'm sure you could use the rest, but you may have missed your chance by then."

"What chance?"

"The chance to teach Holliday a lesson, of course."

Kahn stopped in his tracks and squinted at Samuel. "Who are you, mister? What do you know about Holliday?"

"I know he won't be in town for much longer. I also know he owes me and my partners a whole lot of money."

"Partners?"

"You ever hear of Dave Rudabaugh?"

Kahn snapped his head back and looked around as if someone had invoked the name of a demon. "You mean Arkansas Dave Rudabaugh, the cow thief?"

"Among other things, but yes."

"What's he got to do with Holliday?"

"The particulars aren't important, but he and one of his accomplices cheated Mr. Rudabaugh and some of his partners out of a considerable amount of money. Since Mr. Rudabaugh is a bit more . . . shall we say . . . recognizable around here, it's a little more difficult for him to tend to this matter personally."

Kahn chuckled and said, "Isn't Rudabaugh wanted for murder and rustling?"

"Yes."

"I think Wells Fargo put a price on his head."

"That's a matter of public record," Samuel admitted.

When Kahn looked at Samuel again, he made no effort to hide the fact that he was sizing the skinny man up and wasn't too impressed with what he saw. "I appreciate you paying the fine and all, but I gotta say it's a whole lot to swallow for me to believe someone like Dave Rudabaugh would ride with someone like you."

"I don't exactly ride with him."

"Then what do you do?"

"Is that important?" Samuel asked.

"It is if you want me to believe what you're saying. Plus, it seems like you're about to ask me a favor."

Standing there on the street, dressed in his simple dark suit, Samuel looked more like a banker than someone who would give Henry Kahn the time of day. At the moment, he also looked like a very annoyed banker.

"Whoever my associates may be, the important thing is that I am willing to pay you to do a job," Samuel said.

"Is this to work off my fine?"

"No. That was a show of good faith. In addition to that, I'm willing to pay you to do something you probably were already thinking about doing anyway."

"What's that?"

"Knock Mr. Holliday senseless."

Kahn smirked and looked behind him as if he thought the law might have followed him this far down the street. None of the people he saw were too interested in listening to what he and Samuel were saying and none of them wore a badge.

Lowering his voice despite the fact that there didn't seem to be any suspicious ears nearby, Kahn asked, "You really know Arkansas Dave Rudabaugh?"

Samuel nodded.

"And he's really got a bone to pick with Holliday?"

"There was some business in the Black Hills that didn't go the way it should have. Mr. Rudabaugh doesn't like to be cheated and I don't appreciate being made to look like a fool."

Nodding as if he'd suddenly been enlightened, Kahn looked at Samuel in a new way. "You steered Dave toward a job and Holliday mucked it up," he said. "Is that it?"

Samuel raised his eyebrows as if he'd just heard a mule give a lecture on philosophy. "More or less, that's correct. Once you knock him out, tie him up and bring him to me. I'll see to the rest."

"I've worked with fellas like you before. I hired this one little runt to pull some rich suckers into a card game. He was also real good at getting in close to hear juicy talk that was supposed to be kept under someone's hat because nobody would suspect him of being anything more than a twitchy little weasel."

Clenching his jaw and blinking in rapid succession, Samuel looked like he was ready to take a swing at Kahn himself. "I'll pay you a hundred dollars to do the job."

"Make it three hundred."

"I've been following Holliday since Kansas City and I can follow him for a bit longer if you won't do the job. I'm sure there'll be plenty of men willing to earn an easy hundred dollars."

"Easy, huh?" Kahn scoffed. "Why don't you do it?"

Samuel stared blankly at him, keeping his chin raised and his lips together in a tight, narrow line.

But Kahn didn't need to hear any more. He could see all he wanted in Samuel's face. "You don't ride with Rudabaugh, but you scout for him. You don't face a man, but you hire someone else to do it. Just the silent partner, huh? I'll bet you're real good at your job."

"I am, sir."

"And I bet Dave Rudabaugh barely knows you're dropping his name as much as you are. If he did, whether you're working with him or not, my guess is he'd gun you down on the spot. Sure makes it tough to hide when someone like you keeps bringing him into conversations. But that makes it easier for you to get about, doesn't it? Folks hear you mention Rudabaugh's name and they just start quaking in their boots?"

Samuel's face had become a blank slate. The annoyance was coming back, but even that was buried well below the surface.

Kahn didn't need to see much of anything to know he'd hit a nerve. While he may not have been good enough to travel the circuit, he could read a man well enough to know he was fishing in the right pond.

"Are you going to accept the proposition or not?" Samuel asked.

"I'll take it. Hell, I might've pulled my trigger for free if I saw that skinny piece of shit again."

"No triggers. He's to be taken alive. Walk around that corner and wait," Samuel said as he pointed a bit farther up the street. "You'll see Holliday soon. He's staying at another saloon not far from the Reading."

"I want half my money now," Kahn grunted as he loaded his pistol. "I also got a debt at the Reading. You go pay it up while I take care of this business and we'll be square."

Kahn didn't wait for an answer from Samuel. He knew he'd get an earful if the well-dressed fellow had a problem with the arrangement and he didn't hear so much as a peep in protest.

After holstering his gun, Kahn kept his hand on the grip and his eyes open. Before too much of a walk, he was in sight of the hotel where Doc was staying. Kahn picked up his pace and tried not to think about what everyone was saying about him when they looked his way and snickered under their breath.

Kahn's face was still swollen. It hurt to breathe and it took everything he had to keep from making his limp too pronounced. One of his ribs may have been broken, but he would rather suffer through the agony than see the doctor in Breckenridge just so the old man could spread even more rumors about how much damage had been done by Doc's cane.

Pulling open the hotel's front door, Kahn immediately saw the very man he'd been after.

Doc was standing at the front desk with his bags at his feet. He peeled off some money from the bundle he carried in his pocket and placed it upon the desk. The second he heard the brush of iron against leather, Doc spun around and reached for the .38 under his left arm.

No matter how many times Doc might have practiced the move, Kahn already had the drop on him. A shot roared through the air and raked along the side of Doc's chest. By this time, Doc had his gun drawn and his target picked out. At that moment, Doc caught sight of the man standing behind Kahn just outside of the hotel.

"You?" Doc wheezed as he saw Samuel watching from afar.

Samuel didn't reply. Even if he had, his words would have been lost amid the bark of Kahn's gun as he pulled his trigger again and put another bullet into Doc.

Kahn stayed put just long enough to watch Doc drop. Grinning victoriously, he turned and bolted from the hotel. If he saw Samuel outside, Kahn didn't give any indication. Instead, he ran to where he kept his horse tethered and got the hell out of town.

At the moment, folks were bustling on the street in response to the shots that had been fired. Samuel stepped into the hotel and pushed away the clerk who'd crouched down next to Doc.

"That man's been shot," the clerk said.

Ignoring the clerk, Samuel grabbed the front of Doc's bloody shirt and pulled the wheezing man an inch or so off the floor. "Where's the gold?" he snarled.

Doc hacked and wheezed as he forced his eyes to focus.

Once he got a good look at who was talking, he started to laugh.

"You think this is funny, Holliday?" Samuel asked. "Where's that gold?"

"Y . . . you're a real smart fellow," Doc said. "Knowing . . . Henry would be . . . such a lousy marksman."

"I'll see to it you get to a doctor if you tell me."

"And I'll see to it that you get . . . get . . ."

The rest of Doc's words were lost in a prolonged sigh as he slumped back and became deadweight in Samuel's grasp.

More people crowded around the front door and all of them were taking turns gaping inside. Samuel looked back at them, but didn't see anyone willing to step into the room where the shots had originated.

"Doc," Samuel hissed. "I know where Caleb's hiding. Do you hear me? I'll find him unless you tell me where that gold is. Dave will find him and Dave will kill him. You hear me?"

Doc's eyes were partially open, but they might as well have been made of glass. He let his head drop and passed out.

Samuel let the rest of him fall.

[20]

It was the end of that summer when Caleb heard Doc had been killed.

The bundle was the biggest piece of mail he'd gotten since he'd arrived in Louisiana. It may have been the biggest piece of mail he'd ever gotten in his life. Like a kid who'd somehow earned an early Christmas present, Caleb ripped open the bundle within seconds after it had been handed to him. Inside, there was a newspaper and a piece of unmarked stationery; both were folded neatly down the middle.

Like any kid with two gifts to choose from, Caleb went to the biggest one first. It was an edition of the *Dallas Weekly Herald* from the seventh of that month. For a moment, Caleb didn't know what he was supposed to see. But then his eye caught a single paragraph circled in the section reserved for reports of crimes in the area.

Apparently, John H. Holliday had been shot dead in a saloon fight in Breckenridge.

No matter how much he'd expected to hear something like that at some time or another, Caleb felt his heart twitch within a cold, iron grip.

When he unfolded the piece of paper, Caleb only found a few words printed in a blocky, unfamiliar script. Those words were: Services to be held in Fort Griffin at Beehive Saloon.

It had been a while since he'd been to Fort Griffin, but not so long that he could forget the Beehive Saloon. In fact, he could remember both places well enough for him to get more than a little suspicious about responding to the note. Caleb found himself reading through the simple notice in the newspaper several times just to make sure his eyes weren't deceiving him.

Having spent several years living in Dallas, he recognized the script and layout of the *Dallas Weekly Herald*. The addresses were genuine, as were many of the names mentioned throughout the edition. That only left the letter, itself, to be studied. Since there was nothing more than those words written in black ink, Caleb didn't have much to work with.

After both pieces of mail stood up to what few paces Caleb could put them through, there was only one thing left for Caleb to do.

Caleb packed up some things and loaded them onto Penny's back along with his saddle. The old girl seemed anxious to get going and even started to chomp on her bit as Caleb made the last preparations to leave his new patch of land.

There wasn't much else to be done. Even if everything he'd left behind was rooted through or stolen, Caleb would lose less than ten dollars in replacing it. The shack had been cobbled together by his own two hands and the money he'd stashed here and there was coming along with him for safekeeping. If there was one thing he'd learned from Doc, it was to always keep your money within arm's reach.

Before he left, Caleb took one last look at the shack he'd bought. It wasn't until that very moment he realized it would be a last look. The longer he looked, the more he wanted to put the place behind him and be done with it.

The air was too thick and too hot. Even in what should

have been the cooler months, it stuck to Caleb's face like a wet blanket. For the locals, it was business as usual. Some folks even liked the heat. For Caleb, on the other hand, usual business didn't involve living in the bottom of a stewpot.

He had found himself favoring a few of the local women, but they'd started tanning his hide as soon as one woman crossed paths with another one as they came and went from Caleb's house.

A few of the saloons served some good beer, but a couple of local cardplayers had already learned to steer clear of Caleb when it came time to play.

It was time to go.

In fact, it seemed Caleb had decided that a while ago and just hadn't had the gumption to act on it.

He rode to the home of Gus Wilhemette, who was the man who'd sold Caleb his patch of land in the first place. Gus answered the door on the first knock and showed Caleb a crooked yet friendly smile.

"How do, Caleb," Gus said in his thick blend of French and Southern accents. "What can I do for ya on this fine morn'?"

"I need to sell my land back to ya, Gus."

"Oh, movin' up in the world?"

"Actually, more like movin' out," Caleb replied.

That was enough to snap Gus's head back and bring a flush of red to his round face. "Not too far away, I hope!"

"There's some business in Texas that I need to attend to and I won't be coming back for a while."

"Oh, now that is a shame, but maybe a blessin' since Patricia Hume down the street there has been lookin' for ya," Gus added in a whisper. "She got a fire in her belly about somethin' or other, so maybe it's good you make yourself scarce."

Caleb winced as he thought about Patricia. She was a pretty gal with dark skin and curves that flowed like honey. The last time he'd seen her, Caleb was trying to distract Patricia's attention so Marissa Hume could get away without catching one of the punches that her sister was throwing.

The escape would have gone a lot smoother if Marissa or Caleb had been dressed at the time.

"Yeah." Caleb sighed. "Now seems like a good time to go. You know anyone who's interested in my place?"

"Not so much."

"You wanna buy it back from me?"

"Sure!" Wincing a bit, Gus added, "But I'd have to pay ya a bit less."

Caleb knew he was going to be gouged for trying to unload his property in this manner. He also knew he might be able to haggle with Gus to get a better deal. Unfortunately, Caleb could think of more than one occasion where he'd been on the other end of someone getting cheated out of their money. Despite the fact that he wasn't exactly the philosophical sort, Caleb had always believed in the Golden Rule. Every now and then, when that rule was broken, someone had to feel the bite.

In the end, Caleb wound up taking a thirty percent hit on his investment. He actually wound up walking away from Gus's house with a bit more money than he'd been expecting. Both men were on Gus's porch when the deal was concluded and Gus was about to shut the door.

"Looks like today's gonna be a good one," Gus said. "There's another customer on his way."

Caleb counted up his money and stashed it in a few different pockets. "Give my best to the missus, Gus. It's been good doing business with you."

But Gus didn't respond. Instead, his eyes were focused on something over Caleb's shoulder. "Now he ain't walking this way. Looks like he's just sitting out there. What the hell's he doing in them weeds?"

Glancing over his shoulder, Caleb followed Gus's line of sight to find a dark shape among the weeds about sixty yards away. If Gus hadn't been so intent on staring at the shape, Caleb might not have even noticed it. He surely wouldn't have looked that way long enough to catch the glimmer of a rifle barrel in the relentless sun.

Caleb dove forward with both arms outstretched. His

shoulder caught Gus in the stomach just as the other man had started to say something. Gus let out a loud grunt as he was taken to the floor. Before Gus's back hit the boards just inside his doorway, the crack of a rifle shot drifted through the air.

Holding Gus down with one arm, Caleb looked up to see one of Gus's windows being shattered.

"What in the hell you think you're doin'?" Gus asked in an accent that got even thicker as he became more upset.

"Get away from the door, Gus," Caleb snapped.

"Is that man shootin' at me?"

"Just move!"

Gus crawled away from the open door and didn't stop until he was under the desk where he conducted all of his business.

By the time Caleb was upright and away from the door, his gun was in his hand. He'd cleared leather in a swift motion that barely even made a sound. The weight of the gun in his hand told him that it was fully loaded and ready to go. Neither of the twin .44s had been fired at anything more than a few tin cans lately, but they'd been modified in several different ways during the few times Caleb had been alone in his shack.

"Who d'hell is dat?" Gus asked.

"Just keep your head down and your mouth shut," Caleb replied as he inched his way to the window closest to the door. As soon as he'd stuck his head up far enough to get a look outside, another bullet shattered the glass an inch over the top of his head.

Cursing under his breath, Caleb drew his second .44 from its holster and stood up between the window and the door. He pulled in a deep breath, let it out, and then bolted from the house with his head down and both guns barking at once.

Caleb didn't need to get his sights set upon a specific target, since he was moving too quickly to hit much of anything. But Caleb wasn't out to do anything more than get away from Gus's house and to a spot where he might be able to see who'd fired at him.

The rifle fired back at him once or twice, but Caleb made it behind one of the old trees on the edge of Gus's property before he was hit. Once he had something solid between him and the rifleman, Caleb refilled his pistols with fresh rounds from his gun belt.

Leaning around the left side of the tree, Caleb shouted, "Come on out where I can see you!" As those words were still drifting through the air, Caleb ducked and ran to the right. A shot was fired at him, but it was a fraction of a second too late to hit him before he got behind another tree.

This time, Caleb was close enough to the shooter to hear the clack of another round being levered into place. Hoping he was fitting into the bit of time it took to bring a rifle back up and look down its sights, Caleb ran from his cover to circle around and get a little closer to whoever was pulling that rifle's trigger.

Caleb was feeling lucky, so he leaned around the tree to take a shot before he'd even gotten settled behind his newfound cover. Not only was the rifleman ready to take his shot, but he'd also correctly guessed which side of the tree Caleb would choose. Just as Caleb moved his gun arm, the rifleman sent a bullet through the tree close enough to kick some moss into Caleb's eye.

Rather than make a run for it while squinting, Caleb rubbed his eye with the back of his free hand and shouted, "Whoever you are, you're a lousy goddamned shot!"

Sure enough, that sent another round into the tree and gave Caleb a second or so to find another spot to hide. He worked his way a bit closer to the rifleman while continuing to circle around the man's flank. Of course, there was more than enough undergrowth to make plenty of noise to announce every one of Caleb's steps. But that tangle of weeds sprouting from the damp ground worked to Caleb's favor as well.

The sound wasn't nearly as loud as the stomping of Caleb's boots, but it was strong enough to reach Caleb's ears. As soon as he heard that slight crunch, Caleb knew the rifleman was getting to a better spot as well. Hopefully, Caleb could reach the rifleman before he got there.

Caleb once again took a .44 in each fist and started run-ning. Unlike the first time he'd made a similar charge, he didn't just fire to fill the air full of lead. Most of the shots this time around came from the gun in his left hand. That way, the .44 in his right hand was mostly full when it came time to take the shots that mattered.

The first rifle shot that sped Caleb's way came closest to hitting him. It whipped through the air less than a foot or so from drawing blood. After that, the rifleman was too flus-tered to do more than squeeze off a couple rushed shots. By the time he got a good look at his target again, Caleb was running straight toward him.

After firing the last round from the .44 in his left hand, Caleb pitched the gun at the rifleman. The pistol bounced off the other man's raised arms, granting Caleb a couple more valuable seconds for him to aim rather than fire another wild shot in the rifleman's general direction.

Caleb's bullet drilled through the rifleman's shoulder, spinning the man around while also sending him a few steps back. Before the rifleman could get his bearings, Caleb was close enough to knock the rifle aside and drive his knee up into the man's gut.

The rifleman wore a long coat and had a dark hat pulled down low enough to cover most of his face. After he doubled over from that first kick, the rifleman was knocked upright again as Caleb's knee caught him in the mouth.

Staggering back, the rifleman swung his weapon like a club. After Caleb hopped back to let the rifle pass by, the man let the rifle go so he could pull a pistol from his holster. Before he could clear leather, the rifleman heard one word that stopped him dead.

"Mayes?" Caleb asked. "Is that you?"

The rifleman kept his hand on his gun, but didn't draw. Seeing that Caleb already had him at gunpoint, he looked up and returned Caleb's stare.

"It is you!" Caleb said. "Looks like that arm is still both-ering you."

The arm Caleb referred to was slung under Mayes's coat

so that it remained tight against his chest. It could still be used to some degree, but every twitch brought a pained grimace to his face. Mayes still wore a scowl that was similar to the one he'd had when Doc stabbed him in the arm and twisted the blade back at Creek's claim.

"Still trying to shoot me from a distance, I see," Caleb mused. "Maybe this time, you'll get more than a knife in the arm. How'd you find me?"

Mayes shook his head and gritted his teeth. "That don't matter, asshole. You should be more worried that we know who you are and where to find you."

"Oh, you and Rudabaugh, you mean? Where is Dave? I would have thought he'd show himself by now."

"He's comin'."

"Will he get here after dodging all those Texas lawmen who've made it their mission in life to hunt him down? Or will he get here after somehow shaking off the bounty hunters that are sniffing after that money being offered by Wells Fargo for his scalp?"

Mayes didn't have much to say to that. Instead, his eyes kept darting toward his rifle and his fingers kept tapping lightly against the grip of his holstered gun.

"You're not the gunman you used to be," Caleb warned. "Doc saw to that in Deadwood. You want things to get worse for you, then go ahead and make a move for one of those guns."

"I ain't the only one comin' for you. Even if Dave gets caught somewhere along the line, the rest of us still want that gold."

"You mean Creek's gold?"

"It's our gold!" Mayes snapped. "That judge in Deadwood said so."

"First of all, that wasn't no judge. Second, there's no more gold."

"Bullshit."

Caleb smirked and shrugged his shoulders. "Believe me or not, that doesn't change anything. You think I'd be living in a shack next to a swamp if I was swimming in gold?"

After scowling for a few seconds, Mayes brightened up and said, "Then Holliday's got it! He's got the gold!"

"Doc's dead."

It was the first time Caleb had spoken those words out loud. Although he didn't show much of a reaction to them, they hit him like a fist in the chest.

Mayes, on the other hand, wasn't so composed. "That's not true. Samuel found him in Breckenridge."

"Samuel? You mean that little pecker who testified against me in Deadwood?"

"He found Holliday and I found you," Mayes said triumphantly. "You're full of shit. Probably just to cover up where you're hiding all that gold."

Despite the situation, Caleb had to laugh.

"What's so goddamn funny?" Mayes asked.

"The gold," Caleb replied when he could catch his breath. "All that gold you're after. Doc used most of it to bribe that judge you're so fond of in Deadwood."

"What?"

Caleb nodded and laughed even harder.

"You couldn't have handed it all over," Mayes said. "Nobody would've handed that much gold over."

"Maybe not all of it, but it wasn't cheap to pay for that sorry excuse of a trial as well as the chance for me to escape before Bullock could send me to Yankton."

Mayes started shaking his head and shook it even harder when he said, "Bullock ain't for sale."

"He didn't need to be," Caleb said simply. "Everything around him was crooked enough. Creek took his share, we were given ours, then Rudabaugh came along and swiped most of that. How can you not see the humor in that?"

As Mayes kept looking for proof of a lie written on Caleb's face, he became more and more flustered. Caleb just stared back at him as if the lead hadn't been flying a few minutes ago.

"Go home," Caleb told him.

"What?"

"Are you going deaf?" Caleb asked as he lowered his gun

into its holster. "I told you to go home. I'd prefer not to shoot a cripple."

Mayes must have reflexively tried to swing his bad arm because it strained against the strap holding it against his side and scowled with the pain. Before Caleb could laugh again, Mayes reached for the gun at his hip.

Caleb drew his .44 and fired a shot into the other man's chest.

Mayes's good arm swung out to the side as the impact from Caleb's bullet slammed him onto his back. Most the wind from his lungs was knocked out on impact and the rest of it sounded as if it seeped out from the fresh wound in his chest. Opening his mouth wide, Mayes looked as if he was about to howl. Instead, he could only cough up some blood and spit it onto his own face.

Caleb took a few steps forward so he could look down at the other man. Dismissing Mayes as he would dismiss any other dead animal, Caleb reached down to pick up the rifle.

"Dave's . . . comin' for you," Mayes grunted. "He's comin' for you . . . both."

"Yeah," Caleb said quietly. "I suppose he is."

"And when he gets you . . . I hope he rips your damn . . ."

Mayes was cut short by another shot from Caleb's pistol. The bullet punched a messy hole through Mayes's skull that continued into the ground beneath him.

Caleb was done being threatened by Mayes, Rudabaugh, or any of the outlaw's partners. He was also done hiding in the swamp and hoping folks would forget he was alive.

He had a funeral to attend.

Fort Griffin, Texas
∽ September 29, 1877 ∽

It had been a few years since Caleb had last been to Fort Griffin, but enough had happened to give the place a permanent spot in the back of his mind. He wondered how many familiar faces he might see or familiar haunts he might revisit. At the very least, he knew the Beehive was still alive and kicking.

Although plenty of sights were familiar, Caleb picked up a different scent in the air. He couldn't quite put his finger on it right away, but had somewhat figured it out by the time he spotted the Beehive.

The streets were quiet.

Caleb remembered Fort Griffin as plenty of things, but quiet sure wasn't one of them. What grated against him the most was the feeling that the town's wildness was still intact. It was just being held in check like an animal that had suddenly found itself inside a cage.

He tipped his hat to a few folks alongside the street, but didn't get much in return. When he met the glares coming from a pair of men leaning against a hitching post, Caleb thought he might be in for a fight. Both of the men straightened up and hooked their thumbs behind their gun belts to make it perfectly clear they weren't afraid to draw the guns and put them to use.

Rather than put those men to the test, Caleb shifted his eyes from them and kept riding. The two men settled back into their spots against the post.

The Beehive was just as he remembered it. Caleb smiled when he heard the voices coming from inside the saloon and couldn't wait to get something to drink. Rather than get Penny into a stable right away, he tied the old girl up to the closest post and stepped inside.

Although the inside of the place was more or less as Caleb remembered it, all the people at the card tables and behind the bar were strangers. All of them, that is, except for one.

"Why, what have we here?" asked a pretty woman with striking red hair flowing over pale, smooth shoulders. "Has Caleb Wayfinder found his way back to me?"

"Lottie!"

Within seconds after speaking her name, Caleb had his arms around Lottie Deno. The red-haired beauty hugged him warmly, making Caleb the envy of nearly every other man in the room.

Lottie wore a dark green velvet dress with a matching choker placed around her neck. Her hands were strong, yet very feminine, complete with long nails and a thin diamond ring. Once she was done hugging him, Lottie placed her hands upon Caleb's shoulders and rubbed his arms. "What brings you back to Fort Griffin?"

Caleb's smile froze into place, but he wasn't able to hold it there for long. "I heard about Doc. Didn't you?"

"What's he done now?"

"He . . . uh . . . died."

For a second, her eyes widened and she placed a hand over her mouth. Then she moved her hand away to reveal a guilty smirk. "You saw the newspaper, didn't you?"

"Yeah. It was in the *Dallas Weekly Herald*."

"I don't know who wrote that story, but it's not true. Doc's staying over at the Planter's Hotel. It's right over on the corner of Fourth and Parson."

Caleb could feel the dumbfounded look upon his face, but there wasn't anything he could do to remove it. In fact, the longer he thought things over, the more exaggerated the look became. "But I also got a letter," he said while digging the folded piece of paper from his pocket. "Look."

Still smirking, Lottie took the note from him and read it over. She handed it back to him with an apologetic, yet still very pretty, smile. "I can read the letter, Caleb, but that doesn't change things. When did you get this?"

"Over a week ago. Maybe two."

"Well, I saw Doc this morning."

"Where?"

"Planter's Hotel," Lottie replied with a sly grin. "On the corner of Fourth and Parson. Why don't you just go over there yourself?" Suddenly, Lottie frowned and asked, "Where have you been, anyway? Did you and Doc have a falling-out?"

"No. Not yet, anyway. I guess I'll head over to that hotel and see if I can change that."

As Caleb started to walk away, he felt Lottie's warm hand wrap around his forearm. When he turned to look at her again, he couldn't help but be reminded of why she was always such a popular addition to any saloon where she decided to ply her trade.

"It's been a long time, Caleb," she said. "I'm glad to see you again."

"Me, too, Lottie."

"When you and Doc have a chance to catch up, be sure to come back here and see me. If I'm not at a poker table, I'll be dealing faro."

"I'll do that."

Even after Lottie had let go of his arm, it was difficult for Caleb to leave. Turning his back on Lottie was akin to a starving man turning away from a thick steak. After the first couple of steps toward the door, however, the effort became a little easier. Just to be safe, Caleb didn't look back.

On his way to the Planter's Hotel, Caleb felt like he was closer to the Fort Griffin that he'd left behind when he'd ridden out of town the last time. Music played from several different sources. Voices were raised in anything from laughter to profane accusations. The wild animal was out of its cage and roaming free, which was just the way it was supposed to be.

Although Caleb couldn't recall what had been on the corner of Fourth and Parson the last time he'd been in town, he sure knew it wasn't a hotel. In fact, the Planter's looked a little too nice to be in Fort Griffin at all. It was a good size with a small bar in the back of its first floor. A few card tables were clustered in the same room, all of which were occupied by what looked to be fairly decent games.

Doc wasn't at any of those tables, which immediately struck Caleb as odd. Considering what had brought him to Fort Griffin in the first place, he felt more than a little strange when he went to the front desk and asked, "Is there a Mr. Holliday staying here?"

The man behind the front desk was tall and slender. His build seemed even narrower since he wore a starched white shirt that looked to be at least three sizes too big. His angular face was friendly enough, however, as he met Caleb's eyes and replied, "And who might you be, sir?"

"Caleb Wayfinder. I'm a friend of his."

"Yes, yes," the clerk said quickly as he extended his hand over the desk. "Pardon the formality, but we do try to look out for our guests."

"Guests?"

"Yes, sir. John Henry's expecting you."

For a moment, Caleb thought the clerk was referring to someone else. Come to think of it, he wasn't sure if he'd ever addressed Doc by his Christian name. If he had, the practice had long since been abandoned.

"Room number twelve," the clerk said cheerily. "I'm sure he'll be glad to see you."

"Yeah. Maybe."

Caleb was most definitely glad that Doc seemed to be

alive and well. The surprise he'd felt upon hearing that news was quickly being tempered by another suspicion that nagged at him like a burr under his saddle. When he reached the door to room number twelve, Caleb knocked. A few seconds later, he received yet another surprise.

The door swung open to reveal a dark-haired woman with smooth skin and soft features. Her hair was a mess, but looked undeniably provocative flowing over one shoulder to cover her better than the slip that she wore. Her eyes were wide as she looked into the hall at Caleb with her mouth gaping open in surprise.

Caleb had no trouble looking even more surprised.

"Are you Caleb?" she asked with the subtle hint of a European accent.

"Uh . . . yeah . . . I . . ."

Before Caleb could get another word out, the dark-haired woman leaned forward and grabbed hold of the front of his shirt. She pulled him into the room with relative ease and then shut the door. Caleb was barely able to stop himself before tripping over a chair. Once he regained his balance, he whipped back around to get a better look at where he'd wound up.

The room looked like it belonged in a well-kept house rather than a hotel. The sheets and blankets on the bed were rumpled and Caleb could smell what had to have been a delicious dinner that had been delivered upon the dishes stacked near the door. Getting up from a chair placed next to the window, Doc grinned widely and held open his arms. He was dressed in dark trousers with suspenders dangling around his waist and a plain white undershirt.

"Caleb! How wonderful to see you!"

"I ought to punch you square in the mouth," Caleb snarled.

Raising his eyebrows and extending one arm a bit farther than the other, Doc said, "I'd prefer a handshake."

Caleb let out a frustrated sigh and shook Doc's hand. No matter how much he wanted to hold on to the anger that had boiled up inside of him upon seeing Doc, he simply couldn't. "Please tell me you didn't write that letter."

"What letter?" Doc asked.

"The one telling me to come here for funeral services," Caleb said with the hope that Doc hadn't been the one to put him through all of this after all.

"You mean the letter with the newspaper?" Doc asked.

"Yeah."

"No, I didn't."

The dark-haired woman giggled as she crossed the room to a small table holding several liquor bottles in various states of emptiness. "That was my idea," she said.

"Isn't she a hoot?" Doc asked. "She does have a flair for the dramatic. By the way, Caleb Wayfinder, this is Kate Elder."

She smiled and gave as much of a curtsy as she could manage considering her state of dress. "Pleased to meet you. Any friend of Doc's is—"

"Is a fool for riding all the way across Texas to attend his funeral," Caleb snapped. "Now, if you'll excuse me, I think I'm going to leave."

"Oh, come now," Doc slurred as he strode across the room to keep Caleb from opening the door. "Don't be such a wet blanket."

Glancing back and forth between Doc and the dark-haired woman, Caleb snapped, "I thought you were dead! The newspaper said you were dead!"

"Wishful thinking on someone's part, I'm sure," Doc said. "But completely false. If the world wants me dead, it's going to have to throw someone better than Henry Kahn at me."

"Stand aside, Doc," Caleb warned. "I mean it."

"Did anyone see you come up here?" Doc asked.

"Why? Are you going to shoot me rather than let me leave?"

Kate giggled some more and covered her mouth. She didn't cover it well enough to keep the men from hearing her when she said, "And I'm supposed to be the dramatic one?"

Wheeling around to point a finger at her, Caleb snarled, "You can keep your mouth shut."

"I won't have you talk to her that way."

"That goes for you, too," Caleb said as he shifted his finger to aim at Doc.

Even though Doc had taken a stern tone before, he cracked into a smile now. Waving off Caleb's warning, Doc walked over to where Kate was sitting and poured himself a drink. "Care for anything?" he asked.

"Sure," Caleb replied with exasperation filling his voice. "And lots of it."

Doc filled a glass and handed it over.

Caleb took a sip and gave himself a moment to let the whiskey make its way through his system.

"So," Doc said, "did anyone see you come up here?"

"The fellow at the front desk," Caleb replied.

"What about any of those armed men with the sour faces outside?" Kate asked.

Standing up, Caleb walked over to the window. "Who are those men?" he asked while reaching out to pull aside the curtains.

"They're not welcome to look in here," Doc said quickly. "So I'd appreciate it if you leave those curtains alone."

Caleb stopped with his fingers still wrapped around some of the curtain. He considered pulling the curtains wide open just to ruffle Doc's feathers, but decided against it when he thought back to the shadow those gunmen had cast over an entire section of town.

"Those men are vigilantes," Doc explained. "They were already here when I arrived not too long ago and they seem to be more in charge of these streets than any law."

Kate snorted a laugh into the glass she held up to her mouth. "They call themselves the Tin Hat Brigade."

"Tin Hat Brigade?" Caleb repeated. "What's that even mean?"

"It means they're a bunch of loudmouthed assholes who like to push around women," Kate grunted.

Doc shrugged and added, "I couldn't tell you about their moniker, but I do know they made a sweep of some local cathouses and weren't too kind about it."

Hearing that caused Caleb to take another look at Kate. She must have either been expecting the look or could read Caleb's face because she stared right back at him as if to encourage him to say what he wanted to say. Rather than take that particular piece of bait, Caleb took another drink.

"I hear they cleaned out some local outlaws," Doc said. "But they've resorted to posting their signs on walls and making themselves known around here as some sort of well-meaning gang."

"Great," Caleb said. "And thanks for bringing me out here."

Doc chuckled and nodded slowly. "I thought you'd enjoy the challenge. Besides, I heard that someone might be coming to look for you."

"Yeah," Caleb said. He looked at Kate and then stared intently at Doc. "Someone we met in the Dakotas."

"It's all right," Doc said dismissively. "You can say what you want in front of her. Did Dave Rudabaugh come after you himself?"

Despite what Doc had just said, Caleb watched Kate to see how she might react. All she did was scowl, drag her fingers through her hair, and mutter, "I've heard that man's a cowardly asshole."

Caleb laughed and shook his head. "He wasn't there. It was that sharpshooter you found outside of Creek's claim."

"The one I got in the arm?"

"That's him."

"Where is he now?"

"Probably still lying where I left him," Caleb replied. "And you knew he was coming?"

"I knew that skinny fellow from your trial knew where to find you," Doc said. "Lord only knows how he caught your scent, but my guess was that he'd send word to Rudabaugh and he'd want to catch up with you personally. Apparently, those men are still determined to get that gold."

"Gold?" Kate asked as her ears perked up. "What gold?"

"Don't trouble yourself with it, darlin'," Doc told her in a Southern drawl that sounded as if it had been plucked from a peach tree. "Most of it's gone already."

"What about the gold I gave to you the last time we parted ways?" Caleb asked.

Doc held open his arms as if to embrace the hotel room and everyone inside of it. "I parlayed it into quite a fine little streak. It's been enough to keep this feast going for a few days."

"All day and all night," Kate said with a seductive smile that was aimed directly at Doc.

"Yeah, well, something must have happened to your streak for you to fake your own death just to get out of Breckenridge," Caleb pointed out.

"I didn't fake a thing," Doc protested as he pulled up the front of his shirt. "See for yourself."

Caleb leaned down to get a look at the thick scar that covered a section of Doc's ribs like a splotch of dried paint.

"The animal shot me when I wasn't even looking," Doc said. Raising his glass to Kate, he added, "There's your cowardly asshole, my dear."

She reached out to run her fingers gently along the scar, while staring up into Doc's eyes and curling her lips into that seductive smile.

After pulling his eyes away from her, Doc looked at Caleb and said, "Someone got the wrong story and that's what was published in the paper. Not that I didn't think I was dead at the time, mind you. Especially with that skinny fellow standing over me while I couldn't defend myself."

"Samuel was there?" Caleb asked.

"In the flesh. I believe he may have put Henry Kahn up to the task. Even if he didn't, he swooped in like a vulture as soon as I was down."

"That scar looks pretty bad. How close was he when he shot you?" Caleb asked.

"He didn't have the sand to shoot me himself. If he did, I wouldn't be here right now."

"How'd you make it out of Breckenridge?"

Doc smirked, but wasn't able to hide the shadow that crept over him as he recalled those painful days. "The coward who hired Henry Kahn kept asking about the gold and swore that you and I still had it all. The yellow bastard even stole the baggage sitting beside me where I lay. Once he had it, he ran away. When I woke up, I was laying on a cot in some doctor's office.

"Somehow or another, that doctor figured out who I was," Doc continued. "I remember talking to him, but I don't recall what I said. Apparently, I said enough to get word to my cousin George, because he came to get me out of Breckenridge. Honestly, it's still a bit hazy, but it was good to see George again."

Caleb looked at Doc while shaking his head. "Are you kidding me?"

"Not at all. It's been a long time since I've seen George, so of course it was good to catch up."

"Not just about that. I mean . . ." Caleb trailed off simply because he didn't know which question to ask next. "Your cousin got you up and walking after you were shot?"

Doc chuckled under his breath and nodded. "Not to take anything away from George, but my wound looked a lot worse than it was. Once the blood was cleared away, all I needed was a mess of stitches and some time off my feet. He insisted I go back to Georgia where it was safe, but I declined. There's some unfinished business to be wrapped up between myself and Mr. Samuel Fletcher."

"You said he didn't get any gold from you," Caleb pointed out.

"That's right," Doc replied. "He took my luggage, which consisted of a few spare suits and some new handkerchiefs. As if he couldn't tell from lifting it that there wasn't a fortune of gold inside. What an idiot."

"Yeah, well, that idiot tracked me down all the way to Louisiana," Caleb reminded him. "The least you could have done was warn me."

"I thought you'd be in Texas," Doc said in his own defense. "It took a while for me to find someone in Dallas who knew where you'd wound up. And I did all of that while I was recovering. Although," he added, "it could have been harder. I didn't exactly have to worry about folks waiting for my queries. Being dead has its advantages."

"Well, you don't play the part very well."

Doc smirked and shrugged. "There'll be plenty of time for that later. If you could have seen the look on your face when you first stepped into this room, you would have agreed that this little deception was worth it."

Caleb let out another sigh and dropped himself onto one of the room's chairs. "Now that I'm here, I suppose things will pick up right where we left off."

"Not quite," Doc said. "I did have ulterior motives for asking you to haul yourself all the way out here."

"I came for a funeral," Caleb reminded him.

"And you would have ignored the notice if you thought so little of me." Ignoring the roll of Caleb's eyes, Doc continued. "My hope was that seeing I'd been shot would put you on your toes," Doc explained. "And if anyone else got ahold of that bundle before it was delivered, there wasn't anything valuable enough for them to keep it out of your possession."

Waving his hands, Caleb said, "All right, all right. You got me here. Now what? I know you've probably been spending a good amount of time in this room, but that Tin Hat Brigade is all over this town. We may not even be able to run our business as usual."

"Nothing's so troublesome as a bunch of vigilantes who are actually good at their job," Doc said.

"Good at standing around and waving their guns," Kate said. "Some of them even beat up women. Not me, though," she quickly added. "They don't have the balls for that."

Caleb laughed as he sipped his whiskey. "I can see why you like her, Doc."

She smirked and held Caleb's gaze for long enough that it seemed she wasn't too worried about Doc catching her in the act.

"Actually," Doc said as he leaned forward and lowered his voice, "those vigilantes are why I wanted you here and why I didn't want anyone to see you and I talking for very long. I apologize if I dragged you away from any important business you had, but I simply couldn't afford to trust anyone else with this. Those Tin Hats have spent too much time in these parts over the last year or so."

"All right," Caleb said. "Now I'm really interested."

"I thought you might be. Just know that these men are serious and if we step too far out of line, you may just get that funeral you were after."

"You may just get three of them, including your own," Kate added.

Caleb nodded and set down his drink. "That's never stopped us before. Let's hear it."

[22]

The next day started in much the same way as most others in Fort Griffin. The business owners rose with the sun and got their affairs in order so they could work through another stretch of sunlight. Some saloon owners unlocked their doors a bit later, while others spelled the men who'd been keeping an eye on things throughout the less respectable hours of the previous night.

Doc stepped out of the Planter's Hotel and pulled in as deep a breath as he could manage. It was a good day, since he let out his breath with only a slight wheeze and no hacking cough. Checking to make sure everything was in its proper place, Doc straightened his suit coat and adjusted his diamond stickpin so that it was properly centered. Once that was done, he started walking.

The boardwalk was crowded as always and folks moved past him in either direction. He heard the tap of footsteps behind him, but there was no reason for Doc to become suspicious. That changed real quickly when he felt the touch of iron against the small of his back.

"Good morning," a man hissed from behind Doc.

Doc's hand started toward the holster under his arm, but didn't make it halfway before the iron in his back dug in even deeper.

"I'd rather not make a scene in the street, but I will pull my trigger if you'd like to play it that way," the man said.

Nodding, Doc asked, "Finally doing your own dirty work, Samuel? I'm impressed."

"And I'm impressed you're still breathing," Samuel replied.

"Miracles never cease."

"Yes, well, I doubt I'll miss from here, so I don't think you have another miracle in store. Keep walking."

"What do you want?" Doc asked.

"I want to have a word with you and I'd like some breakfast."

"There's a stable not far from here. Why don't you eat—"

"Move," Samuel growled as he cut Doc short with a jab from the gun in his hand. Stepping around to Doc's left, Samuel dug the barrel of his gun into Doc's ribs.

Doc looked down and saw that Samuel had his hand in the pocket of his jacket. That hand emerged through a tear in the jacket's lining, allowing Samuel to keep hold of a .32 pistol without showing it to the rest of the world. When he looked up again, Doc's eyes were narrowed into angry slits and his voice was a dry rasp.

"You're a cowardly little prick, Samuel," Doc snarled. "After what you did the last time I saw you, I should kill you right here and now."

"You think you can draw and fire before I pull my trigger?" Samuel asked.

"Maybe I don't give a damn if I beat you or not. I'm already dead, so a few days in either direction really don't mean much as long as I take you to hell with me."

Samuel lost enough color in his face to make him almost as pale as Doc. He tried to hold Doc's stare, but couldn't. When he jabbed the gun into Doc's ribs, he got no response. When he looked around at the other folks walking by, he only got a few confused glances in return.

"I've already spoken to a few members of the Tin Hat Brigade," Samuel said. "Perhaps you've heard of them."

"I have."

Since that didn't make a dent in the Georgian, Samuel seemed to be out of words. Fortunately for him, Doc had enough words for the both of them.

"I'd still like to kill you," Doc said, "but you caught me at a good time. I'm hungry. You mentioned breakfast?"

"Get moving before I put you down like a dog, Holliday."

Doc chuckled and started walking. Samuel fell into step beside him.

∽∾∿

As the street became busier and additional places opened their doors, more of the ever-present gunmen found their spots along the boardwalk and planted themselves there like posts. One of these men was a tall, lean figure with a bit of black mixed throughout his white hair and whiskers. Despite the fact that he kept his long mustache trimmed and his hair clipped above his ears, he maintained a somewhat wild appearance.

That wildness came from his eyes. When the man let his gaze wander along the street, he looked as if he was taking measurements for one coffin after another. He wore an older-model .45 on his hip in a holster that appeared to be older than the men on either side of him. Nicholas Graymon didn't have to declare himself leader of the Tin Hat Brigade. That title simply fit him better than any of the younger men who patrolled the streets of Fort Griffin alongside him.

"Are you seeing what I'm seeing, Frank?" Graymon asked the man to his right.

Frank was easily a decade Graymon's junior, but he rarely deferred to the older man. Whether or not that was because of youthful confidence or ignorance had yet to be decided. Either way, it had earned him fairly good standing among the vigilantes and locked him into the Tin Hat Brigade's second in command.

"You mean those two men walking across the street?" Frank asked.

"That'd be the ones."

Squinting at the two in question, Frank lowered his voice and said, "One of 'em's Doc Holliday. I don't know who the hell that other one is."

"I do," said the man to Graymon's left. Paul Wilcox looked a bit closer to Graymon's age and had dark skin that was marred by several scars along the line of his jaw. "He came into town yesterday and was looking for Holliday. I had a chat with him."

"Do you know who he is, though?" Graymon asked.

Paul studied the pair across the street and then shook his head. "Not for certain."

"If he's associating with the likes of Holliday, he's worth watching," Frank said. "I heard Holliday killed a man in Denver."

"I heard it was several men," Paul added. "As well as a few up in the Dakotas."

"I don't care about what was heard," Graymon said through gritted teeth. "If I did, I would've run Holliday out of town a while ago. He's been keeping his head down and his nose clean while he's been here, so I don't have a problem with him. Holliday seems like a smart man, though. He knows we're here and he may just be waiting for someone to back his play before he does anything."

"He's just a gambler, though, ain't he?" Frank asked.

Paul let out a humorless grunt of a laugh. "I wouldn't trust any gambler farther than I could throw him."

Graymon laughed as well. On him, however, the expression was more of a subtle shift in his lip as he nodded his head. "And all gamblers got something up their sleeves. Otherwise, they'd have an honest job and associate with honest folks."

"That whore that Holliday's been keeping company with didn't appreciate us rousting her or her friends one bit," Frank said as he kept his eyes on the two men walking toward John Shannsey's Cattle Exchange Saloon. "She could be whispering in Holliday's ear to try and get him to take a shot at one of us."

"She sure as hell doesn't like you boys," someone added from a few steps to the side of the three vigilantes.

All three vigilantes turned to face the man who'd just spoken. Frank and Paul were the only ones who had their guns drawn, but Graymon looked deadlier than both of them combined. Keeping his hand upon his holstered .45, Graymon scowled at the new arrival the way a wild dog scowled at someone who'd just stolen the bone from its mouth.

"You must be new in town, mister," Graymon said. "Otherwise you'd know better than to stick your nose in where it don't belong."

Holding his hands up, the man said, "I am new in town. Just arrived actually."

"I know," Frank said. "I saw you the moment you got here."

"You're very observant. I'm fairly observant myself. That's how I learned so quickly that you men are the ones to talk to regarding certain undesirable elements that might be among us."

"You just got here and you're already scouting out undesirables?" Graymon asked. "Why don't you go see the marshal?"

"Because the marshal doesn't act as quickly as you do. Besides that, I know of some dangerous men who'll be looking to get to you long before they try to get to the marshal."

"You mean like that whore we were talking about?" Frank asked. "We already know she carries at least one gun under them skirts of hers."

"If you boys could be threatened by a whore, you wouldn't be of much concern to anyone, now would you?"

Feeling the crackle of tension running throughout his two men, Graymon stepped forward before Frank or Paul could make another move. "Say what you want to say and be quick about it."

The man nodded and made sure the other three could see that he was glancing across the street at the two men who'd previously been in the vigilantes' sights. "Holliday can be a problem, but it's that other one you'll need to watch. He'll already know all about you and he'll most likely make a move straight for you."

"How do you know all this?"

"Because I've been keeping an eye on him for a while now."

Graymon turned toward the street, but the two he'd been watching were already out of sight. "Paul, I want you to head on into Shanny's. Check up on Doc as well as that other one and let me know what they're doing."

Paul walked away without another word. As he made his way down the street toward the saloon, the locals reflexively cleared a path for him.

Frank eyed the other man suspiciously as Graymon turned back around.

Eventually, Graymon signaled for his partner to lower his gun. "So you know who we are," he said. "Why should we listen to you?"

"Because I can deliver someone to you that'll go a long way in putting you in the good graces of the law around here."

"Who's to say we're not already on good terms with the law? If we wasn't, we'd be in jail."

"Being tolerated and being respected are two different things."

Graymon nodded slowly. "You got a point there."

"And not only will catching the man I'm talking about earn you some respect, it could even earn you some good money."

"And who might that be?" Graymon asked with a dwindling amount of patience.

Caleb allowed himself to grin, knowing that he'd gotten a real good bite on the line he'd cast. "Ever hear of Arkansas Dave Rudabaugh?" he asked.

"Yeah. He's a thief, a killer, and he's got a hell of a price on his head."

"I know a few things about Rudabaugh that may just get

him captured," Caleb said with a confident smirk. "I'll be in touch with you or your men once I'm sure I can deal with you."

As Caleb started to walk away, he was stopped by a hand that was as fast as it was powerful. Graymon grabbed hold of the front of Caleb's shirt as if he intended on ripping off some flesh and muscle along the way.

Speaking in a low rumble, Graymon said, "You're not going anywhere, boy."

∽∾∾

Unlike many other saloons, John Shannsey's Cattle Exchange was a place that felt wide open and had plenty of room for a man to breathe. Of course, the place could have been built that way just to accommodate the thick, wide frame of its owner. John Shannsey had spent plenty of his younger years in a boxing ring and every one of them was marked by the dents in his face and the crooked bend of his nose. Despite those scars, Shannsey was a good-natured fellow who treated most everyone as his friends. Then again, Shannsey's enemies weren't exactly dumb enough to show their faces in the big Irishman's establishment.

When Doc walked into Shannsey's Cattle Exchange, he nodded to the owner. That simple gesture was enough for the big man to pour some coffee into a large mug and walk around the bar. Although he didn't pour any whiskey into the coffee, Shannsey knew enough to get a bottle ready.

"Who's your friend?" Shannsey asked as he approached Doc's table.

Doc took the mug of coffee and eased into a chair. He had a newspaper tucked under one arm, which he placed flat upon the table. "This is Samuel Fletcher. You'd like him, Shanny. He's tried at least two or three times to kill me."

Shannsey chuckled and cocked his head to one side. "Long as he settles his bill, he's all right by me. What can I get for you, Sam?"

Reluctantly sitting down across from Doc, Samuel looked up at the Irishman. Since his cold, tight-lipped frown wasn't enough to dismiss Shannsey, Samuel said, "I don't want anything, thank you."

"You're not hungry anymore?" Doc asked.

Samuel was still pale as he shook his head.

"Suit yourself," Shannsey said. "Will you want some breakfast, Doc? There's still some flapjacks left."

"I would love some flapjacks," Doc said. "I worked up quite an appetite."

"I'll bet you did," Shannsey replied. "You and Kate still getting along?"

Before Doc could answer that question, Samuel slapped his hand down upon the table. "You're wasting my time," he hissed.

Slowly looking up at Shannsey, Doc said, "I'd better tend to this."

The Irishman nodded and kept his eyes on Samuel as he walked back around his bar and sent one of his workers to fetch Doc's breakfast.

Samuel took his other hand out of his pocket just enough for Doc to see the .32 he was still holding. "We've got business, Holliday," he said as he situated the gun beneath the table so it was aimed at Doc's midsection.

"I'll say we do. After you followed me all the way from my hotel like a lost puppy, there's no way I could forget."

"If you would have answered the question I posed outside your hotel, I wouldn't have needed to follow you."

"Question?"

The hand that had been slapped onto the table now curled into a tight fist. Samuel's knuckles whitened and all the color drained from his lips. "The gold. We want our gold."

After furrowing his brow and taking a moment to think, Doc asked, "There's still a 'we' involved? You were alone in Breckenridge. Well, you were alone after Henry Kahn took off like a scalded dog and I haven't seen hide nor hair of any of your other compatriots since leaving the Black Hills."

"They're still out there. I've even heard that one of them caught up to your Indian friend."

Doc laughed under his breath and took a sip of coffee.

"You couldn't even finish the job when I was shot and bleeding on the floor in Breckenridge. Why should I believe you'd be able to track Caleb down all the way across the country?" Once Shannsey looked his way, Doc shouted, "You know how I like my coffee, Shanny, and this isn't it."

"Just thought you'd like to start the morning with a clear head, Doc," Shannsey replied.

Speaking so loudly had put a scratch in Doc's throat. That scratch got him coughing. Once he had that under control, he lowered his voice and said, "Your concern is touching. Now please bring me one of those bottles."

Shannsey brought over a bottle, but it wasn't even half full. He showed Doc a stern look, which was enough to get him away from the table without another tongue lashing.

Doc pulled the stopper from the bottle and poured a healthy measure of whiskey into his coffee.

"Henry Kahn was an idiot and a lousy shot," Samuel said. "If it makes you feel any better, I didn't intend for him to try and kill you."

After thinking about that for a moment, Doc shook his head. "That doesn't make me feel better at all."

"Well, I won't be pulling any more punches and neither will the men who'll be coming to town any moment now."

"Oh, dear. Not the dreaded Dave Rudabaugh. How will I ever contain my fear?"

"Strut all you want, Holliday, but I've had enough of this. Your Injun friend was fairly well-known in Dallas. We barely needed to ask a handful of people to find out where he was. Certain members of Mr. Wayfinder's family didn't have any problem whatsoever in sharing where he'd gone. The job took time and money, but it's done. You've had our money for a considerable amount of time and we're done fooling with you."

"Good," Doc chuckled. "Because it's become very tiresome."

"Then tell me where to find my gold and I'll be on my way."

Still looking down at his newspaper, Doc shook his head.

"You've followed me long enough to know how I spend my days. Surely you would have seen me hauling a wagon of gold from one spot to another. Is that about how much you think I have left?"

"I know that you're a sporting man and, being as such, you would know to keep some money on hand to back your efforts in whatever game you decide to play."

"You must have lost track of me for a while," Doc pointed out, "because I fell on some hard times in Kansas. Your man Henry Kahn did put a hurting onto me that took some time to shake off."

"Even after I'd thought you were dead, I managed to find you again," Samuel said proudly.

"And with all those staggering powers of observation, what makes you think I can carry a bag full of gold everywhere I go? Not that I don't appreciate your confidence, but most folks don't give me that sort of credit."

"I'm surprised you haven't drunk yourself to death and I don't pretend to know how you survived getting shot. You see, my whole point is that it no longer matters if you have the gold in your possession or not."

"Really?" Doc asked as he turned the newspaper over. "Then I must have lost track of what you were talking about."

"That gold belonged to us," Samuel said crisply. "Of that, there is no question. Another fact is that you, Creek Johnson, and that Indian friend of yours stole that gold out from under us."

"Now that is an ugly accusation."

"Yes, but an accurate one."

Both men fell silent as the young blonde who worked for Shannsey stepped up to the table to put a plate of flapjacks and bacon down in front of Doc. She smiled and was about to say something when she noticed that both men at the table were still glaring at each other. Her eyes reflexively darted to the guns both men were carrying and then she backed away.

"Thank you," Doc said in a smooth voice that still made the young lady jump.

She nodded quickly. "Is there anything else I can—"

"No," Samuel snapped. "Leave."

She left and was quick about it.

Doc clucked his tongue and said, "You're going to have to be more polite if you ever hope to touch a woman."

Ignoring the barbed comment, Samuel kept his eyes fixed upon Doc. "I'm certain that gold is long gone. Your partner's share will be brought back soon enough, Creek Johnson will be dealt with, and you've probably spent your portion on gambling and whores like the one you choose to spend your nights with right now."

When Doc stood up, he moved like a trap that had been sprung and Samuel looked up at him like a prairie dog that had just gotten its leg stuck between a pair of iron jaws. Doc's hands were on the table and a good distance from his guns, but that didn't take anything away from the murderous promise in his eyes.

"If you want to live long enough to walk out of this room," Doc rasped, "you'll refrain from speaking one more word about Kate. If I even suspect you're thinking about her, I'll gut you like a fish."

Samuel swallowed hard and did a poor job of appearing to be in control of the situation. "Fine. Now why don't you sit down and we can finish our discussion."

Doc didn't move a muscle on Samuel's order.

Only after a few tense moments, Doc finally eased back and settled into his chair. When he looked over at the bar, Doc nodded to Shannsey. Only then did the former pugilist let go of the club he kept under the bar.

"You owe us that gold," Samuel said. "And since you claim you no longer have it, my partners and I will accept the cash equivalent."

"How much do you figure?"

"Twenty thousand to start. That will buy you enough time for me to check on the going rate of gold so I can figure out how much will square us up for good."

"Twenty thousand?" Doc scoffed. "Is that all? I would have thought you'd build it up to much more than that."

"Oh, there will be more coming to us. After all, it's only

fair that you pay us back for all the expenses incurred while we chased you down to collect this debt."

Doc kept nodding as he started to pick at his breakfast. "And what if I tell you to stuff your figures, as well as anything else you can find, up your pompous ass?"

"Then we'll see to it that you'll wish you had died on that floor in Breckenridge."

"Still 'we,' is it?" Doc asked. "You're heeled right now. No man in his right mind would run their mouth so much unless they were heeled. Why don't you draw that little gun of yours and settle this debt right here and now?"

Slowly rising to his feet, Samuel straightened his jacket. He kept his hand close to his gun, but didn't attempt to draw the weapon. "You have until this time tomorrow to get the money together. If you need more time, get whatever you can and bring it. We'll see what arrangements we can make."

"That's what I thought," Doc said with a sigh as he dug into his breakfast. "Run along, then. Tell Dave I said hello."

[23]

Caleb gritted his teeth every time he felt the rough hand shove him forward. No matter how much he wanted to wheel around and take a swing at the man who was pushing him, he swallowed his pride and allowed himself to be herded like some sort of dumb animal into its pen. To make the indignity even worse, Caleb found himself in the same stable where Penny was being kept.

As Caleb started to turn around, the rough hands shoved him back the other way so he continued to stare at a dirty wall. Since there was nowhere else for him to go, Caleb knew he could be shot at any moment. That knowledge, combined with the aggravation that had built up during his walk to the stable, brought him around with enough power to swat aside the rough hand before it could stop his progress.

Frank had been the one shoving Caleb and he was also the first one to draw his pistol when Caleb insisted on facing the vigilantes. The moment Frank cleared leather, Graymon and Paul did the same out of blind reflex to cover their partner.

"If I meant to fight you," Caleb said, "I could have done it before I was at such a disadvantage."

One nod from Graymon was all it took for Frank to back off. Even after that, all three vigilantes stood ready to pull their triggers at a moment's notice.

"Just what the hell do you want from us?" Graymon asked.

"I wanted to save you men the trouble of finding Rudabaugh," Caleb replied. "Since the law hasn't had any luck all these years, I figure it was better to bet on a horse that's won a race or two."

"What do you get out of it?"

"A favor," Caleb said. "I'd like to ask a favor."

Frank's eyes narrowed as he nodded slowly. "Here it comes."

After silencing the younger man with a quick, stern glance, Graymon shifted his attention back to Caleb. "What favor?"

"First off," Caleb answered as he shifted from one foot to the other, "I'd appreciate it if you didn't kill me. With all the work you've done around here, don't you fellows ever talk to anyone who's genuinely trying to help?"

Paul chuckled under his breath and said, "Folks aren't usually so civic-minded."

"All right, then. How about this?"

Before Caleb could continue what he meant to say, Paul turned away from the window he'd been using to keep watch on the street. "Someone's coming this way."

Graymon's eyes darted away from Caleb for half a second, but were on him before Caleb had a prayer of moving from his spot. "Who is it?" he asked.

"Looks like that fellow that was with Holliday."

"Go see what he wants."

Paul nodded and backed away until he was certain the other two had Caleb well in hand.

"I told you he'd be coming for you," Caleb said.

"That fellow looks like a stiff breeze would knock him down," Frank grunted. "What the hell's he gonna do to us?"

Although the younger man wore a confident smirk, Graymon wasn't so quick to join him. He eyed Caleb intently and waited for the answer to that question.

"He works with Dave Rudabaugh," Caleb replied.

Graymon slowly shook his head. "I know Rudabaugh well enough. Most folks around here do. He's a killer, a thief, and a rustler. He rides with other killers and thieves. He doesn't think far enough ahead to send scouts or spies on his behalf."

"Maybe not, but you don't think he'd turn down some free advice if it pointed him in the right direction where a good job was concerned, do you? Every robber's got to have some eyes and ears scattered about to look for the good openings. It only makes sense."

"Sounds like you know an awful lot about how Rudabaugh works," Graymon said. "Maybe you're his eyes and ears."

"Sure. That's why I walked straight up to you when I could just as easily have walked by without saying a word."

"So why come to us?" Graymon asked.

"I've been hunting Rudabaugh for too long, chasing after that reward put up by Wells Fargo," Caleb replied. "Rudabaugh may not be the smartest robber there ever was, but he knows how to run. Surely you know plenty about assholes like that who manage to give you the slip."

Graymon shook his head again. "There ain't many men who give us the slip."

"Which is exactly why I came to you. I'd rather split the reward and move on to the next asshole than make Rudabaugh my life's work. I sure as hell can't just give up. That'd play hell on my reputation."

"To hell with your reputation," Frank said. "We're not in the business of throwing in with bounty hunters."

"You don't need to throw in with me," Caleb said. "I just thought you'd like to have a part in bringing in a known man like Rudabaugh."

"We got our hands full. Just get the hell—"

"Shut up, Frank," Graymon snapped. Once he was certain

his partner was in check, he shifted his attention back to Caleb. "Why not go to the law?"

"You are the law in this town," Caleb replied. "Everyone knows that. I thought things would go smoother if I let you know what was happening before I face Rudabaugh. Then I thought you might like the chance to make it known that you men aren't just a bunch of gunmen who string horse thieves up from trees."

The silence in the stable dropped like a hammer and hung in the air like smoke. Caleb wondered if he might have gone one step too far in needling the vigilantes, especially if that step might just be off a stool right before a noose cinches in around his neck.

The vigilantes had known what they were doing when they'd brought Caleb to that stable. Although Penny was also in there, she wasn't in much of a position to be of any help. So far, nobody else had come near the stable or even stuck their nose in to see what was going on inside. If Graymon or his men decided to put a bullet through Caleb's head, there wasn't anyone around to stop or even question them.

"You think you can do us some good, huh?" Graymon asked.

Caleb shrugged and replied, "I think we can do this job pretty good if we work together. After that, we can part ways."

"And what do you think that skinny fellow is saying to Paul right now?"

Although he couldn't see much outside the stable, Caleb could tell that Paul was talking to someone out there. Since Graymon didn't have much of a reason to lie, he figured Samuel was making his case at that very moment.

"Whatever it is," Caleb said, "you shouldn't trust one bit of it."

"There's been plenty of other men who've come around here to try and bend our ears with lies and fancy talk," Graymon said. "Most of them just wanted to get our backs turned long enough to put a bullet into them. Even the law's taken a run at us, but none of it's done a damn bit of good."

"This isn't like that," Caleb insisted.

"I guess we'll just have to wait and see what the next few minutes brings us."

～～～

The plan had been for Doc to stay put so Caleb could have a chat with the Tin Hats before he was pegged as Doc's accomplice. Considering that Doc had already been caught off his game by Samuel, Doc could only hope Caleb was faring better.

Doc was supposed to go about his daily routine, so he ate his breakfast and whiled away some time at one of the card tables after Samuel had gone. John Shannsey might have been a good fellow and an honest man, but he didn't know how to build up his saloon into one of the more popular gambling establishments in Fort Griffin. The Cattle Exchange was a bit too straitlaced for most gamblers. There were more meals than cards served in the place, which meant it wasn't about to wind up on the gambler's circuit anytime soon.

Doc liked the peace and quiet he could find there. That was why he'd started most of his days at one of Shanny's card tables whether anyone else was playing or not. He could eat some good food, have some good coffee, and practice his card handling while getting in the occasional game of gin rummy with an old-timer or two. After that, he would find his way to someplace like the Beehive where Lottie Deno held court like a reigning queen.

It was a good routine that suited Doc very well. On this particular day, however, sitting in one place felt like torture. Just knowing that Caleb was out making moves and possibly getting killed for it didn't suit Doc one bit. After Samuel had left, Doc sat down for all of one minute before getting up to pace near the windows. His feet itched within his boots and that itch soon worked its way up to his throat. As soon as he started to fret about it, the itch became a scratch and then grew into a cough. Before long, Doc was coughing hard enough to fill his handkerchief with blood. Letting out a sigh, he turned and went back to his chair.

"Shanny," he hollered toward the bar. "Is that big fellow from Saint Louis still in town?"

After thinking about it for a second, the Irishman replied, "You mean Bill?"

"That's him."

"Yeah, he's still about. He said he's catching a train back north in a few days."

"See if he wants in on a game. Anyone else around who could play?"

"Ed Bailey was kicked out of the Beehive for something or other. He's always up for a game."

"As long as you'll have him here, that sounds good enough for me," Doc said. "If you can scrounge up at least one more, we'll be in business."

Shannsey nodded and walked back to the bar. Being on such friendly terms with so much of Fort Griffin made it fairly easy for him to put together a quick cash game. Even with that in mind, Doc was still surprised to see the Irishman make his way toward his table only a few minutes later.

"I believe you have a knack for this," Doc said without looking up from the cards he was arranging in front of him. "Now, if only I could talk you into letting me run a faro game in here."

"After that business between you and Kate the last time, I'd prefer it if you stuck to poker. Besides," Shannsey added, "this isn't about the game."

"What else is there?" Doc asked.

"A matter in which you might be of some help. Think you could come with me and have a word?"

Doc looked up to find Shannsey motioning toward a doorway near the bar. "Your office?" Doc asked. "I do hope you're not carrying your shotgun."

The Irishman smiled in a way that should have seemed odd upon such a burly fellow. On Shanny, however, the expression was as easy as it was genuine. "Nobody's in any trouble, Doc. There's a man who came to me for some help and I thought you might be able to oblige."

Since Doc had been itching to get out of his chair again

anyway, he walked across the room to Shannsey's office. Along the way, another coughing fit gained enough steam in him to shred a familiar section at the back of his throat. Doc pulled out his handkerchief and pressed it so tightly against his mouth that it would have suffocated anyone else.

The coughing grew in intensity until Doc was finally able to pull in a breath and hold it for a second. After one last effort to clear his throat, Doc tucked the handkerchief away and lifted his chin so he could meet Shanny's friend.

"Wyatt Earp," Shannsey said, "this is John Holliday. Most everyone around here calls him Doc."

Recognizing Wyatt from the brief glimpses he'd gotten in Deadwood, Doc extended his hand and took a closer look at the man before him. Wyatt was a lean figure with dark hair and serious eyes. It hadn't been too long since Deadwood, but Wyatt's face seemed just a bit more hardened than it should have in that amount of time. He nodded once as he shook Doc's hand. "You're a doctor?" he asked.

"When I practice my trade, it's dentistry," Doc told him. "More recently, however, I've been learning my way around a new line of work."

"Shanny mentioned you do some gambling. Having any luck?"

"Not as much as I'd like," Doc admitted. "Fortunately, luck's not a requirement."

Wyatt sat bolt upright in one of the two chairs inside Shannsey's office. In the corner behind him was the Irishman's strongbox and Wyatt propped one arm upon the battered old desk as if he was guarding that money with his life. "I never thought of gambling as a trade. I used to play some faro when I was younger. I've even dealt a game or two."

"Playing faro is for suckers," Doc said bluntly. To his surprise, Wyatt didn't even bat an eye at the smoothly delivered insult. "Tell me something, Mr. Earp. When you dealt faro, were—"

After stopping Doc with a quickly raised hand, Wyatt lowered that hand before it could be considered rude. "Please, when folks call me Mr. Earp they either want something or are addressing someone else. Call me Wyatt."

Doc had to admit that he was impressed, mostly because he'd never been quieted down so quickly and so efficiently. There was a strength behind Wyatt's eyes that was very rare in a man. It was a kind of strength that was simply there like a storm that didn't need to be summoned and would not be diverted. So many arrogant men with big mouths were so eager to bluster and thrash about in order to prove something. It was truly something impressive when someone only had to raise a hand.

"All right, then, Wyatt. When you were dealing faro, were you proficient in some of the more . . . creative practices of the game?"

"You mean cheating?"

Doc nodded.

For a moment, Wyatt's stony facade seemed to crack. Then the slightest trace of a grin appeared under his mustache. "Yeah," he said. "For a while. But the beautiful thing about dealing faro is that you really don't have to cheat to get ahead. The moment too many folks figure that out, I suppose it'll be the end of that game. What about you, Doc? Do you cheat?"

"Everybody cheats," Doc replied. "The ones who are good enough to get away with it deserve to. I find it's much more interesting to see how things unfold on their own. There's more ways to win than just having the best hand."

"Ahh," Wyatt said with a nod. "You're talking about poker. That's a whole other animal. I've never been good enough at that game to invest much into it."

"Then let me be the first to invite you to a game I'm hosting later this evening."

Wyatt chuckled and eased back into his chair a bit. The smirk didn't seem to fit him, but he was reluctant to let it fade. Doc's next question proved to be enough to do the trick, though.

"So what brings you to Fort Griffin?"

"I'm after a man named Dave Rudabaugh," Wyatt replied sternly. "Shanny said you might know him."

As Doc nodded, his eyes took on a steely glint and he stifled one cough that was just strong enough to lift his shoulders. "Dave Rudabaugh," Doc said before coughing again, "is a thieving son of a bitch who deserves whatever hell is coming his way."

"Sounds like you have some history with him."

"How long have you known the man?" Doc asked.

Wyatt shrugged and said, "I've been on his trail for a few weeks."

"That seems to be more than enough time for you to have come to that same conclusion."

"I suppose it is."

"What sort of business are you in, Wyatt? You don't strike me as a bounty hunter."

"I've been a keeper of the peace here and there. I was assistant marshal of Dodge City, but it was more the sort of job I was roped into."

"Whatever you may think of me, I'm not the sort that needs to hear justifications for what anyone else does. No need to belittle your official career. I may not be first and foremost a dentist, but I still hang my shingle when I can. I worked hard to earn my credentials in that respect and I assume it was the same for you."

Wyatt nodded. "It was."

"Then don't try to jump from one side or another on my account. It doesn't suit you."

"No offense, Doc, but you haven't known me for long enough to know what might suit me or what might not."

Doc grinned and tipped his hat. "I believe I've known you long enough to know you're a man who speaks his mind without fear or the assistance of alcohol. I respect that. Your sort are few and far between."

Accepting the compliment with nothing more than a subtle nod, Wyatt sat quietly as Doc removed the flask from inside his coat and took a sip. When he caught Doc's eye again, Wyatt raised an eyebrow before shifting his eyes toward the flask. "Without assistance of alcohol?" he asked.

Without lowering the flask more than it took to speak,

Doc replied, "That's what I said about you. I, on the other hand, am a consummate hypocrite." Doc took one more swig of whiskey before placing the cap back on the flask and dropping it into his pocket. "How do you know Shanny?"

"I've come through here a few times. Before that, I knew him back in his days as a fighter. I officiated a few of his matches. Hell of a quick left jab."

"And he pointed you in my direction?"

"That's right."

"Well, if you intend on taking a shot at Dave Rudabaugh, I'd suggest you form a line. This might not be a bad place to wait."

"He's coming here?" Wyatt asked.

"He should be somewhere in these parts fairly soon, but I don't know exactly where. I doubt he'll lollygag for long before running away, however."

"He does have a tendency to do that. Do you and he have unfinished business?"

Furrowing his brow, Doc asked, "Why do you ask?"

"Because I'd like to know if I should catch him before or after you two meet up," Wyatt replied without hesitation. "You do seem to have more than a passing interest in finding him."

"Believe me, if I knew exactly where he was, I would tell you. If it's not me that gets to put that wild dog down, I'd be just as happy for you to have the honor. You strike me as the sort who wouldn't make a mess of it."

Wyatt tapped the edge of the desk before getting to his feet. "I suppose that's it, then. I should be on my way since Rudabaugh is still on the move and all. If he is lurking about, the sight of me could be enough to send him running."

"I don't doubt that," Doc said as he got to his feet. "I honestly wish I could offer more help."

"Just knowing I'm still closing in on him helps me quite a bit. Thanks for your time."

They shook hands once more and then Wyatt left the office. Doc took another drink from his flask before stepping out as well. By the time Shanny and Wyatt had said their farewells, Doc stepped up to the bar. All he had to do was place his flask on the bar for Shanny to know what to do once he got there.

"Wyatt's a good man," Shannsey said as he picked up Doc's flask and refilled it. "I appreciate you helping him out."

"Think nothing of it," Doc replied as he picked up the flask and raised it in a casual toast. "Any friend of yours . . ."

~~~

"So," Samuel said as he glanced up and down the street for what must have been the tenth time, "do we have a deal?"

Graymon looked over at Paul and got a single nod in return. Despite that, he let out a slow, reluctant breath when he shifted his eyes back toward Samuel. "We don't take orders from the town marshal," he said. "Why should we start taking them from you?"

"I'm not trying to give orders," Samuel replied. "I'm just trying to alert you to a menace in your town. You men have run out so many of the bad elements thus far, I thought you'd be the most prudent choice for this one."

"Apart from gambling and drinking, Holliday hasn't done much of anything since he's been here."

Samuel raised his eyebrows and asked, "Have you kept watch on him every minute of every day?"

"Of course not."

"Then you can't know what he's been into. He's a cheat, a trickster, and a killer. All I ask is that you allow me to prove that for certain."

"And how can you do that?"

"Like I said before, you'll just need to indulge me for a short while and be ready to act when the time comes."

"What do you get out of this?" Graymon asked.

"Just the knowledge that Holliday and his accomplices are finally getting their just deserts. In fact, there's plenty of folks who've already been cheated by Holliday and the ilk he works with right here in this town who would be mighty grateful to anyone who stepped up to do the right thing."

"Like who?"

"Like the men who could see to it that you get some real power in this town," Samuel said with certainty. "Just think how much more you could do with a little bit of official backing."

Graymon thought it over for a few seconds. When he looked down, he found Samuel's hand extended toward him. Finally, Graymon reached out to shake that hand. "All right. We've got a deal." Tightening his grip, he added, "But you'd better deliver."

"Don't worry about that," Samuel said. "You'll be shown Holliday's true colors soon enough."

Frank watched Samuel strut away. Taking his spot next to the vigilante leader, Frank said, "That fella looks like he should have peacock feathers sprouting from his backside."

"Yeah," Graymon muttered.

"You strike a deal with him?"

The older man shrugged. "Of a sort. If I see him with Dave Rudabaugh, there ain't no handshake that'll save that skinny asshole."

"So we're throwing in with Caleb?"

"Keep him where we can watch him, but don't let him stray from your sight for too long."

"And what if both Caleb and that runt are trying to put something over on us?" Frank asked.

"Then we'll put both of them into the ground."

{24}

The entire day had all but passed and Doc had yet to leave
Shannsey's Cattle Exchange. In fact, Doc rarely left his
table unless it was to answer the call of nature. All in all, it
was a fairly normal day. By the time Kate finally made it
around to check in on him, she found Doc sitting behind a
stack of chips that was roughly the same size as it had been
when he'd started.

"Hello, Kate," Doc said with a smile. "Be so kind as to
get a good look at Bill's cards on your way over here."

Bill Kennebeck was a big fellow, but had the smile of a
little boy. He showed that smile now, but was also careful to
hold his cards so Kate couldn't see them as she sauntered
behind him. "Come on now, Doc," Bill said good-naturedly.
"Let's just play poker."

"Now there's a stellar idea," Doc exclaimed. He raised
his tin cup and then tipped it back to drain the whiskey that
was still inside.

Wincing a bit as Doc set down the cup, Bill adjusted the
thick spectacles that sat upon the bridge of his nose. "Is it
my bet?"

"Most certainly," Doc replied. And in the blink of an eye, Doc turned to his right and spoke in a voice that was the exact opposite of the cordial tone he'd used when addressing Bill. "What are you trying to do there, Ed?"

Ed Bailey held his cards in a grip that was just tight enough to keep them from falling to the floor. His other arm was resting on the table so his free hand was within inches of the pile of discards that had been made during the draw. Snapping his arm back, Ed grunted, "I ain't doing a damn thing, Holliday. Just tend to your own affairs."

Sidling up behind Doc, Kate rested her arms on his shoulders and leaned forward to whisper into his ear. Her steep posture, combined with the plunging neckline of her dress, gave the other players something to occupy them for the few seconds it took for her to say, "Yes, Doc. Take a breath and relax. Remember what we've—"

"I remember just fine," Doc snarled as he shook one of Kate's arms from his shoulder. "Ed's the one messing with the deadwood."

"To hell with that!" Bailey said. "And stop talking to that . . ." Pausing when he saw the look in Doc's eye, Bailey bit his tongue. "Stop talking to her and get back to the game."

Doc nodded and adjusted his posture so he was once again sitting perfectly upright. "You're absolutely right." Glancing over at Bill, he added, "Let's play some poker."

"Sounds like a good idea," Bill replied. "It's still my bet and I call."

The Chinese man across from Doc had already folded. Although he spoke perfect English with only a hint of an accent, he knew when to keep his mouth shut. After he'd fulfilled his duties as the dealer of that hand, he sat with his arms folded to watch the game play itself out.

"I'm raising," Bailey declared as he tossed in the rest of his chips. Looking over at Doc, Bailey added, "Make it another hundred."

"But that's only sixty in chips," Bill pointed out.

"I'm good for it."

As the other players looked his way, Doc cleared his throat and said, "It's poker, Ed. You raise what you can and hope for the best."

"Fine. Another sixty, then."

Doc threw his chips in and picked up a silver dollar from the table. As Bill sifted through his own money, Doc started to whistle quietly and spin the dollar between the table and his forefinger.

Although his face had already stated his intent clearly enough, Bill winced and set his cards facedown. "I'll fold this one. A bit too rich for me."

"Take a gander at that," Ed said as he spread his cards faceup on the table. "Three nines. What've you got, Holliday?"

Looking up at Kate, Doc felt her fingertips brush against the side of his neck as she stepped around to sit in his lap. "What I've got," Doc said, "is not something a gentleman should discuss in public. Oh, and these cards don't help, either," Doc added as he tossed his hand.

Bill snickered and covered his mouth with his hand. When Ed Bailey looked at him, Kennebeck tried to disguise his laughter with a forced cough.

Reaching out with both hands, Bailey corralled the pot and dragged it toward himself. "Say whatever you want. I win. Deal the next hand."

As Kate leaned back against him, Doc kept spinning that silver dollar on the table. His eyes remained fixed upon Ed Bailey and his shoulders shook with the occasional cough that racked his entire upper body.

The cards were dealt and a few opening bets were placed. Doc sipped his whiskey from his tin cup and bumped up the bet by twenty-five dollars. This time, both Bill and the Chinaman folded.

"Just twenty-five?" Bailey asked. "I won more'n enough off you to cover that."

Doc smirked and coughed some more. "Listen, darlin'," he said as he took a cigarette from a polished silver case and lit it. "Ed's feeling his oats."

"That's cute," Kate said. When she caught Bailey trying to stare her down, she giggled even harder.

"How many cards you want?" Bailey asked through a clenched jaw.

"Just one." Doc flipped his discard onto the pile along with the hands that had been folded already and waited for Bailey to toss a replacement his way. The card came, Bailey took two, and the rest of the deck was set down next to his left hand.

Bailey nodded and ground his teeth together as he quickly rearranged his cards.

After rearranging his own cards, Doc kept them lowered and continued to spin the silver dollar with his free hand.

"Do I get to watch you bust him, Doc?" Kate asked with a sly grin and wide eyes.

Doc looked up at her and said, "That's not nice, darlin'."

Kate pouted for half a second and then reached down to take the cigarette from Doc's mouth and place it between her own lips. She took a long pull, which caused the end of the cigarette to flare up, and then slid her fingers along its length.

"Are you gonna bet or watch her smoke?" Bailey snapped.

Reluctant to take his eyes off Kate, Doc slowly met Bailey's gaze and blinked a few times as if he'd just rounded a corner to find Ed staring him down. "Oh. Is it my turn?"

"Yes, goddammit!"

Doc wasn't affected in the least by the rage in Bailey's voice. Instead, he furrowed his brow and looked down at the table. "Mind your hand, Ed."

At first, Bailey looked at the five cards he was holding. Then he looked at his discards, which were lying on the table. His fingers went to the pile of discarded cards and one finger was actually under the edges of a few of the cards.

"Oh, sorry about that," Bailey grunted.

Setting down his cards, Doc said, "Sorry's not going to cut it this time. I've asked you more than once not to fuss with the deadwood."

Leaning close enough for her lips to brush against Doc's

ear, Kate whispered, "Didn't you tell me about a man who put Henry Kahn up to gunning for you?"

"What's she saying?" Bailey asked.

"He's been baiting you this whole time," Kate whispered. "You know that man from Deadwood is here in town. He probably got to Ed and paid him to—"

"That's enough of that," Ed growled.

Suddenly, Doc slammed his hand down upon the coin he'd been spinning so he could reach for the center of the table. "I'm taking this pot," he announced. "You're messing with the discards after you were warned to keep your hands away from them and now I'm claiming this pot."

Hunched forward over the table, Ed Bailey shook his head slowly and said, "You don't got the right to take shit. Who else at this table saw me messing with the deadwood? What about you, big man?" he asked Bill. "You didn't see shit, did you?"

Bill still wore his smile, but there was nothing behind it. He held out his hands and said, "You were warned more than once."

"What about you, Chinaman? What'd you see?"

The Chinese man glanced back and forth between Doc and Bailey, but didn't say a word. Then again, with all the whispering Kate was doing, it was doubtful that Doc would have heard much of anything else.

"He's pushing you, Doc," Kate said. "Just like you said Henry Kahn was pushing you."

Spitting out a frustrated breath, Bailey slapped Doc's hand away from his money and then got to his feet. As soon as he was clear of the table, Bailey reached for his gun.

Doc leapt up as well. He moved so quickly that Kate let out a surprised yelp as she hopped from Doc's lap before she was dumped onto the floor. Doc's hand flashed to his coat and he stepped in so close to Bailey that neither man could take anything close to an accurate shot. Fortunately, Doc wasn't reaching for a gun.

Twisting his body behind his right arm, Doc drove his short, curved blade into Bailey's stomach. Gritting his teeth,

Doc jerked the blade upward until it jammed on something solid enough to stop it. Once the blade was lodged into bone, it took a good deal of Doc's strength to pull it free. He knocked Bailey away from him and finally retrieved his knife amid a fine spray of blood.

The sight of that blood elicited some shouts from others in the saloon. Bill and the Chinaman were already out of their seats, but they backed up a few more steps now that they saw the fire in Doc's eyes. Someone at another table already had their pistol drawn and was bringing it up to get a clean shot at Doc's back.

"You take one more move and I'll make it your last," Kate snarled as she pressed the barrel of her derringer against the man's head.

The man at the other end of Kate's gun had a scar running from his chin and down most of his neck. He shifted his eyes to look at Kate, but wasn't foolish enough to move anything else than that.

"Drop the gun," Kate said.

He opened his hand and let the gun fall.

Ed Bailey was still on his feet. His eyes were wide open and his mouth was agape. When his head drooped forward, he tried to reach for the fresh wound in his gut. Just as his fingers met the bloody spot on his shirt, he lost the strength needed to keep himself upright. Bailey started to wobble and then tripped over his own chair.

Once Ed hit the floor, Doc wiped off his blade and put it back into its sheath. "I believe this is mine," he said as he scooped up the pot from that last hand. When he shifted his attention to the rest of the room, he found Shannsey near the bar with his shotgun in hand.

"My apologies for the mess, Shanny," Doc said. "I'll be going now."

"You won't be going anywhere," the marshal said as he rushed through the front door.

"Sorry, Doc," Shannsey said. "I sent someone for the law as soon as things started getting rough."

"I was right across the street," the marshal said. "I would've heard the commotion on my own anyway."

Judging by the looks on the other faces in the room, nobody in the saloon believed that for a second.

"It was self-defense," Kate shouted. "Ed Bailey would have killed Doc."

The marshal looked over to find Kate still holding another man at gunpoint. "Is that so? Can anyone else in here back that up?"

"Sure," Bill Kennebeck replied. "Ed was messing with the deadwood. Doc was in his rights to take the pot."

Doc grinned as if he didn't have blood spattered on the front of his expensive suit. "There now. That's the end of that. Just to express my civic-mindedness, I'll excuse myself from this town altogether."

"You're not going anywhere," the marshal said. "I'm placing you under house arrest until I straighten this out."

Scowling as if she was going to pull her trigger out of spite, Kate said, "That's a load of—"

"Shut her up," the marshal hollered, "and take him into custody."

A trio of deputies rushed into the saloon from behind the marshal to carry out the lawman's orders. Doc held up his hands and allowed himself to be disarmed, but Kate took a step back and kicked a chair toward the deputy who approached her.

"Calm that woman down, will you?" the deputy said.

Doc kept his hands up and started to laugh. "If I knew the trick to that, believe me, I would tell you."

Looking more than a little disappointed, Kate slapped her derringer against the deputy's chest and turned her nose up as if she'd smelled something rotten. "I won't be held in a cell," she said. "You men don't have the right."

"We're not holding you, ma'am," the marshal said. "Unless anyone wants to lodge a complaint."

Since nobody in the saloon was eager to get on Kate's bad side, nobody spoke up.

"Fine, then," the marshal said. "Let's get out of here before things get any worse. Someone see that this body gets carted out of here."

Doc didn't say anything more as his hands were bound behind his back and he was led from the saloon by the marshal. Those two, along with the deputies, formed a procession that found its way to the Planter's Hotel. Due to all the commotion, Doc wasn't able to see the figures that stood in the shadows between two nearby buildings.

"I'll be damned," Dave Rudabaugh said as he watched Doc and the lawmen rush past the alley where he was hiding. "You arranged for all of that?"

"Not exactly," Samuel said. "There was a man inside that saloon that was supposed to take a shot at Holliday."

"Was it that Ed Bailey everyone's shouting about?"

Samuel shook his head. "No. It was some fellow with a scar running down his chin."

"Well, this looks just fine to me. You think we'll be able to get that lunger away from them laws so I can get my money?"

"Most definitely. I've spoken to some men who should be able to arrange that."

"They damn well better," Rudabaugh growled as he turned on Samuel like a wolf that had just smelled fresh meat, "or I'm making good on my promise to carve the price of that gold out of your ass. Nobody steers me to a dead end without catching some hell for it. The only reason I haven't killed you yet is because of all the times you've come through for me."

"This will be one of those times, Dave. I swear it."

"Well, I can't wait around here for long. I've got too many men after me right now."

"You'll only have to wait for those lawmen to leave Holliday alone for a few minutes. I'll make arrangements to deal with him from there."

[25]

Since there were plenty of witnesses speaking out against Ed Bailey and his wandering hands, Doc was placed under house arrest until the marshal could figure out what else needed to be done with him. Since the closest thing Doc had to a home in Fort Griffin was a rented room, he was sent there and locked up under armed guard.

The Tin Hat Brigade showed up behind the Planter's Hotel less than an hour after the marshal had posted his men near Doc's door and went back to his office. Although the marshal shot a few glances toward the shadow-filled lot behind the hotel, he didn't take any steps in that direction. Instead, he prevented himself from seeing anything that wasn't supposed to be there and put his head back in the sand.

Another three shapes lingered in the darkness behind the hotel. One of them stepped forward so his face could be seen in the sputtering light of a single lantern hanging near the hotel's kitchen entrance.

"Good," Samuel said. "I'm glad to see you men knew to come here."

Graymon and Frank stepped forward, leaving the rest of

the vigilantes in the shadows. "Of course we knew to come here. It's not like the marshal was being quiet about it."

"Yes, well, Holliday's inside. If you could take me up there, I'd—"

"Who's that with you?" one of the other vigilantes asked.

Samuel backed into the shadows, "Just some friends I brought to help you men."

"We don't need any help. Send them away."

"Who is that behind you?" Samuel asked angrily. "The more time we waste out here—"

"Holliday's locked up," the man in the shadows behind Graymon said. "What have your friends got to hide?"

"Yeah," Frank added. "Tell them to step forward. If they're gonna help us, they need to be seen anyways."

Samuel stepped forward as the men behind him stepped back. "We meant to cover you from out here in the event that someone tried to rush in after you went into the hotel. Holliday is known to associate with killers, you know."

"Hey," the vigilante in the shadows said. "That's Arkansas Dave Rudabaugh!"

Letting out a snarling profanity from behind Samuel, Rudabaugh drew his gun and fired a shot at the vigilantes. The other man who'd been lurking in the shadows with Rudabaugh rushed away from the hotel to try to fire at the men from a better angle. It wasn't long before Brad's face could be seen in the periphery of the lantern's glow.

Frank had his gun in hand, but didn't get a chance to pull his trigger before one of Rudabaugh's bullets clipped him in the thigh. As soon as he dropped to one knee, Frank received help from the man who'd spotted Rudabaugh from the shadows.

"Looks like I was wrong about you," Frank said through gritted teeth.

Caleb helped Frank up and drew one of his .44s with his free hand. "Don't fret it," he said. "I'm just glad I was right about that skinny fellow."

"Don't worry about him. He won't be bothering anyone for much longer."

"It's not exactly him I'm worried about." As he said that,

Caleb fired a shot at Rudabaugh before the outlaw could pull his own trigger.

The hasty shot screamed past Rudabaugh's head, causing Dave to reflexively drop down low and back away until his hip hit the side of the hotel. Once he had his back to something solid, Rudabaugh sighted along his barrel and fired at the first vigilante he could find.

Graymon let out a pained grunt as hot lead punched through his torso. The impact of the bullet sent him to the ground and the pain of his landing kept him from getting up.

"Kill those sons of bitches!" Paul shouted.

The air suddenly became thick with smoke and thunder from the vigilantes' guns.

Brad had managed to get around to the side of the group and he fired a shot that hit one of the vigilantes who had been standing with Caleb in the shadows. That man dropped to the dirt and clutched his back where the bullet had gone in.

The bulk of the vigilantes shifted their aim toward Brad, sending a wave of lead toward him. One of those bullets hit him, followed by another and another until Brad was flailing about like a doll in a dog's mouth. He finally crumpled to the ground, where his last breath was sent into the dirt. As the life drained out of him, Brad focused on another nearby source of light.

Caleb didn't notice the light at first since he was too busy looking for Rudabaugh. Now that the shadows had been pushed back a bit, he noticed that Rudabaugh wasn't against the wall where he'd previously been hiding. Samuel wasn't there, either.

"Someone's set fire to the place!" Frank shouted. "Get over there before it spreads!"

"You gonna be all right?" Caleb asked.

"Yeah," Frank replied. "Those assholes skinned out of here. They're probably the ones that set that fire to cover themselves. If they come near this hotel again, me or Graymon will burn 'em down."

Caleb ran toward the source of the light and saw that one of the small shacks next to the hotel was ablaze. Judging by the size of it, the shack was either a large outhouse or a toolshed. After standing there for a second and catching a face full of the foul-smelling smoke, Caleb knew which of those two it was.

Although the fire was quickly consuming the outhouse, it was already being controlled by several men who tossed water or dirt onto it. Most of those men were vigilantes, leaving plenty of options open for someone looking to escape Fort Griffin's justice.

Cursing under his breath, Caleb looked around for any sign of Samuel or Rudabaugh. He couldn't see any trace of them. Rather than take off on a wild-goose chase, Caleb headed into the hotel and to the one spot in town where both Rudabaugh and Samuel may be going.

He shoved past the people streaming outside to get a look at the fire and ran for the stairs. Even before he could get a look at Doc's door, Caleb saw that trouble had gotten there ahead of him.

"Open that door," Kate said to the deputy posted outside Doc's room. She took a quick look out the nearby window and saw that the flames were already being snuffed out. Tightening her grip on the pistol she was holding, Kate straightened her arms to shove the gun directly into the lawman's face. "I said open it!"

"What the hell are you doing?" Caleb asked as he stormed the rest of the way up the stairs. As soon as he saw the fire in Kate's eyes, Caleb stopped.

She turned as if she was going to bite. Since her gun was still pointed at the deputy and her eyes were pointed at Caleb, neither man wanted to put her to the test.

"Those vigilantes are clamoring for Doc's blood," she said. "They're already shooting the place up. If you're Doc's friend, you'll help get him away from here."

"Put the gun down, Kate."

"No! We need to move. The fire's already almost out."

"You set that fire?" Caleb asked.

"You're damn right I did." Shifting the full brunt of her glare to the deputy, she thumbed back her pistol's hammer and snarled, "Now toss your gun and open that door!"

Whether out of pure reflex or survival instinct, the deputy lifted his gun from its holster using just his thumb and fore-finger, tossed it away, and opened the door.

Doc was already standing in the doorway with his coat on and his bag packed. He looked at the deputy and then at the gun that had just been dropped. "I believe that's mine," he said as he stooped down to pick up the pearl-handled .38. Keeping the gun in his hand, Doc wrapped an arm around Kate's waist and pulled her to him.

Judging by the smile on her face and the way she gave herself over to him, Kate may very well have forgotten the deputy was there. She kissed Doc powerfully on the mouth and showed no sign of letting up.

The deputy slowly reached for the backup gun tucked at the small of his back. Just as his fingertips found the smaller gun's handle, the deputy felt the sharp sting of something cracking against the back of his head.

Standing behind the deputy with his gun held more like a club than a pistol, Caleb kicked the gun away from the uncon-scious lawman's hand and said, "I hope you two are happy. I just did more than enough to land me in jail."

Doc smirked and replied, "Only if they catch you. My vote is to put this town behind us."

"I've got horses waiting nearby," Kate said. "Let's go."

The three of them rushed down the stairs and out of the hotel. Although the fire was mostly out, everyone in the vicinity was watching the smoking heap of wood too closely to notice Kate leading Doc and Caleb around to the opposite side of the building where three horses were wait-ing.

"I hope I got it right," Kate said to Caleb. "If that's not your horse, we'll be wanted for horse theft."

"You got it right, Kate," Caleb said as he rubbed Penny's nose.

Doc wrapped his arms around her again and dipped her as if they were on a dance floor. "She sure did. I didn't even own a horse."

Letting out a tired sigh, Caleb was about to hurry the two

along when he saw three figures on horseback who weren't so transfixed by what was left of the scorched outhouse.

Dave Rudabaugh already had his gun drawn and ready to fire. A few paces away from Dave, Samuel and the man with the scar on his chin were also taking aim.

There was a split second before a shot was fired. For Caleb, time seemed to grind to a halt. When he tried to take a shot before Rudabaugh or the others fired at him, Caleb's gun arm moved as if it was trapped in cold molasses. Within that fraction of a second, Caleb realized he wouldn't be quick enough to shoot first.

A shot blazed through the air, but it wasn't the shot Caleb had been expecting. Instead, it was fired from the rifle of another man who'd gone unnoticed until this very moment. Rather than waste a second in looking for the source of that shot, Caleb brought up his own gun and fired at Rudabaugh.

The outlaw flinched in his saddle and fired over his shoulder as he pointed his horse to the south and snapped the reins.

More shots were fired by Samuel and the scarred gunman, creating another round of confusion in an already tumultuous night.

Caleb and Doc returned fire. Even Kate sent a few pieces of lead through the air. Before long, the gunman fell from his saddle, leaving Samuel alone.

The man who'd fired his rifle at Rudabaugh rode forward in pursuit. Rather than rush off after the fading sound of hooves, Wyatt Earp pulled back on his reins and took stock of the situation. "You folks all right?" he asked.

Without saying a word, Doc raised his gun, aimed, and fired in a motion that was almost too quick to see.

Wyatt brought up his rifle out of pure reflex, but realized he hadn't been hit. Glancing behind him, Wyatt found that the man with the scarred chin had been one twitch away from putting a bullet into Wyatt's back. No longer possessing the strength to pull his trigger, the scarred man dropped his gun and fell from his saddle as blood spread from the fresh wound in his chest.

"I think we have this well enough in hand," Doc said as he spun his pistol once around his finger and dropped it back into its holster.

"All right, then." Tipping his hat to Caleb and Kate, Wyatt added, "Best of luck to you. And you, ma'am." After that, Wyatt snapped his reins and headed south after Rudabaugh.

Doc and Caleb strode forward. Kate kept one arm wrapped around Doc's midsection and her other hand tightly clenched around her gun.

Watching them approach, Samuel shook his head frantically and then threw his gun so far that it disappeared into the night. "I surrender!"

"Too late for that," Caleb said in a low, growling tone.

"But I'm just a partner," Samuel insisted. "Dave's the one you want! Even Brad spilled more blood than me and you got him already. Please . . ."

"You made all the arrangements for that blood to be spilled," Doc pointed out. "You may not have fired every shot, but you sure as hell made certain the guns were aimed in the right direction."

Slowly reloading his gun, Caleb asked, "If we let you go, will you just convince someone else to come after us?"

"N . . . no!" Samuel whined. Waving toward the man that Doc had shot from his saddle, he added, "That fellow there already had a grudge against Mr. Holliday. He would have come after you whether or not I arrived."

"And what about Ed Bailey?" Doc asked.

The confusion on Samuel's face was too thick to be anything but genuine. "Who?"

Doc glanced over to Kate. "You wicked girl."

She shrugged and showed Doc a sexy, if somewhat apologetic, smile as she climbed into her saddle.

"Surely there's money to be made in coming after us somewhere along the line," Caleb continued. "After all, you know not all of that gold went to Farnum."

Samuel kept shaking his head. "That's over now. We're square."

"He's lying," Kate said with disgust.

"I know he is. He couldn't even fool those vigilantes and they were itching for an excuse to string us up."

"Forget about the gold," Samuel pleaded. "There's no more debt between us."

"Oh, you're right about that," Caleb snarled. With that, he sighted along the barrel of his .44 and pulled the trigger.

That single shot caused the pistol to buck against Caleb's palm and punched a hole through Samuel's head.

After wavering a bit in his saddle, Samuel slid off one side and landed in a heap.

Doc let out a low whistle. "My goodness, that surprised me."

"Why?" Caleb asked. "I've lost track of how many times that asshole tried to get us killed. He only would have tried again some other time."

"Not that," Doc added as he fixed his eyes upon Samuel's lifeless body. "I thought I'd be the one to shoot the little weasel."

Gripping his .44, Caleb pulled himself onto Penny's back as more commotion reached his ears from the town behind him. "Sounds like those vigilantes have gotten to their horses."

"Or it could be the law," Doc added with a gleam in his eye. Beside him, Kate showed that very same gleam. "What do you say, darlin'?" Doc asked. "Shall we take our leave of this town? There was plenty of action to be had in Kansas."

"I'll go where you go," she replied.

Caleb rolled his eyes and shook his head. "How about we just go before we get shot down or strung up?" he asked impatiently.

"A splendid idea," Doc grunted as he mounted the horse Kate had stolen for him. "I believe I've enjoyed about as much of this place as I could stand."

With that, the three of them snapped their reins and dug their heels into their horses' sides. It was a long way to Dodge City.